DOUBLE
TAKE

For unemployed actress Olivia Quinn, it was just an opportunity to go on television. Not that it would help advance her career; she wouldn't have done it if she hadn't been rotting from inactivity.

But her involvement in a television news item about a missing girl generates a series of dramatic events with Olivia as their target. Intrigued with Rita Dale's disappearance, Olivia starts to question neighbours, relatives, friends about the missing girl's whereabouts. In return, she is subjected to harassment, violence and prejudice. Then her room is ransacked, just as Rita's was before she disappeared ...

June Oldham is a former teacher living in Ilkley, Yorkshire. She has held several writer-in-residence posts and has also been director of the Ilkley Literature Festival. Recently she has held an Arts Council Fellowship in Creative Writing based in the two Derbyshire villages of Normanton and Pinxton. As well as her acclaimed novels for teenagers, she also writes for adults.

Other books by June Oldham
ENTER TOM
GROW UP, CUPID
MOVING IN

JUNE OLDHAM

DOUBLE TAKE

PENGUIN BOOKS

PENGUIN BOOKS

Published by the Penguin Group
27 Wrights Lane, London W8 5TZ, England
Viking Penguin Inc., 40 West 23rd Street, New York, New York 10010, USA
Penguin Books Australia Ltd, Ringwood, Victoria, Australia
Penguin Books Canada Ltd, 2801 John Street, Markham, Ontario, Canada L3R 1B4
Penguin Books (NZ) Ltd, 182–190 Wairau Road, Auckland 10, New Zealand

Penguin Books Ltd, Registered Offices: Harmondsworth, Middlesex, England

First published by Viking Kestrel 1988
Published in Penguin Books 1990
1 3 5 7 9 10 8 6 4 2

Printed and bound in Great Britain by
Richard Clay Ltd, Bungay, Suffolk
Filmset in Melior

For Judith Beattie

Chapter One

With legs soaking in four inches of tepid water and trunk upright, Olivia attempted to savour one of her lodgings' more neglected antiquities. Fashioned like a hip-bath, its deep belly supported on wide, clawed feet, it stood majestic in the middle of the room and beguiled with the promise of an opulent wallow. But this was spurious. As soon as she had climbed in, hopeful for total immersion, the brass tap shaped like a well-nourished mermaid bearing an H tattooed on her tail, had been taken by a paroxysm of belching, emitted a final squirt and dried up. Fortunately this disappointment had a compensation for when Olivia had paddled through the shallows and closed the valve, the pipes along the route from the basement had halted their rattle, the shudders under the floorboards had been reduced to mere quivers and the house was at last still.

Quickly, before the surface could harden to ice, Olivia smeared soap on that half of her body grounded above tide level and rinsed it off in a pool between her feet. This done, she rested her nape upon the lip of the bath and contemplated the fluff which whiskered the plaster-rose in the ceiling, looped the electric wire and topped the glass shade with a felt cap. Now that the bathroom had been opened up for her use – her landlady declaring a preference for a strip wash at the sink – Olivia wondered whether cleaning it were her responsibility, though she did not imagine that was an issue to have engaged Mrs Winterton's thoughts; she had an almost devout tolerance of dust probably because, as she would

1

remark, it was the simple matter to which we shall all be reduced. Nevertheless Olivia thought she might have a go at removing it. That would be one way of passing the time. To have a bath was another, but there was a limit to how long she could bear to sit marinating her legs in a trough of lukewarm, slightly moist silt. And there was a lot of time to pass.

The possibility of a reprieve was signalled by the telephone's clang in the hall and, over the last six months programmed more acutely to its sound than she had ever been to an alarm clock, Olivia was out of the bath before the second ring. Bibbing her front with a towel and forcing wet feet into pumps gave her just enough time to acknowledge the convenience of a bathrobe behind an uncurtained window, and the sprint down the passage and stairs provided another two seconds for listing the callers: Yorkshire Television ('Emmerdale Farm', five lines); Video Training Film (waitress); RSC (Dorcas, shepherdess in *The Winter's Tale*, and unspecified understudying); Octagon Theatre (dance-tap in new musical); The Monstrous Regiment (community tour). The half-dozen steps along the hall to the telephone allowed her to work out, in the event of a choice, her preference: the last, she decided, as picking up the handset she gave her number.

'I'm pleased that I've found you in,' her mother greeted.

'I'm not,' then hastily clarified with: 'I'd rather not be hanging about.'

'Still resting, then?' The inverted commas round the second word were as arch as a trendy expression from the pulpit. Though not wholly reconciled to the occupation of her daughter, Mrs Quinn could not resist some of the reflected glamour she believed it conferred and she had been quick to adopt its vocabulary. *Resting* gratified her; it was so much more admissible than *unemployed*.

Irritated, Olivia said, 'Yes; I'm still out of work.'

'Didn't the part in television come off, then? I was phoning to inquire the time. I thought you said tonight.' The tone was alarmed and slightly resentful. As soon as this conversation was over she must dash round to neighbours, telephone friends, contact the milkman, paper boy, Olivia's former headmaster, cancelling all the excitement she had spent a week drumming up. Her daughter was tempted to let this happen but the desire for fame, however parochial, won.

'Yes; it's going out tonight after the local news, but it doesn't count.'

'Your first television appearance, and you say it doesn't count!' Her mother pretended bewilderment, and there were crackles and thuds. Olivia could see her at the other end, lifting the telephone off the table and sinking to the floor, weak with relief. 'I'm surprised you can be so modest, Olivia.'

Not so long ago you had advised that. 'There's nothing to boast about. It's not a *part*. I don't have anything to say.'

'That doesn't matter, dear. Being there on the screen is what's important. Who knows, somebody might see you and say, "That's just the young woman I want for such and such." '

It was necessary to suppress the hope. 'I've told you what it is, Mother: not a part, a representation.'

'And that's enough. Thousands of people will be watching. I can vouch for several dozen myself.' Olivia had been right. 'We shall all be switching on at seven, waiting impatiently for them to get through the boring bits until it's "Mystery of the Week".'

'It's a very short mystery; it takes all of two minutes.'

'A person's future can be decided in less,' Mrs Quinn philosophized. Then predictably, 'It's a shame you couldn't visit. We could have all watched it together and gone for a little celebration afterwards.' Showing her off.

'You can do that anyway. I must go back to the bathroom, Mother.' She knew better than to mention that she was standing there with only a towel between her and two clear panes of glass in the front door, incongruous replacements within the bowing and cracked mosaic of leaded lights. 'I have to smarten up for Judy. She's coming this evening.'

'I see.' A mistress of the pregnant monosyllable, Olivia's mother conveyed what she saw: that, despite her offer to pay the fare, her invitation had been declined in favour of an evening with a friend. 'Well, as we settle down we'll think of the two of you watching.'

'I shouldn't bother. I'll be meeting Judy at the time.'

'Fancy making you miss the film! We'll record it for you, then you can see it next time you're home.'

'Thanks, but I've just started to rent a video-recorder. According to Equity I can set it against income tax.'

Mrs Quinn laughed. 'That's a good idea. And you'll be subject to tax soon, with many more film parts like this!'

Eighty pounds.

'Is that all? Mervyn picked up two hundred and twenty-five.' Outside the coach station Judy paused beside a bin lapped by the rubbish of other travellers and deposited the gnawed peel of a grapefruit and a crumpled tin of Coke. Unimpeded, they hit the bottom.

Olivia said, 'This was only a morning and it wasn't Central. Mervyn's was a speaking part, too.'

'Don't remind me. One line. You'd have thought it was Hamlet, the fuss he made of it. Look, I argued, given that you have to do it straight, there are no more than ten or twelve ways you could possibly deliver it. "The boss wants to know, Mrs Hinckley, whether you've settled on Passion Pink gloss with a hint of purple on the ceiling or Mirage Mist with a touch of sand on the walls." For example, I told him, you could do it like Brando: "The bors he, ugh, ugh, wanna sorta, ugh ugh, know, ugh, Mrs . . ." '

'Or Gielgud, mellifluously: "The boss wisshshsehes to knooooooooow . . ." '

'Exactly. A pity the actual line was: "I've brought some colour cards for you to choose the paint, Mrs Hinckley," but he enjoyed the anguish.'

'Oh, Judy!' After the past weeks the other's company was refreshing. 'Anyway, I would have enjoyed some anguish. All I had to do was dash out of a house, down the path, slam the gate and disappear up the street.'

'You could have tried one of John Cleese's funny walks.'

'No chance. There was nothing to go on; no character, no situation. Nothing. I was there merely as a look-alike of another woman.'

'Spooky.'

'Not at all. The whole thing was a non-event. They didn't even provide the clothes. I had to wear my own. It's their attempt to jazz up the local news. Pathetic. Some hick producer with no budget but ambitions to film the next John le Carré decides to practise with a sort of down-market "Crime Watch". Did you see any of that series? Well, think of it without the banks of telephones or the operations-room policemen selected by Scotland Yard's casting director for their appearance of integrity and compassion, and imagine it without the research, presenters or important story, and you've got "Mystery of the Week".'

'I can't wait to see it, particularly since your account doesn't square with Alan's. He was in raptures getting the job. Rang me straight away. He must have blown the fee on the call.'

'He had more latitude.'

'Which no doubt he took.' They giggled. 'Why?'

'Because he wasn't representing a named person. When the agency sent in my photograph – Claire was in the office that day – she suggested Alan for the Telecom fellow who's supposed to be the last one to have seen me – the woman. She's called Elizabeth Drew. The casting assistant was only too happy to have another locally based actor since that cut down travelling expenses. Alan could play it more or less as he liked, whereas I had to keep the character neutral otherwise I might have prejudiced the viewers' response.'

'Sounds difficult and hardly worth it for such a crummy programme.'

'A matter of professionalism.'

'I hope it was appreciated. The job's not the kind to attract ecstatic notices, is it? You were just a cipher. Like being part of an identity parade.'

'Not a part; all of it. And that's what I've been saying. I was employed merely in the hope that some people would be reminded of somebody else. Worse than being an understudy. I wouldn't have done it if I hadn't been rotting from inactivity.'

'I know.'

'There's been nothing since last October, Judy. I've been put up for several parts and I write round to remind directors of my existence, after which I can't think of anything more I can do. You were – what? – three months, before this Assistant Stage Manager job came up.'

'Correct. I was beginning to wonder whether I had chosen the wrong occupation.'

'What's the alternative?'

'Haven't you heard the rumour that the theatre's not the only way of earning a living? Or, in the majority of cases, of not earning a living. I've thought that some time we ought to test the truth of it.'

'We both have: waitressing, charring. You did that courier job.'

6

'I'm ignoring those because they're automatic. There are so many out-of-work actors serving bars you'd think bar-tending was an apprenticeship for the stage. If it turns them to drink, it is. No; we should be more imaginative and, as well as that, find some way of cashing in on our talents.'

'You're not suggesting Strippergrams?'

'No, but something along those lines, something where we could go in as actresses, supplying a need. There must be thousands of needs waiting to be tapped.'

'Yeah. Let's think . . . My Aunt Fay used to complain about the necessity to attend parent–teacher evenings. Having five children, she was obliged to turn up at some school or other almost monthly. What about HIRE A MOTHER? We wouldn't have to know anything about the kids concerned but just dress marvellously and flirt with all the male members of staff.'

'You've got it! "RENT-A-MUM . . . and forget those tedious evenings showing a brave face in the school assembly hall. Instead, put your son's future in the hands of England's answer to Jane Fonda." We could offer a real service to women here, Olivia. It's not help with the housework they want because they can find ways of avoiding that; nor is it help with the cooking and ironing because there are always frozen fish fingers and radiators that'll dry a shirt reasonably flat. It's the social chores that are less easy to evade and all the duties to Janet and John's education: cubs and brownies, football and violin, extra French and dancing classes.'

'We could do RENT-A-MUM for school prize-givings, swimming galas, sports days, birthday parties, hospital visits, carol services, school plays.'

'We're on! If ever we're out of work at the same time we'll have a go. Which reminds me. Fran says that Common Weal are looking for jugglers. I thought of you but decided you couldn't meet the requirements: male and black. Quite apart from the fact you can't juggle.'

'That does seem to cut me out, but thanks for the thought.'

'Any time. Olivia, I know you aren't exactly flush at the moment but couldn't we take a bus?'

'There aren't any. Which allows you more leisure to savour the town's distinctive features.'

'I've seen them all before, elsewhere. One town's neglected back streets are pretty much the same as another's. These houses haven't deteriorated naturally, you know; they were specially built like this as suitable habitations for students, first-generation immigrants, one-parent families, supplementary benefit claimants and out-of-work actresses. It's a reproduction of where I live. Apart from the distinctive feature of – don't look round,' she hissed, 'a kerb crawler.'

Though her experience of stage crises was small, Olivia obeyed this directive with the phlegm of an old trouper left holding up the set. 'I hadn't noticed. Why not look?' she demanded.

'I think it's best to seem unconcerned.'

'It sounds to me that you make a habit of this.'

'Formed in France, as a matter of fact. Summer evenings, instead of exercising the dog. Except in some notable areas, I find it less popular in England, don't you? Have you come across this nasty on wheels before?'

'I haven't come across any in this town. Somehow it doesn't seem its style. However, we're only four doors from home.'

'Don't stop. Go past it.'

'Whatever for?'

'Haven't you any sense? So that he doesn't find out where you live.'

'And we walk the streets till he runs out of petrol?' She realized that they were speaking in whispers. 'You're mad, Judy,' she shouted. 'Wonderfully, wonderfully mad. Come on.' Released by the ring of her voice, she grabbed the other's hand and pulled her swiftly along the cracked pavement, round the slumped and rotting gate, up the five feet of path and the four abrupt steps. 'Now give him the two fingers,' she yelled.

Flushed, their shoes rocking on the eroded stone, backs flattened against the creaking glass of the door, they looked down, but the car had gone. Leaving the throb of its engine in their ears and a dryness in their throats.

Olivia opened her handbag and trawled for her key, conscious that she fumbled. Judy said, 'A pity we didn't get his number.'

'I'm not likely to want to look him up.' She felt ridiculous now; the sprint had been childish.

'It would've been a useful check if it happens again. You could report him.'

'You seem to have developed a taste for the sensational.' Her words were pitched to the squeak of the key as she scratched round the lock. 'This is Brick Street – not a tatty thriller.'

Judy sucked in her cheeks and examined the chipped dado along the passage walls, the marble-topped washstand on which stood the telephone, a constellation of finger-marks on its dulled surface. And Olivia thought, she's anxious and I'm snapping, because of a kerb crawler.

'Forget him,' she said. 'Feel like spaghetti lightly smeared with mince? I'm down here, in the basement.'

But as she followed her, Judy added, 'It's significant, isn't it, that we both say "him"?'

'I'll say it is. It signifies the practice of certain men.'

'But neither of us saw. In spite of that, we make the assumption. Which is as sexist as a man's taking it for granted that Nurse Smith is a woman.'

They had reached the bottom of the steps. Above their heads a pane of glass tufted with moss sieved the light.

'Hardly. Have you met any women kerb crawlers?'

'Not as far as I know.' She hesitated as if there were

more she wished to say, but seeing Olivia's hand round the knob of her door she was recalled by her sense of the occasion to: 'I hope you can rustle up a couple of glasses. I've brought a bottle of plonk. Courtesy of our very own artistic director. Or it might have been had he known about it. There's to be a reception for civic dignitaries on Thursday, first night, and I reckon it's stage management's duty to ensure that they don't stumble home to their beds pissed out of their tiny minds. This place would make a marvellous set, Olivia,' looking round the room. 'It's like a crypt. All it needs is a coffin.'

'Don't mention that to Mrs Winterton; she might oblige. I see it more as a dungeon with a few arbitrary mod. cons., i.e. a cooker but no sink; an ironing board but no iron; a kitchen table but no stool. Help yourself to the sofa. It's improved since I extracted its single spring.'

'Thanks. Christ! I can feel you're keeping up with your hobbies. Whenever I'm requested to level up an old settee I ask, "Do you want me to stuff it or gut it?" The latter because of you.'

They laughed and thus the pulse of the car at their backs was silenced.

Much later, at the end of a quite different topic, Judy conceded, 'I don't expect there can be many women stupid enough to invite a man into their car.'

'Judy, stop brooding! Any woman capable of doing that must surely also be capable of looking after herself.'

'I wasn't thinking of quite that situation, though.' She paused, then, 'But yes, I suppose you're right. Which poses the question, am I capable of looking after myself? It was through my giving Alan a lift in the theatre van that the thing with him started.'

Olivia grinned. 'When is he collecting?'

'Half eleven, which is four hours after he wished.

Where do you wash up?' The offer was made not in order to tidy the room but to resist the scurrying time.

To Olivia the crusted soup bowls and plates, the empty bottle, wine glasses and used pans were mementoes of her guest to be hoarded. 'In the kitchen. Tomorrow.'

'In that case, why don't we look at the recording of this "Mystery of the Week"? Round off the evening with some light entertainment.'

'If you insist.'

Switching on the machine she pressed the review button and they peered at the figures tugged backwards across the screen, the limbs jerked in a slapstick race: Alan, his lighted cigarette doused by his companion's match before his feet hauled him to the front of the Telecom van; Olivia, her hair swinging at her nape and heels going like pistons pulled towards them, her hand lifted to a gate which closed loudly before opening for her to back in, her face to them now, intense, and her body sucked up the path and into the front door of a house in which furniture rotated; another face staring; then a wink, more furniture static and polished.

Olivia stopped the tape. 'There you are. You've seen it.'

'Very enjoyable, but I'd like to study the way you bang the gate. Do you mind running it through forward, normal speed?'

'I'll let you have my autograph, too, if you like. I've been practising it for my fans,' but she complied. At last accepting that she must watch herself, Olivia felt her bowels contract as if she were going on stage. Such nerves were incongruous to this fleeting appearance.

'You've seen yourself on video plenty of times,' Judy remonstrated above an advertisement for Unbeatable Bargains in Bedroom Accessories. 'We learned a lot from it, especially in the second year.'

'I shan't learn anything from this except not to do it again.'

'You're not likely to be invited. You can't be many women's double. I'm not taken with this voice-over, are you? I certainly wouldn't choose it as a bedroom accessory however much of a bargain it was.'

Tittering, Olivia felt the muscles relax and was grateful.

The display of bedroom furniture snapped off and the same voice continued, 'Pennine News now brings you "Mystery of the Week".'

'Did they have to use him again?'

'Of course. He's Ron Hawksworth. Never off the job.'

'Well, his talent's thin enough to spread easily. Looks as if they spread the advertisements as well,' Judy observed as, reminiscent of a promotion for brown bread, the title sequence of cobbled streets came up. 'All it needs now is a creaking inn sign. I'm really gripped.'

Ron Hawksworth's voice was intoning, 'This week's mystery centres on the whereabouts of a young girl aged seventeen. Here is a photograph taken several years ago.'

Dropped on a wet cobble, a transparency curled to its shape, expanded, flattened, took on opaque colour and filled the screen as the street disappeared.

'The director's got style,' Judy approved.

'Yes; but no script.'

Information was sonorously listed: her name, the town where she lived, the street where she was last seen, not far from where they sat; while the face regarded them as it had regarded a school photographer four years earlier, suspicious, sullen, defying the camera's eye.

'Had you seen that?'

'No, of course not. I just filmed my bit. They didn't even tell me what she's called.'

The tense privacy of the face accused them; watching, they were associated with its loss.

'He says her name is Rita Dale.'

'Yes,' and Olivia was touched with the useless impulse to lean forward and give the girl hers.

The face receded and its stillness was replaced by a frenzy of whirling objects, the film accelerating to a carousel spin, conveying vertiginous panic, before it slowed down and jumped about the debris of a fractured bedroom, its abrupt cuts suggesting haste; then tracking round more leisurely, the camera closed upon details, nosed out their damage, withdrew but unsatiated returned, no longer recording but engaged in a complicity with the violence of the knife that had sliced into a cushion, with the invasion of the hands upon bras and panties dangling from open drawers.

'Clever but horrible,' Judy gasped. 'You'd have thought her parents would have tidied up before this lot reached it.'

'This isn't their house. It's where she was living with Elizabeth Drew. Here.' The room slid away and a terrace of stone houses took its place.

'It was in this street that the scene you have just witnessed occurred,' Ron Hawksworth stated, underlying the director's intention that they should believe they had seen the actual incident. 'It is thought to be connected with Rita's disappearance. Though there is no evidence, to date, of any attack, there is someone who might be able to help clear up our mystery of the week.'

'It belongs to them, does it? How desperate can you get?'

'Exactly,' Olivia agreed. 'It's their attempt to introduce a little drama into the local news, and I don't suppose they'd get police clearance if what they've shown had any importance.'

The camera had selected one of the houses and was

skidding up a short path towards the front door. It climbed the steps, reached the knocker, then swung down, resting on the ground below like a glance from someone standing on the top step. Because of the slope of the land, the ground floor at the front of the house was four feet above the path and, level with the middle step, the cellar window reflected the weeds not a foot from its glass before descending into a narrow twilit well slimed with leaves.

'Like your place,' Judy remarked.

'They're all the same round here,' and Olivia discovered that she had looked over her shoulder at the dark window behind.

'A Mrs Elizabeth Drew rents this house where Rita lived,' they were told as the camera returned to the door, 'so her assistance could be crucial in the search for Rita.' Just short of being subliminal, RECONSTRUCTION winked on the door as it opened. 'Mrs Drew was seen leaving the house two weeks ago but has not yet returned.'

Olivia came through the door, pulled it closed, checked the lock, walked down the path and round the gate. For a second there was a close-up of the gate swinging home, then a cut to Alan, head raised at the sound, and the camera went back to Olivia hurrying away up the street.

'That was masterly,' Judy congratulated. 'Rather like ghost writing. What shall we call it? Unrecognizable acting?'

'Perfected by an unrecognized actress. I warned you.'

'But I didn't believe you could do it.'

Laughing, they watched Alan shake his head, feel a pocket in his dungarees, walk to the back of the van and accept a cigarette from his mate.

'Nothing unrecognizable about that!' Judy whistled. 'He must have got wind of a new trophy: Walk On Actor of the Year. Let's see him again.'

14

On the second repeat they played it with him; on the third they imitated; by the time they came to the fifth they were taking him off. Their heads snapped up with cartoon suddenness, their eyes widened in pantomime astonishment, their hands squeezed pockets in a burlesque of frustrated search, their fingers grabbed at the proffered cigarette and cupped the match against gales in a parody of nicotine dependence, and they savoured its taste with the critical deliberation of connoisseurs testing a new brand.

While the video-recorder continued with the next programme, the 'Mystery of the Week' past, a mere sequence of pictures, touching or pretentious but inconsequential, their brief impact dissolved by the satire and fun.

'I've a feeling that wasn't quite admissible,' Judy said as they flopped on to the sofa; 'bitching my boyfriend.'

'I thought you'd forgotten.'

'Momentarily.' Judy frowned. 'I hope I was going for the actor, not the man.'

'Is there any difference?'

'Not a lot, but that doesn't worry me.' She shrugged, amused at herself. 'I think he'll relax when he gets work again. Without it, he has to keep reminding himself he's an actor. You're different.'

'Yes. As far as I'm concerned, I'm an actress only when I'm in work.'

'And a good one, Olivia. You'll lose confidence in yourself if you talk like that. You've a profession; it's simply that at the moment you're not engaged in it.'

Olivia nodded, wondering why Judy had chosen to ignore her meaning: that she separated the fictions of theatrical life from the actuality of the everyday.

Which was disrupted by knocking on the front door.

'That'll be him,' Judy said. 'Hell. He'll have your Mrs Winterton complaining if he goes on like that.'

'He won't. She's partisan, and in any case she's away for the week-end. I'm by myself.'

'Sad how years in bed-sits condition you to fear the wrath of landladies,' but she was at the window, peering up the dank shaft, shouting to Alan that she had heard and was on her way, then rushing round the room, picking up handbag, coat, looking for shoes, transforming their quiet into a rattle of departure.

To delay it, Olivia asked, 'Won't he come in for a cup of coffee?'

Shod, one arm sleeved, the other holding back the door, Judy paused. 'He anticipated that and said not. He wants to get straight back to his place. I've only twenty-four hours and he's piqued already by my spending four of them with you. It's worse than if you were a man.'

'Well, thank-you-Alan. But you don't have to humour him.'

'By galloping off? I haven't seen him, either, for five weeks. This isn't humouring Alan, darling; it's lust.'

Outside she crouched on the steps, dangled a hand at the cellar window and shouted, 'Before I depart, I'll give you a ring.'

'Do that. I'm never far from the phone.'

She was the width of her room away, plus twelve rises of cold stone and a causey of warped linoleum, when it sounded. Her sleep ruptured, wisps of dreams still clinging like the warmth of her bed, she rose, passed through the angling light, up a dark tunnel and into the bleached hall. Fuddled, stumbling towards the imperious phone, she felt the moon's presence, flinched at its glitter stinging her eyes, at its shaft pricking her nakedness and, as her hand reached out, she recoiled from its touch stained by its reach through the door's coloured glass and blotching her flesh.

She recited the number and waited. 'That you, Judy?' she asked and, more alert now, wondered at the hour.

'Judy, this is a damned silly time to call.' But already she knew that it was not Judy who had called her.

She waited, hearing nothing in the silent house but her own breaths and the contrapuntal echo against her ear. She waited, shivering under the moon's thrust, and saw transfixed upon the wall the silhouette of her breasts.

For some minutes she stood there, then she lowered the handset. In place again, it had a curious sheen in the moonlight. Because its waist was girdled with sweat.

Chapter Two

It was not until she had removed the sheet from her face and found that the morning's unaccustomed light came from the bedside lamp that Olivia remembered. She had been grateful for the lamp. Once such a light had corralled her against the night ogres of childhood; last night it had blunted the moon's edge and muted the hustling silence of the wire. The action, Olivia told herself, of a pervert flipping through the directory for women listed, dialling and listening, getting a thrill from the alarm in the voice and flesh goose-pimpling under a diaphanous night-gown. The absence of the latter she might mention, if he phoned again; the knowledge would drive him mad. On the other hand, his particular fetish might be of the Mrs Winterton variety, combinations under layers of winceyette. Olivia was pleased that she had not been bothered, but had to admit that, toughened by the bombardment of seventy years, Mrs Winterton might have found the call distressing only because she was denied stuffing her brolly down the man's throat. In her middle years a vigorous and probably just magistrate, she had a direct approach to punishment coupled with a militant defence of citizens' rights. Aspiring muggers fled from her path.

'He caught up with me on my left and began pulling at my handbag,' she had recounted to Olivia, 'but I was carrying my umbrella in my right hand so I swung round and jabbed him in the chest. He didn't like that, the scoundrel, and whined that he was only trying to attract my attention. Such boldness! I pointed out that he'd

18

succeeded and would attract more if he didn't make himself scarce. It is advisable to act promptly and decisively, Olivia; in a tight spot one doesn't waste time asking questions.' Whereas Olivia would have liked to think that she might.

Deflected by the serried roofs, a halting peal of bells summoned the devout. There was no scurry of answering feet outside, but Olivia drew herself higher in the bed, stood a pillow against the headboard and leant upon it in saving pretence that soon she would get up. Such lassitude, with its laboured deceptions, was the main symptom of 'resting', the word which her mother had trilled so gaily, shying away from the question: resting from what or what for. Neither did she think herself inconsistent when she deplored the insecurity of the theatre yet used the gentle and protective euphemism that no other profession had coined. She might even have convinced herself, Olivia thought, that 'resting' was a kind of convalescence from work, while to Olivia and her colleagues it was the other way round.

Watching a blackbird pecking for worms five feet above her, Olivia considered how to occupy the day and decided wryly that, unlike the enviable employed, she could not justify it as one for leisurely recuperation. Many alternatives were closed to her, however: the Monday excitement of reading the Sunday papers in the library; the Wednesday run-through of her latest choreography for trolley and Muzak in the supermarket; the treat in collecting supplementary benefit; the invigorating walk round the museum, a way of keeping fit whatever the weather; the drama of the shift at the actors' agency, soliciting theatres, submitting photographs, checking availability, welcoming a call for a member to join a queue of fifty for an audition, suppressing the old theatrical chestnut, 'Whom do I have to sleep with to get the part?'

In a minute or two she would rise, wash in the

bathroom and dress. Perhaps she should dress first and stoke up the boiler; senile, and low-pulsed despite Mrs Winterton's brisk ministrations, it had probably taken the opportunity to expire in her absence. Resurrection would be sluggish; it could take all morning, after which there might be a few grudging pints of lukewarm water for washing up the previous night's pots. She ought also to wash the yellow sweat-shirt she had worn yesterday evening. There was still a smudge of grease on the sleeve where it had rubbed against the gate, for the cameraman, no doubt flouting union rules, had been liberal with oil to make the hinge move smoothly. The result was a mark on a garment that was almost a second skin. 'Not that again!' Judy had said.

After that, tidying her room, reading, preparing a meal, she would give the day a busyness though prompted by neither interest nor appetite; she would try to ignore that the busyness was artificial, that the difference between a day spent supine in bed and one spent supinely was merely a gesture at activity, feeble and tweaked.

The weeks had no urgency or distinction, the days level without perspective when she was not in a play. Rehearsals and performances did not reduce vitality but increased it, so that then every hour was crammed. Blithe, improvident with pleasures, she would entertain after shows, read until dawn, swim before performances, and bring a sprightly efficiency to mundane tasks. The days had a wholeness then, and so had she. But when there was no work, neither she nor they had substance; she was not entire. It was as if, by working on a part and projecting a character, she discovered her own, what she was capable of, or in what ways she was inadequate. It was a chastening process at times, but always valuable.

Whatever occupation she contrived while she was 'resting', she felt empty. A cipher.

Judy's word. To describe the first part she'd had for six months. Except that it wasn't a part and had provided no stimulus because it had not engaged her. The demands of the programme had prevented that. There had been no text to work on, no situation, no clothes; not even a false eyelash or a touch of blonde rinse. Idly Olivia wondered what she would have done had more been required of her; built on observations of people who knew the woman, she supposed. There must be plenty in the town; the casting director must have found someone with a photograph or able to match Olivia's with the remembered face. The research might have been quite enjoyable, she reflected, slipping out of bed at the thought, like collecting material for an improvised play. Had she been offered more scope, she could have created an interesting role for herself, enough for someone to notice.

'Excuse me,' he began, a finger plucking the newspaper under her elbow.

She pushed the *Sunday Times* across the library table while she turned to the next page of advertisements in *Stage*.

Again the finger approached. It tapped. Olivia looked up.

He examined her face swiftly, the frame of her hair, then blushing, fixed his eyes on the neutral Formica between them. 'I'm sorry to interrupt but I had to speak,' breathless. 'I thought it was you. I saw you on television on Saturday.'

Her first fan! Brown eyes slightly bloodshot, off-white complexion, lantern jaw flecked by clumsy shaving, but transforming the dim lamp above her into a sun making vibrant the drab, patting her shoulders with restoring compliment. The dismissive attitude she had adopted with her mother had no place here.

'Kind of you to mention it,' she said, but it was inadequate appreciation for what he had done for her day.

Shy, as if unprepared for her warmth, he stared down at the table. 'You won't remember me, I suppose.'

He must have been among the clutch of bystanders who had watched, well away from the film unit and outside its magic ring.

'No; I'm afraid I don't. I hadn't much time.'

He nodded. 'That's right. You were generally busy.' Then, in a rush to articulate sentences which might disappear with the courage he had temporarily coerced: 'I didn't visit her often, in any case. Not many did. That's why I'm pleased you're back. Rita's missing, you see. My reason for approaching you like this. They thought you might be able to help.'

Astonished, Olivia felt like an actor wrongly addressed when coming on stage and who has to improvise a correction on behalf of the character not present.

'You've made a mistake. I'm not Elizabeth Drew. What you saw was a reconstruction.'

Somewhere in a back room a librarian keen on economy switched off the lights.

His diffidence was aggravated by her words but with an effort peering, 'You're right,' he stuttered.

'Absolutely. Inside information.'

For a moment he remained sober, then grinned. 'You must think me a fool.'

'Don't push me.'

'No, better not; but I am. Watching the programme, I knew it was a reconstruction, then when I saw you, I thought, She's come back. But by the time I introduced myself I was thinking it was her I'd seen on the box. I can't understand it.'

'You haven't introduced yourself.'

'Stephen Crayshaw. Steve.'

'I'm Olivia Quinn. Am I really so like her?'

He hesitated. 'I ought to say, yes. The features, shape,

colouring – they are all practically identical; but then, as soon as you speak, there's a difference. The vivacity changes everything.'

Through a window she saw the sun glint round a chimney, ready to light up the vivacity. She smiled. 'In that case, I'll have to keep talking.'

'It's true. I wasn't making a pass.'

'I know, but do carry on. Reconciling oneself to flattery is part of the job.'

Embarrassed, he muttered, 'I suppose so.'

To return to *Stage* now would be uncivil; she felt obliged to restore his brief ease. Casting round for a subject for chat, she could think of only one. 'How well do you know her?'

'Mrs Drew? Hardly at all. I can't remember ever speaking to her. She'd be about, but I didn't really want to get into conversation with her. It was Rita I was visiting so I tended to just slide by.'

He looked a natural for sliding by. Olivia's lips twitched. 'Like that, was it?'

'Not really,' he corrected. 'She wasn't the sort of landlady who lurks but I don't think she was overfond of men.'

He seemed an undeserved target for dislike. 'Well, you've managed to speak to her this morning – I'll be as bad as you soon – to her proxy, I should say.'

They laughed. 'Because I'm worried about Rita. I haven't seen her for some weeks, then suddenly there was her photograph on television. It was eerie, like seeing a ghost. I keep telling myself that they are making a lot of nothing; Rita never stays long in one place. But I can't forget that room. I had to switch off. Luckily you came on before I got to the button.'

She wondered why he considered her appearance to be lucky. 'I know nothing more than you.'

'You didn't pick up any theories?'

'They weren't interested in theories; that's for the police, and I was just doing a job: two hours' messing about and thirty seconds of filming. I wasn't included in any discussions, if there were any. I simply did as I was instructed, and as far as the acting went I could have been part of the set.'

'You did fine! Except that I can't imagine Mrs Drew banging a gate. They got that wrong. I think they got something else wrong, too. There was something wrong about the room, but I can't work out what it was. Of course, it's a bit since I was in it so the memory's blurred. The cutting didn't help, either. You were never given an overall view, just details in close-up. It was sickening.'

'Yes.'

They were silent, thinking of the scene.

'I suppose we have to accept that kind of obscenity,' he concluded. 'If something has happened to Rita, then that programme can only do good. People will be keeping their eyes open, looking out for her. I thought of looking, but where? If there's anything you can do, you will, won't you?'

Surprised, she raised a shoulder in negligent assent. 'Of course, but I can't imagine what. I don't know this place or anyone who lives here. At present it's convenient for me to be near my agency; it's a co-operative and we run it in shifts, so it's easier to lodge in the district. When you have work, of course, you move where it is. A case of: have Equity card, will travel.'

He nodded, sympathetic. 'For your sake, then, I hope you move soon.'

Had he been someone from the agency she would have asked, flirtatious, for whose sake would she *not* move soon. To Stephen, however, she murmured acknowledgement and waved to his, 'All the best, then,' as he left her, a strange young man, bashful yet steady, nervous yet firm in condemnation of the programme. It was odd that, clearly no cretin, he should have addressed her as Mrs Drew. Perhaps, tuned to the chance of meeting someone who might help him find

Rita, he had allowed anxiety to translate hope into belief.

She could hear it ringing as she walked up the street and her neck was greased by memories of Sunday bells chiming through the silence of the lifted phone. Repeated and repeated. So she pretended it belonged to a neighbour and lingered by the gate feeling for her key, sure of its place yet letting her fingers prolong the search. But like a petulant child demanding attention the ringing continued then, the door tardily opened, it ceased as she entered the hall.

On the ebb of its sound Mrs Winterton shouted from the kitchen, 'If they would wait, I could lay my hands on it. They stop the minute I get close.'

Along the linoleum footprints in mud indicated how far she had come to proximity. She followed them. Feeling the squeeze of clay under a boot, she bent down, peeled off the lump and dropped it into her pocket. The action was not occasioned by a fleeting interest in cleanliness, Olivia decided, but by a reverence befitting the substance from which they were both derived.

'I'm out at the back,' Mrs Winterton explained and added impishly, 'tilling.'

As usual charmed, Olivia smiled back. 'A pity you haven't more to till.' Six feet of soggy clods under a verdigris elder.

'No. I'm a realist. My ambitions are modest. I wouldn't ask for any more.'

'Did you have a good week-end?'

'A week-end, Olivia, is never good with my sister Dorothy. It is spent listening to tales of woe. In middle age she looked forward to her declining years in the expectation of being cosseted by her adoring husband. Unfortunately he displayed a singular selfishness and died before taking up duty. So she is left to nurse her hypochondria alone and I'm afraid that she hasn't the stamina for it. She has, however, a television set which she calls her life-support machine. In that case, I told her, we must equip her with an alternative in the event of a power cut, and switched it off. The alternative was not the peace I had hoped for; depressing one button merely released another. Dorothy talked all week-end, without ceasing and with a good deal of repetition. With the result that I may consider obtaining a contraption against her next visit. It would stem the flow and allow me to nod off. All this, Olivia, is not to demonstrate that Dorothy's loquacity is contagious but to explain why, though in the presence of a television set, I did not see your brief appearance. How did it look?'

'Adequate, I'd say; which was all I could aim for. It won't bring a job.'

'I suppose not, but you can't be sure. It might bear fruit; large oaks from little acorns grow. Looking back, I'm surprised how often the important things in my life have arisen by accident from what seemed an insignificant event.'

Olivia nodded, aware that she had been contemptuous of similar sentiments expressed by her mother.

'So you mustn't grow down-hearted, Olivia. It may be that being on television has had an effect because people have been clamouring for you all morning. There have been at least five calls,' charitably discounting that any could have been intended for her. 'When you ring your agency, would you please ask them to be a little more patient? Tell them that, if I'm answering the phone, they have to allow for the halt, lame and blind. Being of the theatre, they will be able to imagine that.'

Watching her return to the kitchen, noticing how she fitted her boots into the prints of clay like a child who avoids cracks in the pavement, Olivia reminded herself that the calls might have come from the agency as Mrs Winterton had assumed.

'Yes, we have tried to get you,' Earl answered. 'There's

been an availability check for the Piccolo Theatre for July. I said I'd have to find out whether you are free; that was in order to introduce a hint of healthy competition. They're auditioning in London the end of this week. Will let us know by tomorrow if you're called. I decided it was in nobody's interest to quibble about the short notice, or to ask why they couldn't arrange an audition straight off. She was obviously some timorous little mouse delegated to flick through the files and come up with a list for the director to stab his pin into.'

'What's the play?'

'Sorry; I didn't ask. Miniature, I expect, since it has to fit in that theatre.'

'I don't know it.'

'Neither do I. Another joke belly-flops into the sewer.'

'Oh, I see. Sorry.'

'I can take it, dear, wiping the egg yolk off his face. You're rather short on enthusiasm, Olivia. I know this check isn't the most marvellous thing that could happen, but it's better than nothing.'

'Yes.'

'Feeling neglected?'

Mrs Winterton had said that the telephone had rung five times. 'A bit.'

'My shoulder's free for crying upon.'

'Thanks, Earl.'

'Good. Unfortunately I'm playing squash tonight but do you fancy tomorrow? If you starve till then you might be able to face one of Greasy Len's hamburgers.'

'All right. I'll slot it into my appointments diary. Earl, did you call me about anything else? I've been at the library and my landlady was out in the back yard. The person always rang off before she could reach the phone.'

'We'll have to remember that. Yes, I have another item to report, ma'am, clicking his heels. It's rather odd. The parents of that girl who's missing have been on asking if they could have your number. They were given this one by Pennine News. I didn't know what the policy is on that, but Alan had popped in – our very own strong, decisive though slightly muscle-bound Alan after a day with the nubile Judy – and he whispered instructions. So I didn't give them your number but agreed to pass on a message. They're anxious to speak to you. How's it feel to be an instant celebrity?'

'Not so hot. Why should they want to speak to me?'

'I don't know; they didn't say. More precisely, the father didn't. It was him on the line, and a man of few words, somewhat uptight. Not one to give much away.'

'I don't feel like ringing him.'

'You can't do that, anyway. He only left the address: 24 Cattlegate, near the glue factory, which figures.'

'Does that mean that he is asking me to visit them? I can't possibly. What would be the use?' Stephen had said, If there's anything you can do, you will, won't you?

'*Use*? How do you mean, use? I assumed that he wished to thank you for taking part in the film.'

'That wasn't to do him a favour. And he could have said that to you, couldn't he? I've no wish to go round and collect.' Her voice had leapt higher, tight with control.

'Now careful, love; it's not a summons from Peter Hall. Ignore it. I told him it was unlikely that you'd have the time.'

That really was a joke. 'Thanks, Earl,' she said, but without bitterness.

'All part of the service: protecting our stars from the public. Only please don't do the same for me some time.'

'I promise. Has anything else come through?'

'Isn't that enough for one morning? Must return to the typewriter. Be with you tomorrow evening. About eight?'

'Yes.' If Earl had tried to speak to her only twice, then the caller's total had reached yesterday morning's fig- ure, but she could not ask him to recall the number of attempts he had made. The request would oblige her to give reasons for it and she would not be able to conceal her conviction that she was the person's deliberate choice. She did not wish to hear herself say that. Describing the silence on the telephone, giving it an intention, would grant it, like a character on stage, a definite substance; it would be fleshed out, truly exist.

'Look, Olivia,' his voice was saying, 'I wish you'd co-operate. I'm trying to put this down but I can hear you thinking. On the count of three, girl, will you please replace the handset. And forget the father. He must be going frantic, I imagine, but that doesn't oblige you to sit and hold his hand. It's not as if "Mystery of the Week" is a popular series and you have to be nice to the fans. In the circumstances, I should ignore it. Curtain. One, two . . .'

The circumstances were a girl disappeared and a father going frantic.

Cattlegate was a street of corroded houses, windows nailed close against the rattling gusts and the stench of the factory behind. Doors, their thresholds elevated by precipitous steps, opened straight on to the pavement divided into unstaked but confidently held strips in which were set a pram or a tricycle, a plastic rack for milk bottles, a wheelchair, boot scrapers or tubs sprouting flowers. Number 24 had a window-box screwed to its sill and an iron handrail to assist the feeble up the two steps. Olivia held it as she listened to the movements startled by her knock. The door opened, offering a stripe of face.

Across the anchoring chain Olivia said, 'I understand that you've been trying to get in touch with me. I'm from On Cue – the actors' agency. Olivia Quinn.'

The woman frowned. 'Oh, yes. I thought for a minute it was her. I've been hoping ever since that programme, but nothing's come of it. He's in the bathroom.' Her gaze lifted over the other's shoulder and her lips puckered as if she were trying to work out what she should do.

Embarrassed, Olivia considered offering to visit again later, and not go back, but the woman recalled civility and began fiddling with the chain.

'You'd better come in. I'll go and fetch.'

The room was the 'best' one, the show-piece for strangers, preserved in polish and sealed from the odours and steam of the kitchen at its back. The arms of the three-piece suite were covered in sleeves which, matching the upholstery, camouflaged the wear, and the empty grate had been stuffed with paper then concealed by a screen. A plastic vase containing artificial flowers stood on the sideboard between two photographs: Mrs Dale younger, shivering under scarves, one hand clutching a bouquet and the other hooked through the arm of a man already balding who had raised his chin to receive the camera, and was sombre and stiff; the other photograph was of an earlier period and a different man. Dressed in the uniform of the Royal Artillery, he lounged on a bench outside a pub and his dishevelled hair, his hand flourishing a bottle and his laughter were the only source of vivacity and spontaneous enjoyment in that circumspect room.

'Reginald Dale,' the first man introduced himself, pushing his wife in front of him and proffering his hand. 'Please sit down.'

They sat opposite each other, separated by the screened hearth. Mrs Dale stood by the window and twitched the curtains, snagging the net. His glance moved her to a straight-backed chair by the door and she sat tensely like someone waiting to be summoned.

'She's not herself at the moment,' he said. 'She's very upset. You must excuse her. No one cared for a daughter more than Mrs Dale.'

There was a sniff from the chair. Olivia dared not look.

'She'll pull herself together, given a bit of time. It's no

good pining. Better to square up, occupy herself, not moon about waiting for news. It could be weeks before that comes, if it ever does, and she must prepare herself for the worst. That's sensible.'

Horror dried her mouth; her breath stopped. Sensible to anticipate Rita's death. That's what he's saying, Olivia told herself, and aloud managed: 'She'll turn up.' But, coming in a whisper, the words confirmed his and drifted across the room tidied for mourners.

'If she does, then we shall be the more thankful. But it's wise not to rely on it. We know what that can lead to.' His eyes were on Olivia but she knew he was addressing his wife. Finished, he looked quickly towards the straight-backed chair, his expression a warning.

She wanted to get away. She couldn't think why she had come. She had expected anxiety, not this resolute denial of life. It was grotesque and chilling.

'I must go,' she said.

'The young man in the office said you were busy.'

She waited, giving him time to explain why he had wished to meet her. Soot in a damp flurry grazed down the wad of paper and splattered over the hearth.

'It's raining,' he said. 'I'll get an umbrella.'

He had gone before she could prevent him. Standing by the door, she had to speak to the wife. 'I'm sorry about Rita.'

'You're an actress, aren't you? Rita always says she doesn't know how they can do it, up on a stage.'

After the man's conviction, the change of tense was shocking; it was like the resuscitation of a corpse. Grasping the knob, Olivia tugged at the door but it was damp and would not budge.

'She can have her room again any time,' Mrs Dale went on, her voice almost inaudible as if engaged in a private chant. 'The bed's always made, she knows that, I've told her often enough. There's no need for her to go elsewhere. Nobody can replace a mother.' The final sentence was an appeal.

Mesmerized, Olivia found herself shaking her head.

'Of course not,' the other agreed, satisfied. 'You're supposed to look like her, aren't you? I wouldn't know about that but I can tell that's as far as it goes. You wouldn't do it, but we can comfort ourselves that in the end folk get their deserts. All the same, I have to admit that Rita is very impressionable.' She faltered at the last word, rolling it in her mouth as if practising a new description.

It was meaningless raving but Olivia could not stammer out palliatives; they were stopped by 'get their deserts' and the accompanying malice in the woman's face. She pulled at the door.

'I've found you an umbrella,' the man said over her shoulder. 'There's no need to return it. Mother and me have got ours.'

She was trapped. She couldn't get out. She was in a set where all the doors were locked and, with lines used up and role completed, she was forced to continue the scene.

'I'll manage, thank you.'

'It's a bit on the common side, to my way of thinking, but it's in good condition, almost brand-new,' and he opened the umbrella out. The flare of scarlet dotted with yellow trefoils challenged the room. 'I'd like you to have it.'

Unable to escape, she turned, saw the pleading and, no longer practical, the uncovered grief.

'It belonged to Rita.'

And she recalled from a decade earlier a friend's death and she, not yet eleven, sent to visit at the mother's request. They had sat without speaking; there was nothing to say. Until finally the woman had given her a ring. 'You recognize it? I'd like you to have it. Now you may go.' It was as though Olivia's visit had brought her for the last time near the dead girl and, seeing this other to the door, stroking her arm with an absorbed obsequial gesture, she had bad her daughter farewell.

'Thank you,' Olivia said.

But out of the house, with another street between them, Olivia let down the umbrella she had obediently unfurled and allowed the rain to wipe across her face. For she had not been Rita's friend; she had never known her, their only connection a woman Olivia resembled and had represented in a two-minute film. She had never met this girl whose father was prepared for her death. That was preposterous; there was no suspicion, no hint.

The rain was coming faster. It bounced on her cheeks, filled her hair and washed along her throat. Vigorous, assertive, it repulsed the joyless sepulchral place she had just left and drew a response from her flesh. Then she was running, running as she had that day from Pam's mother, feeling the spring of muscles, knowing the race of blood, assured by the pumps of her breath; because she was alive, licked by the rain, flushed by the swirling air, her feet gliding over tarmac and her eyes brushing colour over the damp sepia streets.

She ran without slackening, given over to sensation, unimpeded by Rita's umbrella wedged in the crook of her arm, oblivious of strollers and shoppers and school-children. And taking vitality from the rain and combing draughts, she was surprised and elated by a purpose which began to flicker in her mind.

So she had reached the door of her lodgings and had inserted the key before she heard the car. Without turning her head she listened to it idle for a second then pass on.

Chapter Three

'You're crackers!' From anyone else, the sentence would have expressed astonishment or disapproval. Alan made it into a statement of fact.

'Gives me something to do.'

'So would bug hunting.'

She could not understand why Judy went for him. It could only be his beautiful body – alleged. Had she known it was Alan she was speaking to she would not have mentioned it; but when she came in from her search Mrs Winterton had been holding the telephone, and her greeting, 'It's that nice young man from the agency' had been such a relief that she had rushed straight in with: 'Earl, remember that Rita Dale? Well, I've begun to look for her.' She had forgotten it was another day, Alan on rota.

'With about as much sense,' he added.

'Perhaps I'm not sensible.' Not in the way the father suggested. 'Any news your end?'

'Have you really blown your mind? This is an actors' co-operative, not a bloody detective agency.'

She grinned at the misunderstanding. 'A brilliant deduction, my dear Watson. I was thinking along those lines myself. Heard from the Piccolo?'

'Not yet; but if nothing comes through by five I'm going to give them a ring. They should have let us know before now if they want to see you on Saturday, which is a bloody silly day to audition anyway. Apparently the director's in Edinburgh the beginning of this week, so he can't start auditions till Thursday.

Anybody would think actors don't qualify for a week-end's leisure.' As if many of them would not have enjoyed that all week! 'They should have phoned earlier. It's Tuesday, for God's sake.' Alan the high-powered tycoon. She wondered whether the City were conscious of its loss.

'I think they'll have a calendar, Alan.' When he tele-phoned them, however, he would make a switch. She had heard him: cool, businesslike and discreetly flatter-ing, practising his young but immensely experienced civil servant, executive grade. 'All the same, I'd be glad to know, but their silence almost certainly means that they have decided not to call me.' She felt less forlorn than usual. Six months' disappointments must have anaesthetized the nerves.

'That's no excuse.' He paused. Olivia sighed. Some crummy director had once told him to count out his pauses and she could hear him now – on his fingers. 'Heard anything from Judy?' he finally enunciated his line.

'No. It was only Saturday that she was here.' She would have liked to add, 'Remember?' Alan was the sort of man you were under contract to provoke.

'I thought you two were in touch. Constantly.'

'You know, Alan, there are two large panes of clear glass in this front door. They aren't as nice as the leaded lights that fell out but they do allow an uninterrupted view of the hall where I'm standing.'

'What?'

'So all you have to do is run over, take a peek and check.'

'You don't have to be offensive. All I asked was . . .'

'Whether I'd heard from Judy and the answer was, no. That didn't merit a sarcastic comment.'

'You're being very touchy, Olivia. Sorry I inquired. All I wanted to know was whether she had got back to base safely and you are the obvious person to ask.' The waspish tone had been smothered in diplomatic urbanity. 'When she rings you, would you mind asking her to telephone me?'

'I don't expect she'll ring. It's a busy week. You know very well that it's her first night on Thursday. Anyway, she's on the phone.'

'Yes, technically. The theatre doesn't like private calls, however, and she was in the bath or something when I rang her place last night. Also this morning. Very devoted to personal hygiene, at the moment, is Judy.' The laugh was forced.

'You're not telling me you've had a row?'

'You'd like that, dear, wouldn't you? But don't waste your powers of detection on us. You'll need them all for little Rita Dale, God help her,' and the handset clattered down.

Judy had said that he had been cross because she wouldn't go straight to his digs on Saturday; now that for some reason she was avoiding him, he was venting his frustration upon Olivia. He was blaming their friendship and suggesting that she desired the undivided attachment that he claimed for himself. Still holding the telephone, Olivia felt his spite stitch along her arm as the wire burred on, not silent but, again, wordless. When she replaced the handset she found it necessary to wipe it upon her sleeve.

Down in her room she hung up her jacket, stood Rita's umbrella in a basin to drip, and made herself a cup of tea. By these small unremarkable tasks normality was resumed, and sitting under the submerged window with its ragged canopy of weeds, she considered the day. It had begun well, pulling her out of bed by the skid of the paper boy's boots, whisking her into the bathroom with a teasing intention, rinsing sleep from her eyes with the reminder of what that was. It had not mattered that she had no idea how to carry it out. It had not mattered that the light, rusted by rain, dropped into the basement and dulled her clothes' individuality and colour as she dressed. It had not mattered that she could not brush off the mud from her denims still damp from the previous day or that her trainers remained sodden and she had to go out in pumps. It had not mattered that the task seemed impossible, that the inquiries which now occurred to her: at bus station, Job Centre, to neighbours, would already have been made. All that mattered was that she leave her basement room, climb up into this town which she had never bothered to explore or be more than casually acquainted with, and begin her search.

And unbelievably, not expecting a reward, she had received one.

Approaching the bus station and trying to calculate how long it would take to speak to every driver – number of drivers employed (unknown) times frequency of shifts – she heard the rap of stiletto heels behind her and a panted, 'Hi!'

Olivia turned to a girl who, blushing, dropped the hand outstretched to detain her. 'Sorry,' she said and made to pass on. 'I thought you were a friend.'

Another mistaken recognition. 'Do I resemble her from behind as well?' she demanded.

Halted by Olivia's astonishment, the other echoed, '*As well*? You aren't like her at all. I wouldn't have thought anything about the pumps and denims – hers are generally mucky – if it hadn't been for the umbrella.'

'It isn't mine. Wait a second.' She had to adjust. 'Look, are we talking about Rita Dale?'

'Who else do you think you might look like from behind? You a friend of hers, too?'

'I haven't met her, but I was lent this umbrella. Do you know that she's missing?'

'Do you mean missing proper or just bunked off?'

'I'm not sure. I want to find out.'

'Why're you so interested? You're not from the DHSS, are you?'

'No. I've never been invited across the counter.'

The girl smiled. 'You sound like Rita. I don't see how you've got her umbrella if you don't know her.'

Karen herself did not know Rita well; their acquaintance was limited to random meetings in a pub: 'You know how it is, recognize a face you remember from school and you wave and maybe have a quick chat if there's nothing else doing.' This casualness had affected their conversation; interrupted by pedestrians weaving round them, abbreviated by Karen's need not to miss a bus, it was disconnected and superficial. Under the sheltering umbrella, recollections would begin strongly then drift, refracted by the rain. Accustomed to seeking even in the most circuitous dialogue the movement towards its goal, Olivia, as she sat in her room and squinted up the dim shaft, tried to give their talk coherence.

Rita always seemed happy enough and the mention of Stephen had brought a laugh: he was one of God's own worriers. As far as Karen knew, he'd never been Rita's boyfriend, not properly, and she didn't need him to fuss. Karen reckoned she was all right now. The question, 'Now?' had been answered by a tart, 'She's got her own place, hasn't she?' followed by wariness. Karen didn't like to say, but she reckoned there might have been some bother. Rita was upset one night and got drunk. No, she didn't know anything about the state the house had been left in, sharply reminding Olivia that she hadn't watched 'Mystery of the Week'. 'Do me a favour! It's the disco down at the Palace on Saturday nights. You took off her landlady, did you? So why're you asking me?'

This latter question was repeated at the Job Centre, an assistant inquiring suspiciously why, if Olivia wanted to know what her friend was up to, she didn't ask her herself; and bus drivers, bolting for cover in the form of a tea break, mumbled, 'Never look at a face, love; I've got enough on my plate watching the traffic and seeing to tickets. The inspector's your man.' Who said, after two hours' invigorating warm-up jumping the routes, 'Your best bet is to ask your friend's mum, love. She'd know.'

'Why didn't you say you were a journalist?' Earl asked as they waited for Len to grease a hamburger. 'People love to think they're going to be in a story. They'd have talked, whether they knew anything or not.'

'No doubt. But fantasies won't solve the problem.'

'Not solve it, no; but they might by chance give you a line as you sift through. It's not so far from the way we work sometimes, is it? Particularly if there's not much in the part. We find a possibility and fill it out. Some even start from the clothes. God knows what they do if they're playing Adam.'

She laughed. He had not said she was crackers. 'I'm after a situation, not a character, Earl, and I'm not playing one, either. As a matter of fact, that's why I didn't pretend to be a journalist; I did consider it. But somehow I didn't feel the part.'

Earl rolled his eyes and took another sip of his beer. 'Olivia, you don't have to *feel* a journalist when all you have to do is ask a few questions. "Good afternoon. Would you mind giving me a moment? I'm from the *Gossip* and I'm investigating the disappearance of a young woman from a house in Hackney Street. I should like to ask you a few questions. You'll find them absolutely painless and you don't have to bother about details such as fact and truth; I'll see to all that. You may remain perfectly anonymous if you prefer because that's at the discretion of the editor." If you *felt* it, Olivia, you'd be doing more than the journalists themselves.'

'Cynicism is not permitted. You're supposed to have a spontaneous, natural and trusting approach to life, remember. It was simply that I doubted whether I could do it, just cold, striding in, especially after yesterday.'

She had already told Earl of her visit to Cattlegate.

He winced. 'That was disgusting.'

'Yes, but . . . thinking about it, what Mr Dale said seems so bizarre that I can hardly believe I got it right. He did talk in exactly the way I've told you but it wasn't really to me but to his wife, as if he were telling her more than she must not rely on Rita's being found. And he was holding something back. That makes me wonder if he were trying to suggest something quite the opposite when he gave me the umbrella. Do you suppose he did in the hope that it might lead me to Rita? It's collected one friend, sort of, already.'

'That's too far-fetched. OK for a pot-boiling thriller to pull in the coachloads but people don't behave like that in real life. You didn't think that at the time.'

'Because it reminded me of Pam's mother.'

'Right, so trust your instincts. As I'm supposed to do.' They grinned.

'All the same, I think I shall go back.'

'To that loony bin?'

'Ostensibly to return the umbrella, but I should be less agitated the second time; I shall be prepared. So I may be able to get the family line on Rita.'

'You might. And that's the right way to express it because their line won't be the only one.' He groaned, shading his eyes with a fist. 'Imagine what my lot wouldn't say about me!'

'That's if they knew it all. Loyalty would keep them quiet, wouldn't it? As it does my mother. In this case though, I might learn a lot from what they don't say.'

'But you won't find the girl that way, Olivia. As you've

said, you're after a situation and that's character stuff. Which could get at you. Sure you can cope?'

He was still puzzled by her inability to play a journalist. Soon he would make the connection. Quickly, because she was not ready for that, she evaded. 'Now who's going over the top? Anyway, tomorrow night I may find out where she is. I'm meeting some of her mates in a pub. Karen turned up again, mid-afternoon, leaping off a bus as I lay in wait for its driver. "That was a real crappy interview," she announced, " 'bout fitted the job, but I'll take it if offered. I'm sick of living like money had gone out of fashion, though why I sweated for five O levels just for packing boxes, you tell me. Him who saw me couldn't. But coming back, when I'd finished working out what would be left after my stamp and that, I had a think. About Rita. It's a bit of a mystery, in' it? I'll ask round. We'll be in the pub tomorrow night, the Gate, by the market. Come if you want. Might as well. You never know what you might pick up. Only not Wayne. He's mine." '

'Shall you go?'

'Yes.'

'I hate to sound discouraging, Olivia, but isn't this a job for the police?'

'I suppose it is, but they don't seem to have got very far, do they? They haven't been questioning Rita's friends. Karen didn't even know she had disappeared.'

'They may not consider there's a case to be investigated. That "Mystery of the Week" seems to have dealt with a totally spurious piece of news. If there were anything in it, the police would have started looking not only for Rita but for the landlady as well, and the Dales would have been told. They would have to have a reason for beginning a search, one that was worth the use of police time.'

'That's not a commodity I'm short of.'

'It's not the time you may spend on it that worries

me,' but he did not ask her to justify her decision. 'Len's signalling. No, you sit tight. I'll collect.'

The day's Hot Rod Hamburger came with lashings of diesel oil, a washer of carbonized onion and a mesh of burnt chips. Earl stripped his down with the tissue provided and added mustard to weaken the taste. 'I can't take it straight,' he told her. 'That would be flying in the face of nature.' The joke, however, was automatic to fill in a pause.

'You may ask me,' she said. After his patience it was unfair to hold out.

'Not if you don't wish. I'll just put it down to stage fright, off stage.'

'It was because I couldn't do it like that. It was too . . . artificial. It didn't fit.' The meat was tough; it had to be chewed so much it blocked off the breath. 'I couldn't frame the questions in a way a journalist would have done, with that kind of prodding inquisitiveness. I could only inquire as if I were a friend.' She had said it. She had admitted it to them both.

Earl made a pass at his hamburger, snapping chips. 'And you've never met her. Well, I'm hardly the one to comment on that. It's extraordinarily emotional but,' he shrugged, 'so be it.'

'I feel I must find her.'

'I hope not in order to contradict her father's ghoulish prediction.'

Earl is sharp, she thought; never misses a trick. 'No; at least, not entirely. That accentuated a feeling already there, though I had tried to dismiss it. Probably that's why I visited them. I can't account for this, but I feel committed, and not in a rational way. How's that for a piece of sloppy professionalism? Do wonders for my acting, this will, won't it?'

'Stop that, Olivia.'

'It's the whole thing: that memory of Pam, and the mother suddenly hissing that people get their deserts —

42

Heaven knows what she meant – and Alan bitching over Judy. They all have the same effect on me. It doesn't matter to me whether the police think there is a case to investigate, Earl. I can't pay attention to quibbles like that. Because I feel as if something very vulnerable and fragile is under attack and I must save it. I feel drawn in. Ever since making that film I've felt drawn in, though I pretended that I didn't. Two hours' work, Earl, the first time I've earned money in six months, and this is what it does to me!'

'Well, you might say, dear, you've got more than your money's worth. I've never been lucky enough to get a non-speaking part that gave me all this lovely passion, gratis,' playing camp. His facetiousness was deliberate and, because he was Earl, it did not pain her. The mask he had chosen had a chink; anxiety peeped through.

She nodded. 'I'll try,' meaning: try to steady up.

'Good.' He staked a chip on a tine of his fork and began carefully, 'Talking of films . . . Raymond came into the office yesterday and told me about that bit part he had with Granada. Would you like to hear? OK. It is rather choice. I told him it was absolutely made for his next circuit of the clubs, but he brushed that aside. Ever since Granada spotted him and gave him that small part as a bruiser, he's had the bug. As he confided, he wants to concentrate on going straight. Seems a perverse ambition for a stand-up comic, but there we are. All he had to do – one episode in the series – was walk up to a VIP who's just alighted from a train and say, "Welcome home, Fred." Fred being a local lad who's made good, is now an international name and is returning from some celebration, so he's being met by civic dignitaries, brass band, etc. Our Raymond, luckily without mayoral chains, is one of the welcoming party.

'The week before the take he assured wardrobe that

43

he had an appropriate suit, and the night before he went into training for stardom by limiting his ale intake to five pints and rejecting the overtures of his missis so that he was not, as he said, played out on the day. Isn't he gorgeous? The call was for nine o'clock on Huddersfield station. Arising in good time, he took down his suit on which he had not laid a hand since he got wed fourteen years ago. "But you've got a fifteen-year-old daughter," I protested. "She came a bit before," he defended. And before ale and laughs in working men's clubs. Because, as you will have guessed, the suit didn't fit. However, the trousers had been on the big side, so a discreet snip at the waistband sorted them out, and the jacket didn't look too bad if he left it unfastened. The waistcoat, though, was more problematic, but Raymond and Mrs Ray aren't a couple to be defeated by a four-inch gap. They simply transferred that to the back. She sliced up the back seam, he buttoned up the front and she stapled the open edges to his shirt. Thus costumed, Raymond sallied forth.

'It took him some time to get into Huddersfield station, of course. He hadn't reckoned with the amount of parking space a television unit takes up. Neither, I suppose, had the innocent public. In the end he slipped his car into a place reserved for the disabled and got past a policeman by dragging a paralysed leg. So he was only twenty minutes late. Fortunately the brass band were complaining about the acoustics, so nobody noticed. The rehearsal went perfectly. The fanfare started up; the home side shambled down the platform; the assistant director stepped down from a stationary train; Raymond moved forward, grasped his hand and bellowed his line. He did it to perfection, he told me. They were all over him. According to Raymond it is very unusual for anyone to sustain such a line without making a fault or even forgetting it. He was insistent about that. Further rehearsal was deemed unnecessary and the cast was given an hour to cool down. Raymond managed to evade the close inspection of the wardrobe mistress by warning her that she'd provided the chap playing the mayor with the wrong sort of chain, signed three girls' autograph books in the name of Charles Bronson, borrowed a stapler from property, performed running repairs in the lavatory, joined the party in the snack bar and consumed six polythene beakers of British Rail tea. That was, sad to say, his undoing. Raymond was very insistent about that. When the gut's used to beer, it's dangerous to change. That can upset the chemical stability of the whole organism, in which generous bulk Raymond includes his head.

'The call came for the take; the sheet was removed from the red carpet; banners were dusted; the brass band negotiated a note; the welcoming party lined up; the director retreated; the cameramen adjusted their sights and the train inched into the station. Fred and his entourage had been put on at Leeds and though it was impossible to disguise their business from the legitimate passengers, they had been asked to ignore what was happening and to alight in their usual fashion from the train. It pulled up. The crucial coach was opposite the civic party. They slid forward. The door of the coach swung open. Raymond strode across, grabbed the chap's hand, pumped it heartily, leered into the camera and recited, "Welcome home, Fred." "I appreciate the thought, mate," the other answered, "but the name's Sam." '

It was many minutes before Earl could continue. His story relaxed tensions and their laughter was wild and anarchic. Customers glad of the respite from chewing turned in their chairs and stared. One shouted, 'Let's all share the joke.' Grateful, loving Earl for such restoration, Olivia put her arms round his shoulders and gently butted his head.

'So they had to take it again,' he concluded. 'They had to ferry Fred and his party back to Leeds and put him on another train; they had to keep the brass band on for another three hours; they had to pay the whole cast for another half-day. Must have cost a bomb. And do you know what Raymond said? That it was pretty good, having only the two takes, because some actors are so thick it's necessary to do it over and over again, whereas, come tea-time, they had finished. Unfortunately he didn't manage to get in a word about future engagements; the director was busy and kept waving him off but he's confident he'll get more. Apparently the casting secretary when approached admitted that she had liked the way he had moved. Incorrigibly.'

And they were shrieking again. Finally Olivia gasped, 'But Ray can't be serious?'

'That's the trouble. You're never quite sure whether he is or not. He went through all that with a completely straight face while I was creased up. So he's left us to think that he might really expect he'll get more work after that, just as he's left us undecided whether the joke is on him or on us. He ought to keep to the clubs; he's wasted anywhere else. Now I'm going to buy you another beer and then you're going to tell me what you've chosen to take for audition on Saturday.'

She had not yet decided; the call had reached her late that afternoon. Then, tired by her unsuccessful quest and trying to coerce a utility in Karen's invitation, she had been stirred to nothing more than a limp interest, inquiring about the London trains, ordering the ticket with the agency, repeating a routine which was as stale and dispirited as the hope. Earl had altered that; he had made her laugh; he had re-established a perspective in which the occurrences of the last three days shrank to a manageable size.

So now as she sat at the table, Earl waiting at the counter which Len called his bar, she anticipated with more enthusiasm the Saturday audition, its brief replication of an appearance on stage, and she felt the characteristic excitement which was a paradox of enjoyment and fear. The occasion became not a useless chore but a pleasure generous with promise, creating a condition in which both her own problem and that of Rita could be resolved. For the day's energy had been wrestled from the hold of her private dejection; now it sprang up without restraint, it rippled with optimism and sparkled her brain. As stretching back, she contemplated the audition, she was eager also to renew her search. No longer was she noosed by the father's behaviour. She was capable, ready; she winked across at Earl and smiled at the attentive customers. She no longer blanched at the memory of Alan's spite.

Neither did she blanch when the man caught her eye. He was sitting alone at a táble, a large man, one hand clenched by the side of an empty plate. Unaccompanied, isolated from the talk and clatter, he swilled the beer round his glass then drank from it mechanically without removing his look from her face. And struck by his slumped loneliness, by his appearance of having been cast off, Olivia had smiled and nodded before she had registered the quality of his stare.

He was up immediately, the abrupt lunge causing the table to rock and his chair to sway then snap obediently straight at the thrust of a knee, which in a second had jabbed at a leg of the table she occupied, upon which were crunched two red, knuckled fists. Jerking back, Olivia heard the smack of her shoulder against the unplastered wall and saw his thrill at her pain. 'You bitch,' he sneered.

She was aware of silence and halted movement, of a film stopped and holding postures incomplete which gradually uncoiled as the reel resumed, bringing people towards them but slowly, languorously, arms outstretched but floating, delicate in a mockery of haste. While gasses of grease and beer smothered, adding the words: 'Filthy cow' and '. . . tell us what they do.' Then the fists scraped back, the face shot up, the chest was hooped in ridged arms and Len was whispering, 'Right, mate, the door's open. When I put you down, you're out of here in one second flat,' followed by curses, the scratch of shoes on tiles, the crash of stools, the thud of a slammed door, Len's face telling her the man had been seen to, Earl holding her hand, murmurs of sympathy, the dawdled retreat and resumption of talk speculative and curious in which everyone shared.

'I was paying, so I didn't see,' Earl told her. 'Len did, though. He pushed me back and vaulted over the counter as if it were a five-bar gate. Incredible. Wonder if anyone from Granada spotted it.'

She tried to smile but her lips described the imminence of tears.

'I heard what he said, though. I'm sorry. You got what should have come to me.'

She shook her head.

'Yes. It's happened before. Some men are quite sincerely revolted; they say it's not natural, rationalizing a kind of primeval fear. Which is a laugh, isn't it? When they are just sufficiently inhibited not to insult me, they spit their venom over the girl.'

'He wanted to know what you did.'

'Exactly. A pity you didn't have time to explain.' His grin cajoled but she could not respond. 'I haven't heard it put quite like that before, but it's the usual assumption – that blacks are permanently and gigantically tumescent.'

'I wouldn't know about that,' trying to giggle.

'That's better.' He put his arms round her. 'Sorry I can't oblige.'

'That's twice you've apologized for nothing.'

'I meant it both times, Olivia. You're the nearest any woman has come to causing me regret.'

'Regret! Don't say that, Earl. Not tonight.'

For tonight it was harder to be forsaken. She needed his warmth, his body tucked round hers, shutting out the sight of the man's face. And as he kissed her cheek, there in view of Len and the rest of his customers, the tears finally gushed. Because she was the wrong sex.

Chapter Four

It had been ridiculous to behave like that, Olivia repri-
manded herself over breakfast. Her feelings for Earl had
stabilized months before when she had finally accepted
his preference. Silently, because she did not wish him
to suspect a hope that he had never encouraged. So an
infatuation that might have developed into an emotion
more solid had passed into a friendship generous and
almost as affectionate as any she had. However, it
seemed that the pangs of love had not been entirely
quietened, she acknowledged satirically; they could
produce the occasional twitch. For the previous evening
she would have staked everything – their unspoken
agreement and friendship – to have brought him to her
bed. Which astonished her. She had no desire for intimacy with Earl.

'Even were that offered, I wouldn't want it,' she had
once confessed to Judy. 'Kissing, the usual touching, is
fine, but merely the thought of anything more fills me
with disgust. It's the idea of men with him that bugs me.
I'm as bad as the population at large.'

Judy had laughed. 'In this instance I'd stay with them
since an attempt at seduction would definitely be a
waste of time! You're disappointed, that's all; a touch
of sour grapes. I imagine you'd be just as much bugged
by the idea of a woman with him.'

But Olivia had not agreed.

Ten hours earlier she had not felt squeamish; she had
wanted him to help her through the night. It was a
simple need, the urgency to repair self-valuation splin-

tered by the man's words, to prove that despite them she was desirable. Again she was astonished. She had been harassed before, and though never so viciously or in such terms, she was dismayed by this episode's effect. It was like a physical assault, and Earl's explanation had heightened not soothed the bruise.

She was disappointed in herself. Her reaction to the man had been his success; his power had been endorsed by the sight of her fear. But, shocked, she had been unable to summon a detachment. As she looked back, the whole evening had the tempo of a cardiograph's needle describing a feverish pulse. She must cure this; there was the audition on Saturday. For which she must rehearse her pieces, be calm and relaxed.

Olivia finished her breakfast, stacked the crockery on a tray by the electric fire, collected towel and clothes. She knew that the most valuable preparation for Saturday would be to find Rita Dale.

On the landing Mrs Winterton met her with: 'I think I should mention, Olivia, that our telephone is very popular suddenly, even allowing for agency business. Someone called three times while you were out yesterday evening.'

'The same person?'

'I was given no opportunity to inquire since the caller put down the telephone as soon as I answered it. I'd be grateful, my dear, if you would issue a gentle rebuke. I don't know what is the current practice but I consider it discourteous to ring off without an apology for bringing the wrong person to the phone. I'm always ready to take a message.'

She was certainly the wrong person, Olivia thought. 'I'm sorry. I don't know him.'

'A prospective young swain or an unidentified bad lot?'

'If the former, he's so smitten he's tongue-tied. I had hoped that you wouldn't be bothered.'

51

'Since I live here, that was not very likely. If I'm right in deducing that you wished to protect an old woman from unnecessary annoyance,' she deduced correctly, 'then I'm touched but a little irritated. I am not yet senile. I can still contemplate, though with repugnance, the affairs of this world. When did these nuisance calls begin?'

Chastened, Olivia explained.

'I'd say that on the first occasion the choice of number was totally random,' Mrs Winterton reasoned, 'but after that it was remembered and became automatic. To imagine that the selection was deliberate is somewhat extravagant. Though admittedly the improbable is not impossible. Ten years on the Bench taught me that no abnormalities are . . . impossible. But I cannot understand why you should think this is directed only at you.'

'I have the feeling it is.'

The other tutted. 'You have too much free time, which encourages brooding, Olivia. It will be a good day for more than your pocket when you get work.'

She smiled agreement. Faced with the woman's robust sense, her conviction was irrational, an egocentric indulgence. Perhaps, after so long without applause, she wanted attention.

'Few people can know this is your number,' Mrs Winterton pointed out. 'Neither is your name in the directory.'

Through the open door of the bathroom and beyond its window marbled by rain and grime Olivia could see sheds, plank gates crooked between high brick walls, the pewter-grey dust of an alley; then mirroring this, the back of the next street whose windows looked across, their stealthy regard lidded in net. Which hers, this bathroom neglected but for her use, did not have. Unfrosted, the glass reminded her of the discrepant panes in the front door and her stomach was twisted again by the threat of the telephone's silence within the colluding moon. 'If he knew I lived here – knew which house – how could he get the telephone number?'

Impatient, Mrs Winterton leant forward and slapped her wrist. 'Drat you, girl, for being so foolish. I'm certain the calls are merely chance. Why should anyone wish to upset you? You've done nothing to provoke such nastiness. And though I have quite a reputation in these parts and from time to time excite a good deal of antagonism, unbridled criticism of the management of the Old People's Home scarcely merits systematic and anonymous vexation.'

If she's so well known, Olivia thought, plenty of people could tell him who lives here, then he only had to look up the name in the directory. He would know that the younger voice was hers. Or he might work for Telecom.

'No doubt the caller will grow bored shortly or find some more satisfactory way of occupying his – or her – time,' the other went on; 'but if the tiresome business continues I shall ask the exchange to intercept incoming calls. The disadvantage about that is its effect on the innocent. Asked to state the number she required, my sister Dorothy would be struck with incurable amnesia. However, that is a risk I may have to take. Should we receive any more of these calls today, I will attend to them before I leave – late this afternoon. I'm going to visit my nephew and shall insist that he take his wife out while I look after the children. I shall pack a nightgown to prevent argument. I enjoy a treat occasionally,' referring to a weekly habit. 'The dust can wait until I get back.'

It was very patient, Olivia thought, smiling; it had hung about so long that it had probably forgotten, along with Mrs Winterton, what it was waiting for.

There was no dust in the front room of the house in Cattlegate and the soot had been washed from the

53

hearth; but unrefreshed by a breeze from an open window and not rumpled by the movements of living warmth, the air lay musty and flat.

This was acknowledged by the woman who invited her in. 'We come in the back as a rule,' she said, bolting the door and replacing its chain. 'Charlotte likes this kept tidy. She's out at the minute, roaming, and he's at work, so there'll not be repercussions if we go into the kitchen. The kettle's on low, ready, always is, but if you'd like a cup of tea I can soon put it on again, after. I'm Dora Booth, her mother.'

Charlotte's devotion to polish was more reticent in the kitchen. Concessions had been made, presumably reluctant, to its use, and though very clean it bore signs of occupation: knitting poked from under a cushion; the toes of shoes peeped from beneath the sideboard; ironed clothes reached down from the rack above the hearth; a line of unripe tomatoes knobbed the window-sill, beckoning the sun.

'I see you've got our Rita's umbrella,' the woman said from the scullery.

'Yes. I've brought it back. That's why I've come.'

'Well, we don't see much of her nowadays but I'll keep it till she's next round, or leave it out for her. She's got a key so she can always get in. Are you a friend of hers, then?'

Unprepared for a woman who appeared not to know that her granddaughter was missing, Olivia floundered. 'Sort of.'

'Sort of? Doesn't sound like much of a friend to me.' Water swilled in the sink then she was at the door, nursing the teapot. 'But our Rita's never do. Never seem to stick, except now and again. I tell her you can't expect the earth, only I do reckon she would have done better than those she's had.'

'But I'm not one of them,' Olivia defended. 'I'm just returning this.'

'At least you're honest. I must say not many would bother. It's like Rita to lend out to strangers.' She scooped tea from the caddy and went back to the kettle.

'She didn't. Mr Dale lent me the umbrella on Monday.' It was a small point to struggle over but she wanted to clear it up.

'That's right,' Mrs Booth answered serenely. 'Now I think on, they mentioned you'd been.'

'And I've never met Rita,' she persisted.

'Haven't you now? In that case, I've been speaking out of turn.' With a swift change of tone, the woman discarded accusation. 'Between ourselves, you haven't missed a lot, not if you like company. I'll not have persons say anything against Rita, she's my flesh and blood, but it's my opinion she hasn't got the way with folks you need. Not like her mother's uncle Charles. That's why I called her Charlotte, you see, hoping that a bit would rub off. Life and soul of the party, he is. People loved him as a lad; give him their last shilling if he asked. I've brewed it strong so it'll take more water after the first couple of cups,' carrying these and saucers to the table.

'Are you saying that Rita is shy?' She must make herself ask questions even if they did not seem pertinent to her search.

'She's not so much shy as not easy, on the awkward side, won't let herself go. Don't tell me you're another young 'un that refuses sugar; to my mind tea's like slops without. Have a biscuit; there's nothing like a spot of tea and biscuit of a morning if you're allowed.'

Permission granted by Charlotte's absence, they both selected a biscuit from the tin. Mrs Booth sighed contentedly. 'Nice of you to call round. Are you visiting?' She's already forgotten, Olivia thought, but before she could, mistakenly, remind her, the other added, 'I can see you're not from these parts.'

'How?'

'By the way you talk. But I've nothing against it within reason. Not like some. I'm ready to keep an open mind even if a body does talk posh.'

Not discomforted by this candour since in a comparable situation she could have employed it herself, though without the regional conceit, Olivia answered, 'I'm not necessarily a visitor because I talk like this. Most people that I've met round here do.'

'Funny I don't meet them; but then, it's bingo for me, not bridge.' Her look was hostile, placing Olivia amongst those who occasioned her resentful contempt.

Again there had been no warning for this abrupt shift of tone and, annoyed at being for a second time unjustly accused but anxious to restore their former amity, Olivia resorted to a spontaneous performance. She took a gulp of her tea, wiped her mouth with the back of her hand as if rehearsed by Alan, and pronounced in an accent woven from mill smoke, fell mists and dyed-in-the-wool yarns: 'As I say t'wife, for them after nowt butta comfortable flutter, bingo's handy.'

There was a moment's quiet, that dreadful hiatus for the decision between bouquets and rotten eggs, then Mrs Booth's cup clattered in its saucer as she rocked back and the room took the blast of her trumpeting whoops.

'You're a rare one,' she said at last. 'Just look what you've made me do,' and after a number of false starts tipped the tea in her saucer back into the cup. 'You're as bad as my brother Charlie; he's a card, he is, and never better than when taking folks off. Should've been on the halls, but they were before his time. You ever thought of anything like that?'

'I'm an actress.'

'Get away with you! You're having me on.'

'No; I'm not.' Encouraged, Olivia talked about her profession and, because she assumed that Mrs Booth wanted only the excitements of grease-paint and lights, the thrill of an expectant audience and the noise of applause, she censored the rest: the apprehension, the fatigue, the present emptiness, so that for a brief space those did not exist. Sitting stage centre, surrounded by meticulously chosen props, placed before the window's cyclorama and with a rack of clothes forming the tabs above her head, she enjoyed a solace in the deceit. But it was short-lived.

The other questioned, 'Did you act in that film they made about Rita?'

So she did know that Rita was missing but had not admitted it, taking the umbrella with no word or sign of distress. Her description of the girl had been unsentimental, not falsified by an anticipated grief. She was confident that Rita would be found and though this optimism was matched to Olivia's need, she found it disturbing; it was complacent and facile. Convinced that Rita would reappear in the future, Mrs Booth accepted her unexplained absence without curiosity or alarm.

'Well,' she prompted, 'did you take any part in it?'

'Yes; I did,' and Olivia heard herself stuttering because by 'part' the other did not mean a theatrical role; she charged complicity. 'I was Elizabeth Drew.'

'Her Rita lives with? Waste of time, I'd say.'

'It was a job; the first that's come up for months.'

'And we've all got to eat,' the woman conceded. 'I can see it's not all roses, being an actress, if it's like that. But they had no business putting it on telly, poking their noses in. I wouldn't watch it, but Charlotte and him did, and they told me.'

'It might help to find her.'

'Not if she doesn't want. She's biding her time, takes after Charlie in that. Until she's ready wild horses won't drag her out.'

Olivia took another mouthful of tea; lukewarm, it was blamed for the nausea in her throat.

'Won't drag her out of where, Mrs Booth?' She had to humour her.

'Out of where she's hid. She's stubborn, is Rita. You wouldn't have said so when she was little, always did as she was told, but that's how she's gone: stubborn. Look how she left here. Not long finished schooling, and she's up off. Her father would have kept her, he's not a bad one in that respect, he'd have seen she wasn't short. But no, would she be doing with that? Not Rita. She's got the supplementary benefit, she says, so she can do by herself. Living in the same town, with a proper home here for her! Charlotte'll never live down the disgrace.'

'It's natural to want to be independent.' But she was beginning to like Rita.

'Ay, and it seems it's natural to ride roughshod over them that are older, with not so much as a sorry when you've hurt. But young 'uns are always the same.' She paused, rubbing an arthritic knuckle, then more calmly, 'I can't pretend I was any different. I was the second in a row of nine and my mother always promised herself a rest when I'd left school and could help out. But I didn't think much of that and was soon looking round. Married my Bob no more than three months after he'd popped the question and had four of my own inside five years. Talk about out of the frying pan!' She cackled harshly. 'Served me right. You'll have another cup? Topping up'll not drown the pot.'

'Thank you.' Waiting, Olivia considered how to return the conversation to Rita while avoiding reference to her disappearance. She did not wish to hear again the assertion that the girl was biding her time. It was a piece of lunacy glinting from the bedrock of practical sense.

'I expect your mother got used to your leaving home,' she said as casually as she could manage, stirring her tea. 'Just as mine has,' and did not blink at the lie. 'And eventually Mrs Dale won't mind as much, will she? If

Rita is anything like I was a few years ago, I reckon there'll be a lot of compensations.'

Mrs Booth laughed. 'A bit of a harum-scarum, were you? I'd not be surprised. But Rita wasn't, not till this blew up, and I'd be telling a lie if I said I didn't sometimes feel like giving her a push; she was altogether too quiet, seemed to lack spirit, but it seems I was wrong. She had spirit enough when she'd made up her mind. Or perhaps it was a case of the worm turning. It was the way she did it that wasn't right, in my view. Got all her bags packed and stacked on the pavement, then comes into this kitchen and announces she's off. And she didn't mince her words, either. They didn't bother me. I know when I'm right; but Charlotte is a different matter and was cut deep. It was a long time, too, before they found out where she was. Rita has a crafty streak and she kept herself close, but Charlotte was always out looking and one night when she saw her leaving a pub she followed her and got the address. She didn't visit but she was able to keep tabs on her. That settled her down a bit.'

Though she sat in the path of the tunnelling sun, Olivia shivered. A woman thrown off by her child was a desolate figure, but she was a wretch possessed as she travelled the streets. Which she was doing once more: roaming, as Mrs Booth had said, her steps paced by the hope of a chance sight. Because she had found her daughter on that other occasion and would do so again. The belief was irrational and its intensity terrible, leaving the woman no resource against disproof. Frightened, Olivia was suddenly gripped by doubt.

'Until this last lot, that is,' Mrs Booth continued. 'She'd have been better off not knowing about it, in my opinion. Rita'll turn up again when it suits. But some busybody next door saw the milk and went along to the police station, so a constable came round. How they got this address, I'll never know; you can't keep anything to yourself nowadays, but round he came and before long Charlotte was in a state again, what with having to say that Rita had left home and the questions. I went after him when he was going and told him not to put himself out; it's a family matter. He said it was only a routine visit and he wouldn't be taking it any further unless something suspicious turned up. He wasn't there to get persons who'd flitted because they couldn't pay the rent or such. Will you have another biscuit?

'Of course I didn't know whether he meant our Rita or the other one, but that didn't bother me; and I reckoned him saying that settled the business and I told Charlotte as much; but then the telly got on to it – tongues must wag sixty to the dozen in that street – and they must have got licence to go into the house. Charlotte didn't like that but she gave them a photo, they were that pressing and telling her all the time they'd find Rita for her. Left her room in a state by all accounts, too, cheeky buggers.'

'That's how they found it.'

'So they say but I wouldn't put it past them to mucky it up if they were after a show.' Her description fell short of vandalism but Olivia did not correct it; there was enough general truth in Mrs Booth's prejudice to discourage argument. 'Do anything, some folks will, to get others hotted up. Take that reporter. If I'd had my way I'd have shown him the door and as things turned out I'd have been right.'

'I didn't know that the press had got on to it.'

'Only the *Evening Chronicle*; the *Post* wouldn't condescend. We're not important enough for them,' indicating an ambivalent attitude to publicity. 'The young man was nice enough, seemingly, but he got round Charlotte with his sighing and clucking and put ideas in her head which would have been best left out. She was upset as it was, being told Rita had gone again after months spent looking, but she was in a real state by the time he'd left.

Doing a follow-up, as he called it, of the telly, asking questions, only not like the constable. All he wanted to know was things like dates, when she left and the last time we'd seen her. This newspaper man wasn't satisfied with that. No; he wanted what he called the story. I told him there wasn't one but he took no notice of that and claimed the state of Rita's room looked fishy. "I've known tidier than our Rita," I told him but that didn't stop him.'

'Was he suggesting that she had been attacked or something?'

'He wouldn't go as far as that but he did say that some person must have it in for her. "You should've seen her bedroom here," I told him and he gave me a look like I was three sheets to the wind. "It's you that's barmy," I said. "Our Rita's not the sort to provoke such nastiness." '

It was strange to hear this echo of Mrs Winterton but not really surprising, Olivia thought; the argument was obvious. Unfortunately, nastiness often had no excuse for being provoked. She thought of Alan. It was true that she had risen to his sarcasm over her friendship with Judy, but surely that should not have incited him to speak so maliciously.

'So he went off that and asked about her landlady,' Mrs Booth was saying. 'You know her, that Mrs Drew.'

'No, I don't know her. I represented her.'

'Of course. I was forgetting. Charlotte said you looked very like.'

'I didn't know she'd met her.'

'She was going on the telly.'

About to inquire when Mrs Drew had appeared on television, Olivia realized the muddle. Incredulity gagged an attempt to clear it up.

'Charlotte hadn't anything against her, that is to say, personally, not till that chap from the *Evening Chronicle* came round. He was a sly one, asking questions in a way

61

that put words in her mouth. As I said to Charlotte, no landlady throws a lodger's things about, she wants the place kept respectable, even if there is something going on.'

'What sort of thing?'

'You might well ask, my dear, and he wouldn't come straight out with it. Mentioned a journalist's instinct, something to do with his nose, though I wouldn't have drawn attention to that if I'd been him, never seen such a conk on a man, took him round in circles and us with him, too, asking what footing they were on and whether we were happy with Rita living with that type. I asked him what he meant by that and I must say he had the grace to blush. "I'm afraid I'm not at liberty to answer that," he says, "but I appreciate how a mother must feel when her daughter gets a pull to leave a nice home like this." Smarmy young know-all.'

'Mrs Drew has gone away as well.'

'That's what he said. "And what's so funny about that?" I asked him. "We've come to a pretty pass if you have to stick up a notice every time you leave the house." That's what two wars have done for us – identity cards, numbers by your name, reporting to them behind desks if you've earned a few extra bob to give a bit of spice to your pension. Might as well be locked up, I sometimes think, for all the difference it makes. But there's some that give it the slip.' She paused. Slowly, her voice low but vibrant, she continued, 'Ay, there's some that'll not have tabs kept on them. They're the lucky ones. They were blessed with the fairy touch.' Again she paused and, smiling, her face changed; its severity was smoothed into gentleness; its lines recalled dimples and the look she gave Olivia was a girl's, winsome, carefree, lit by the unbarred sun.

'Here,' she said, rising, and tapped her guest's arm. 'I'll show you.'

Opening a door in the corner of the kitchen, she led

Olivia up a funnel of narrow stairs lit by a skylight above. At their head was the bedroom looking on to the street, and four steps along a passage barely a man's width was a door to the room over the kitchen. 'Rita's,' her guide said as they passed. The third bedroom, above the scullery which projected from the main structure into the yard, would be smaller, Olivia knew, and in such terraces these were sometimes converted into bathrooms with the help of council grants. They rarely offered enough space for a full-size bed. Neither did the one she was looking in now, but it was impossible to determine whether its dimensions were at fault; the immediate reason was what it contained.

'Go on in.' The woman drew Olivia past her and into the tiny well at the centre. 'I keep it dusted. You have a good look,' she urged from the door.

Unwillingly, feeling like a trespasser, Olivia let her eyes skim round the room, over tables, chests, shelves, cabinets, anything that offered a surface for hoarded possessions, faded, yellowing, threadbare, warped and curled by years of the changing seasons and the fingering light but laid out with affection, brushed or cleaned with vigilant love. Her glance arrested by a pair of knitted bootees felted by washing but threaded with new ribbon and placed in a nest of lace, Olivia began to examine as the other wished and saw the wooden rattle impressed by small teeth, the hoop, the stringed whip and the top chevroned with coloured chalks, the birds' eggs neatly blown, a bicycle clip, a pile of cigarette cards, then the cigarette packets themselves, Gold Flake still lustrous but empty, a football, a collar stud, a cigarette lighter, its brass buffed to gold, then letters, magazines, a time sheet, the progressing memorabilia of a man.

'There's more in that trunk,' Mrs Booth told her; 'things that 'ud soon spoil if left out, like what he was christened in. And I keep his watch safe in a box, it was his granddad's, he wouldn't take that with him. Solid gold it is, and he wears it as meant with the chain across his chest when he gets himself up. I haven't let anything go.' She waved round the room. 'Though there's some that wouldn't think twice about getting rid of it, given half the chance, but Charlotte always backs me up. Takes a good picture, doesn't he? I've got an album full in that drawer and I change them over the end of every month so they all get an airing.'

Nodded towards a cabinet, Olivia looked at the photographs. Not knowing which face she should praise, she skirted a group of footballers and peered at a young man astride a motor bike, grinning, slightly impertinent. He reminded her of someone she thought she should know.

'That bike wasn't his,' the other interpreted. 'He'd borrowed it for a lark. Allus doing something to give you a laugh.'

By the side of this there was another in an ornate silver frame; it showed him dressed as a soldier, a man little older than herself, laughing across the years.

A third photograph of him was on the sideboard in Charlotte Dale's front room.

'Is he your son?'

'Mine were all girls, more's the pity. That's Charlie. Of course, there's a lot here'll be no use to him: he's a bit big for rompers!' she chuckled, happy. 'But there's his civvies in the trunk; I wash them every Whitsun so they stay fresh, and when she was a little one Rita would clean his boots but she got so's she wouldn't, I'll never know why. There's not another that could have a great-uncle like him.'

Great-uncle. Olivia leant against the table trying to calculate, but she knew that was not necessary.

'When do you expect him back?' she asked, forcing her voice to remain even.

'Any time. I can wait. I've been waiting this last forty year or more. I've the patience; he'll not catch me out.

The kettle's always on the hob and his best togs ready. You like what I've done, then?'

Her stomach lurching, Olivia nodded obediently but could not look into the woman's eyes. They were blind to the knowledge that she had brought Olivia to a private shrine.

' "Don't you be worriting, Dora," he said on his last leave. "I'll be out of this lot sooner than you think." He wasn't cut out for the Army, didn't like being at anybody's beck and call, so I knew what he meant. When he was reported missing I didn't take any notice. Missing, was the way They put it, believed dead. Well, Charlie wasn't made to stop bullets. No; he'd taken a chance when he saw it coming, but then, you see, he had to lie low. Stick him in prison if they found him and that wouldn't suit. Always as free as the wind is Charlie. As I said, it's granted to some and he's one of the lucky ones. He'll not be cooped up. Not like Charlotte or me.'

Chapter Five

Reaching a low wall by the side of the supermarket, Olivia sat down to recover her breath. For a second time she had fled from the Dales' house; for a second time they had offered her an experience with which she could not cope. She was appalled by her inadequacy. She was nearly twenty-one; her life had not been particularly sheltered; she had come across eccentricities, neuroses, the disintegration in the clamp of failure or loss, but she had never met anything like this: a woman sensible, astringent, vigorous yet animated by an insane belief. Perhaps this wasn't so abnormal; perhaps lots of people had this in some degree which accounted for extravagant conduct. Such as Alan and the man the previous night. But this must be different. A forty-year vigil! She wondered how it had started. From the error that 'Missing, believed dead' concealed a hope? From the adoration of a sister that refused to be bereaved?

She flattered herself that she had perception and sympathies but Mrs Booth had defeated her. Brushed by the relics of a man long dead, she could not talk of his homecoming; only condolences would wrinkle her lips. So she had stood silent, wishing she could stop her ears to the woman's plans: banners across the street which had welcomed back others, the outings, the parties in honour of a hero returning, handsome, rollicking, ungrizzled by time. Until finally she had escaped on the back of excuses which had been accepted as truth but were an expression of cowardice.

She must buy food, go home and make a sandwich. That might calm her stomach. She felt sick. No wonder that Rita had left home. She was seventeen. Seventeen years of that! Acquiescent when she was a child, cleaning his boots, but as she grew older less patiently deferring to the intrusion of a woman who waited on a ghost.

'There isn't much room left for you,' Olivia had said, trying to restore the commonplace.

'I don't need any more. His are enough for me. I wouldn't mind sleeping on the sofa in the kitchen but Charlotte won't have that so I climb in with Rita.' In order that his cenotaph should remain undisturbed.

Mrs Booth had said earlier, 'She didn't mince her words but that didn't bother me. I know when I'm right.' Presumably Rita had at last had the courage to denounce her grandmother's obsession. Which her mother may share, for Rita's words had 'cut her deep'.

This must explain Mr Dale's ghastly insistence that his wife 'prepare herself for the worst'. He knew what the opposite 'can lead to'. He spoke out of the haunting of years as he sat in a room whose funereal atmosphere was appropriate to his choice. While upstairs in that divided house was a woman devoted to an impossible resurrection. Olivia did not know which scared her the more.

But Rita's mother refused to be coerced by her husband. She was out, roaming; Rita had been found once and would be again. And now Olivia was grateful for this persistence; it affirmed life, though she was revolted by the suspicion that Mrs Dale was influenced by her mother's faith in another's return.

She had nothing to prove that, however, only hints that Mrs Dale was sympathetic towards her mother's delusions. Earl had warned her against theories that were far-fetched. Olivia got up from the wall and strode into the supermarket, thinking: the reasons why Mrs Dale continues her search are irrelevant; what matters is that she is doing it. She hoped that the woman was making more progress than she. All she had come across so far was a friend called Karen who didn't even know that Rita was missing, Stephen who said that she never stayed long in one place, and a soldier's monument.

She had learnt something about Rita, though, but she must be careful about that, she warned herself as she picked up a basket. If she began to create a character, discover the feelings, the attitudes, the motives behind the behaviour, she would become immersed in it and that would be dangerous. Rita wasn't a girl in a play, a fictitious person bodied out for the length of the performance, given a truth dependent on art, wholly absorbing and alive for a small space, then shed. Rita existed. She wasn't born in the imagination of a dramatist then realized by the skill of an actress. She wasn't confined to a three-hour show; she belonged to the same cycle of hours as did Olivia and their re-creation might take over Olivia's own. Fearing this, she told herself that she must concentrate upon the situation. To find that, to discover what had happened and trace the girl was more scientific; it was a job she had undertaken and it would be conducted more successfully if she were detached. But she knew that was already denied her because from the moment she had opened the door of Elizabeth Drew's house and had run down the path, she had felt involved. It had begun then, as she had tried to tell Earl. Perhaps it was the house, she argued to herself, so similar to Mrs Winterton's though she had seen only the hall, and Alan hanging about waiting for his cue, stopping her before the take of her scene to ask when was Judy's next visit. It was as if that morning's work had been a piece of make-believe, as if it were not a film she was taking part in but a segment of her own life that she was hurrying through. And though it should have been humdrum and unmemorable, it carried a hint of crisis, a warning that something of value was at risk and

68

the swift pinch of personal danger. Did it seem like that at the time? she asked herself. Or has the occasion sprouted all that in the memory, a poisonous fungus whose spores are a kerb crawler and a phone's silent threat?

There was no sense in dwelling on those; she must apply herself to her task. Over lunch she would be systematic; she would try to recall all the comments of people she had met and see if they were related. As, thinking of this, she regarded a row of tins without seeing the labels, Olivia felt the tug of an examining stare.

'I thought you were someone else for a minute, but you're not a bit like her, when you look close,' the woman stammered. 'Sorry,' and moved away.

'That's all right. Do you mean Elizabeth Drew?'

The other stopped. 'Yes. It was just that I haven't got my glasses; they got broke. I should've known first off it wasn't Elizabeth. She wouldn't let me pass without a word.'

'How long is it since you've seen her?'

'I don't know.' She expressed no surprise at the question, just as it appeared quite natural that Olivia also knew the woman. 'It could be three weeks or more. It's not easy to get round.'

'Do you know she's not living in her house at the moment?'

'A neighbour over the way told me it was in Monday's paper, on account of the young girl: I can't remember her name.'

A small child wedged in the trolley's stocks began to whine; fatigue dragged at the woman's face.

'Rita Dale. I suppose the two of them disappearing near the same time must be simply a coincidence?'

The woman took a dummy out of her pocket, wiped it on her sleeve, sucked it and pushed it into the child's mouth. 'Coincidence?' she repeated. The word was effortful, too long; it measured the distance between them. 'I wouldn't know about that. Maybe it was best getting out of the way for a bit.'

'Out of the way of what?' She was conscious of the interrogation, that she was subordinating the woman with the authority of health, articulateness and freedom from ties.

'Everything. She always says she's lucky. She can clear out, but when ructions come I haven't the chance.'

'I don't understand what you're talking about.'

The other looked at her. 'No, I can see that,' she answered with a flick of bitterness. Then, 'Let's hope you never do.'

When you reach a dead-end, Olivia advised herself, just turn back and try another route. 'Have you any idea where Rita Dale might have gone?'

'Why should I have? I expect there was a reason. We never talked but I knew she was there.' The hands on the trolley began to shake. 'If you're from the police then I'm telling you I know nothing about it.'

'I'm not from the police.'

'That's just as well. If I was seen talking to one of them, it 'ud be taken wrong. I'll have to go. I've been longer than I ought and it'll be noticed. There's the baby outside in the pram and she'll need feeding.'

Clumsily she slid the trolley into a tight arc and followed it towards the till, her back humped inside the shiny pilled cardigan, her scraggy thighs silhouetted under the flimsy transparent skirt, the sandals broken and white legs prematurely veined. Watching her, Olivia saw that the neglect was not only that of poverty but of defeat; and thought, could I ever become like that?

She stood by the shelves of tinned meat and looked about her, considering for the first time the nature of what she saw. Since coming to the town she had shopped there weekly, using the place as a quick convenience. Absorbed in her own affairs, a transient, someone who did not belong to the town, she had hurried through purchases and had left with no more acute sensation than one of distaste. Now she gave the shop her attention. It hardly qualified as a supermarket; the name was a hopeful make-believe for three corridors of shelves on which were stacked tins, dried milk and sliced bread. At one end a concession had been made to less restricted diets by a rack of bruised onions, a few rotting carrots and wizened potatoes sustaining pallid shoots. At the other end a more realistic understanding of customers' requirements was indicated in a heap of sanitary towels, a card of children's dummies almost empty, tablets of aspirin and, by the till, packets of cigarettes. Even had the dust been removed from the tins, the place would have been irrevocably squalid: a packet of biscuits, staved in, leaked a gritty scurf; a dispenser of strawberry sauce, experimentally squeezed, still oozed red; bags of sugar, their stay too brief to justify shelving, remained in cartons on the floor; and rashed densely over the curling linoleum tiles were the jet scabs of discarded chewing gum, tufted with hairs or sticky with spills. And Olivia thought, did Rita come here? Did Rita, after leaving the neat cleanliness of her home, having to live as I do on the dole, come here and feel smirched by its ugliness, be revolted by the dirt and depressed by the apathy which make it such a horrible place? Perhaps she had come but, like Olivia, had not noticed; or had resembled the shuffling customers who seemed not to care. Or more likely, reared in the town she had simply received this as a natural feature. She would be no objective observer. Yet Olivia was taken with an irrational impulse to protect and, striding to the till, asked, 'Does Rita Dale shop here?'

The man put his finger under a sentence in the magazine, looked up and considered while she willed a negative.

'Was she the one on the telly?'

'Yes.'

'I thought I recognized you.

'I'm asking about the other one, the girl in the photograph.'

'That wasn't much use, was it? Must have been taken years ago, working it out from what they said in the paper. But I knew it was you the moment you came in. Have they found her yet? They was hoping you'd come forward.'

This time she did not pause. 'I'm not the woman she lodged with. I just pretended to be her.'

'Funny sort of job, going round taking off someone else. Wouldn't do for me. I'd soon get myself in a pickle. Still, there might be something in it,' he reflected, 'if it's bigamy you're interested in.'

'I'm not.'

'Takes all sorts. You want this checked out?'

Olivia wondered what else he imagined she might want done with the goods, but nodded.

'Not as much as usual,' he commented.

'I don't generally buy any more.'

'See what I mean? Like I said, if you set out to be two folks, you can get so you don't know t'other from which. You lose track. Mostly it's ten or fifteen quid.'

'Not for me,' she insisted. 'You must be thinking of the other one.'

She immediately regretted the correction. He glared resentfully. 'I'm not thinking of any on yer,' he snapped, punching the keys of his machine. 'I'm here to take the cash, not waste time admiring the mugs of customers. So don't blame me if a couple on you look the same. And if one has the habit of putting me to the trouble of ringing up no more than a miserly three pounds seventy, then don't be surprised if I don't recall it chapter and verse. The other one, or you, depending on which way the wind's blowing, was a proper customer. They can say what they like, that's nowt to do with me, because she paid on the nail and never let out a word of com-

72

plaint, though now and again they'd forgot to deliver the new bread. "You feed them too well," I used to tell her, though it wasn't in my interests. "How many you got?" "Just the one," she'd say, "but still growing. At least, that's the excuse." '

So, whatever was implied by the reference to gossip, Elizabeth Drew had been a satisfactory customer and had not stinted Rita. The arrangement between them clearly went further than letting a room. Remembering the photograph's pathetic defensiveness, Olivia reflected that the other woman must have responded to a need. And though she had not eaten that day, or probably because of that since hunger induced a kind of somnolence, Olivia turned from the direction of her lodgings and walked though the unfamiliar streets towards the house of Elizabeth Drew.

It was not until she had reached it, private again after the inquisitive cameras, that she wondered why she had come and, feeling suddenly shy and discomforted by this involuntary inspection, she excused her hesitation at the gate by closing it gently, then turned to go. A tap on a window prevented her. Looking up, she saw a woman in the adjacent house beckon.

'I thought it was her for a minute,' the neighbour greeted her from the door, 'but then I saw it was you. When my hubby was watching that programme he said, "You've done a nice job there, Laura." It was my description, you see, that the television went for and when they brought round your photo I said, "That's the one. To a T." '

'Thank you,' Olivia said since that seemed expected. Also, the woman was responsible for providing her with half a day's work.

The neighbour preened herself. 'I didn't mind being put out a bit. Do you get called upon much?'

'Not as a double. That sort of work's limited, I hope.'

Unsmiling, the other nodded. 'You could say it's a

73

waste of time and money if nothing comes of it. It hasn't fetched her back, or found little Rita.' She lowered herself down the steps then bustled the four paces to the gate. 'It's her we have to worry ourselves about. The moment she came, I said to my hubby, "Next door's no place for a young girl." '

'Why was that?'

The woman glanced up the street and checked for eavesdroppers. Seeing none but a mangy dog methodically refreshing his territory, she leant over the gate and whispered, 'Men.'

It was clear that some horrified answer was required. Unable to comply, Olivia merely contrived to look startled and stammered, 'Did Rita have a lot of boyfriends, then?'

The other shook her head impatiently. 'Not Rita! *Her!*'

'Really?'

'Round knocking every verse end. In the middle of the night mostly, and drunk as lords. Disgusting. Woke all the street. Funny-looking oddities, too, for the most part. They hadn't seen water for weeks. As Frank said, the nearest they'd ever got to water was beer. He's a comic at times, is Frank.

'I went out when it first started to ask them to show a bit of consideration for others but they didn't take any notice and Frank said better keep out of it else they'd start knocking here, so I took to banging on the wall.'

Reluctantly suppressing the obvious comment, Olivia nodded.

'Got a reputation for herself up the street, one way or another,' and before Olivia could frame a request for definition of the various ways, she went on, 'but nobody interfered, of course; there was no proof. Rita wasn't the only one either, you know. I could have put their minds at rest about that, but naturally I didn't go round telling tales.'

I bet you didn't, Olivia commented silently. 'Wasn't she?'

'Not a bit of it.'

It wasn't that her talent for interrogation was improving, Olivia told herself, but that there was an understood convention: prompts were required not to encourage the speaker but to maintain the suspense and give a semblance of dialogue.

'There were others coming at all hours. "I can't understand what any decent young man can see in half of them," I said to Frank and he pointed out the callers were hardly decent so perhaps they weren't so choosy; none of them in the house were what you might call oil paintings.'

'Weren't they?'

'Except *her*,' she added hurriedly but conceded only that Elizabeth Drew would pass in a crowd. 'You flatter her. When the television brought the photo I told them, "She's like, but the drawback is, she's better favoured." '

Irritated but controlling her tone, Olivia remarked, 'It will be interesting to compare, if we ever meet.'

'Well, you live here, don't you? One from the telly said. So you might; she's never away for long. Except that I wouldn't be surprised if after this little lot we hadn't seen the last of her. I saw her going off, you know, cool as a cucumber, as well as that lad from the telephone exchange, but they would choose to put him in the picture. After all I'd done! I thought it best to report it, after hearing that car one morning – only it shot off before I could get to the window; but as my hubby says, I can't be expected to be responsible for the whole street – and then what with her going and the milk piling up on the step, it looked suspicious to me. As I said to Mr Garbutt, "That Mrs Drew must have left little Rita there by herself for a bit because she'd have been sure to remember to cancel the milk if the house was going to be empty, whereas a young one is more feckless." Only it wasn't my business to stop other folk's milk – I'd not get any thanks for that – so I went to the police.

'They came round grumbling and fetched in Mr Catchpole who lets this row but they all slipped in and out without as much as a word in my direction. First thing I knew about the way Rita's bedroom had been smashed up was watching the telly. "Well, did you ever?" I said to Mr Garbutt. "They can come here asking me to judge photographs but they don't think that puts them under any obligation to give a hint of what it's for." "You'll know what to do next time, Laura," he says; "you'll keep quiet and let them shift for themselves. See what a job they can make of that." And then when Monday night's paper came out and it said that about violence, I said to him, "They should've come and asked me. I could've told them about that." It could've happened any time, the way she carried on. All that knocking! And them so drunk! If anything has happened to that young girl, it'll be her fault. If little Rita's hurt or worse, she'll have to take the blame. She wasn't fit to be in charge of a youngster. And she should never have left her by herself, a prey to any undesirables that turned up.'

An hour later, revived by a tuna-fish sandwich and a mug of tea, Olivia sat on her bed and tried to remember all she had heard. Since Stephen had approached her in the library on Monday, the number of people she had met either by chance or intention had multiplied rapidly: four already today and it was only Wednesday afternoon. Their knowledge of Rita ranged from family intimacy to the shop assistant's hearsay, so not all had information and none could assist in the search, but each had at least one comment or opinion about her or where she had lived. It was impossible to estimate their accuracy but, accustomed to studying a play not only for its surface meaning but for the undertones and to discover the line of the sub-text, Olivia examined what she knew.

Discounting for a moment the fanatical convictions of the Dales and Mrs Booth since they defied relation to anything else. she decided that there was some agreement in Steve and Karen's references to Rita's disappearance since he had mentioned that she never stayed long in one place and the latter had inquired whether she had simply bunked off. Both considered her to be reasonably happy where she lived and according to the man in the supermarket she had been looked after well. But the neighbour's account seemed to contradict this and supported Karen's idea that Rita must have been in some trouble since one night she had got drunk. All the details from Karen and Steve were reliable, Olivia decided; she had sensed no dissembling and she could imagine no reason for it. The neighbour's claims, however, were more in doubt. Yet the disorder she had described seemed to fit in with the girl's wrecked bedroom; and that was a fact.

It was the only uncontroversial one she had. Steve had been mystified by the room, she remembered, feeling that there was something wrong with it, but that was unimportant; its state was beyond question. Everything else was a hotchpotch of conjecture and insinuation. These had to be considered cautiously but she could not ignore one feature they shared. Though coming from apparently unconnected sources, they were disturbingly consistent in their references to Elizabeth Drew.

She went through them. The journalist from the *Evening Chronicle* had asked what 'footing' she had enjoyed with Rita and had called her 'that type' and, since Mrs Booth had argued that no landlady would damage a room in her own house, he must have implied that Mrs Drew was responsible; but he would not explain the hint that 'things were going on'. The neighbour had been more explicit; what she had described was probably nothing more than noisy parties occasioning the envious disapproval of a puritanical street, but they had earned Elizabeth Drew a notoriety which had reached the man at the till. This seemed the most sensible explanation but it left her uneasy. Perhaps 'sensible' was not the criterion; it could not encompass Mrs Dale's hope that Elizabeth Drew would get her deserts. Finally, the stooped woman in the shop had been nervous about the police and had thought it had been wise for the other to get away for a while. Which confirmed the neighbour's assumption.

Olivia paused. During the last three days she had listened to voices tuned to anxiety, surprise or irritation, but now they were smothered by others. Sifting through the garrulity of Mrs Booth's report, the neighbour's self-importance, and finding the relevant details, she heard only prejudice and dislike. But for that, she might have been ready to consider the neighbour's accusations, though it was difficult to believe she was seriously claiming that Mrs Drew kept some sort of brothel. The idea was so fantastic that Olivia felt ridiculous applying the word to it, and it was not likely that the neighbour would wait for proof before complaining to the police. Perhaps she was hinting other practices, wife swapping or blue films, for example, secret things not exactly illegal but balanced on the edge of the law. Recalling the woman in the shop, however, Olivia could not imagine her taking part in any such activities.

Again Olivia was perplexed; such a situation was beyond her understanding. Extraordinary, exotic, it was incongruous in that street and her instinct was to reject it. Yet was it so bizarre? Though hardly a regular feature of small-town society, it happened. It was more comprehensible than Mrs Booth's revelation. When she had embarked on the search for Rita she had not expected anything like this.

Above her in the hall the telephone began ringing.

She was tempted to leave it but professional habit was too strong.

'I've been trying to reach you all week but you've been out or engaged,' her mother complained. 'Now calls are being intercepted. Whatever is going on?

'How disgusting! Are you all right, dear? Were they obscene?' Mrs Quinn gabbled after Olivia's explanation.

She answered, congratulating herself on her patience.

'But why should anyone decide to upset you in this way?'

'I'm not upset, Mother. The number has been chosen at random.'

'I hope you're right; but you can't be sure, so I should take precautions.'

'Mrs Winterton already has, as you'll have gathered.'

'I don't mean reporting it to the exchange. I mean being careful. You never know what some people will get up to. If you go out at night you really shouldn't walk back by yourself.'

'Please don't fuss.' Were she to tramp at midday over a ploughed field her mother would warn that the furrows were populated by brigands. 'I've told you – the calls are not directed at me.' She made the insistence so positive that she was almost convinced.

'Very probably not, but you can't depend on it,' the other was equally insistent. 'There are some very strange people about, Olivia.' She didn't know the half of it. 'So you'd be advised not to take chances. Have I ever told you about your father's cousin Gillian?'

'I expect so.'

'She married a few years after us but we couldn't attend the wedding because you had the measles. Well, immediately she and Alex returned from their honeymoon, the telephone calls started. In the middle of the night. They couldn't get a wink of sleep and the moment they answered it, the person cut off. It went on for weeks. Then they put the Post Office on to it and it stopped. Years later the mystery was solved. Somebody sharing digs with the person at the time told Gillian. And do you know who the caller was?'

Her sense of drama is predictable, Olivia thought. But it worked. 'As a matter of fact, no; I don't.'

'An ex-girlfriend of Alex.'

'That's incredible!' For the first time her voice was warm, interested. 'Fancy going to all that trouble! She must have disturbed her own sleep as well. I'd have to be far gone before I did that.'

'Hell knows no fury like a woman scorned,' Mrs Quinn answered, pleased with the quotation. 'You see, she couldn't bear the thought of Alex . . .'

'I get the picture,' Olivia interrupted. 'Has anything of note happened your end since you last phoned?'

'No, I'm afraid not. We live a very quiet life, the two of us,' suggesting riotous revels when there had been three. 'I wanted to tell you how much we enjoyed the programme.'

She couldn't mean that.

'Seeing you on television,' she corrected, rightly interpreting her daughter's silence. 'Have there been any comments?'

'Not as far as I know.'

'I wouldn't be surprised if some director has seen it and has you stored in his mind. We all know that getting your face on television is half the battle.' She had learnt her part well. 'I've been thinking how that must affect you. It must be exciting to go out and have everyone recognize you.'

If her name were up in lights on Shaftesbury Avenue, her mother would bribe the management to keep them switched on during the day.

'Of course everyone has not recognized me, Mother. You talk as if I'd had a star part! And those that have mentioned it have confused me with the woman herself.'

'Surely that's a great compliment! It shows you were very convincing, Olivia, which must give you a lot of satisfaction. I'm delighted. Does this mean that you are meeting a few people? Apart from the others at the agency, you seem to know hardly anyone. One can be very isolated in a new town but if you get to know only a handful of people, you soon feel less miserable.' Her mother's universal cure prescribed for all disorders from compulsive eating to tics. Olivia wished she could contradict it without reservation.

'I don't know how you've formed the impression that I'm miserable. And I'm not a stranger at all; I know dozens of people. There's a fellow called Steve I see every Monday in the library hunting through the Situations Vacant. He's not a boyfriend,' she stated to discourage, 'but we look out for things for each other; and there are all the gossips in the local supermarket where I'm well in with the manager; and there's a couple who invite me to their house – they've a fascinating old mother living with them; and there's Mrs Winterton and neighbours. I could spend my time, if I wanted, just going the rounds. For example, I'm meeting a friend, Karen, in a pub this evening and since others will quickly gather we're bound to have a good time.'

'I'm pleased you've settled in so well. I hadn't realized. But don't forget: whenever you want to get away from it all,' Mrs Quinn said without sarcasm, 'your bed's always made up.'

They had said their farewells and replaced handsets before Olivia recalled that she had not mentioned the audition at the Piccolo Theatre.

Chapter Six

In the Gate, by the market, the peremptory thirsts of the first hour had been quenched and there was a lull for consolidation before the last frenzied provision against the overnight drought. This gave leisure for expressionless scrutiny of a newcomer and heads, swivelled at Olivia's entrance, creaked back to follow her walk to the bar. Not altogether displeased at commanding this public attention which with a little effort could be likened to an appearance on stage, she smiled at the nearest rank of customers and, quickly assessing the form, ordered half a pint of the local brew.

'That'll put some muscle on you,' the barman approved, his position requiring a civility not attempted by others for he added, 'Josh, give the lady a bit of room.'

Josh leant a grudging inch nearer his companion. His back, broad as a door, had been swung in her face when she reached him and she had to squeeze round it to pay and pick up her glass. Almost brushing the grey nylon shirt wealed by the rhombus pattern of the string vest, she flinched nervous, dismayed that she had come.

This surprised her. Though she rarely went into a public house unescorted, she was accustomed to visiting other places alone and had frequently scorned more dependent women who relied upon a companion's shelter, but now she had an intimation of their fear. Standing by the bar, sipping her drink with the convincing poise gained from her training and temperament, she knew that the cold glass slipped and, putting it down, wiped her clammy palm. Across the room, faces, every one male, regarded her; a few were indifferent, others puzzled, some ostentatiously calculating her aggregate of sexual points, all placing her as that other, the woman who had dared to intrude on their patch. Without intention she had challenged a code which admitted women only on sufferance, as invisible appendages of men. Even so, they were not openly hostile. They didn't need to be, she thought, because they had an impromptu champion: Josh.

His face distorted by a look which came near to revulsion, he was watching her image in the mirror behind the bar and as she attempted to lift her glass he leant sideways, pinioning her against the next customer, using his great back as a wedge and crushing her breasts. Still holding this position, he bent his neck towards his companion and said something which drew an answering obscenity. At this they both spluttered, then jetted out vapours of beer and showered spittle in loud mocking hoots.

'Let's hear it, Josh,' the barman pleaded.

'Some other time, Bob, when it's your missis' night off,' offering a slight acknowledgement to a woman replenishing the stock of crisps while giving a sideways nod towards Olivia. Again his eyes scratched down her reflection, and nudged, his friend shared his jeers.

Clamped against the bar, the beer welling vomit in her throat, Olivia felt the panic of something trapped, the desperation of someone cornered in an alley watching the relentless approach of boots that will soon bruise and break. She put down her glass again and began to edge back but, trembling, caught her heel against the leg of a stool. As she apologized to the man who occupied it, she saw across the broad back the leer on the mirrored face. And suddenly defeat was vanquished by anger. She raised a hand, tapped the mocking shoulder and, as the head screwed round, demanded in a voice that carried the length of the bar, 'If you have any remark to make about me, would you please say it to my face.'

The silence was immediate; a few residual echoes tinkled like ice against glass; shocked faces bobbed on the perimeter of her vision but at its centre was his, at first fourteen inches from her own, then six. The eyes jerked among those behind her, recruiting uncritical support, while damp, tufted nostrils distended and the lips drew back over nicotine-grained teeth.

'What's up wi'yer? I've no "remark" to make on you. Don't push yourself. If business is slack, then get outside and wait. Only, I'm fussy, so I'd need a few more inside me first.'

Hedged by a swell of sniggers, Olivia dredged for breath and, with it, words; but another voice said, 'Hi! We've only just seen you. We're round the other side.'

'You've forgotten your drink,' Stephen added, while groping as through a mist she began to follow.

Obediently she went back; the barman pushed her glass towards her; and as she sensed an apology in his gesture, some of her composure returned. She glanced round the circle, still silent, like that one on the telephone who for four days had waited for her to break. And drawing herself up, she looked down at the carious mouth, the clogged nostrils, and keeping her expression calm and lips steady she stared into the eyes until, their triumph faltering, they blinked and slid away.

When she rejoined him, Stephen fussed, 'I hope you haven't been waiting long, but you seem to have struck up a conversation, more than I could manage.' This indicated that he was oblivious of what had occurred and, its repulsive scum still on her, she had no wish to disabuse him. Leading her down two steps and into what must once have been the back parlour, he added, 'They're a rough lot in the bar. In here's more select.'

'Listen to him,' Karen exclaimed, and made a space for Olivia on the bench. 'It's so select you have to be on sup. ben. to get in. She's an actress,' she told the rest, 'with no job. So she can have a free pass.'

'Do you know Meryl Streep?' one asked.

'She's Nick's pin-up for the moment,' Karen explained.

'I'm sorry, no; I haven't met her.'

Nick frowned, disappointed. 'I suppose it was a long shot.'

'There are a lot of us about.'

'You're the first one I've spoke to,' another commented.

'Ask her for her autograph, then, Wayne,' Karen suggested. 'But Trudi's sister's been in a picture, hasn't she, Trudi?'

'Anybody could've been! I could've got a hitch there, no hassle, only they didn't want blokes. Dinner and thirty quid a day! Just for standing in a queue outside a butcher's!'

'What was it?' Olivia asked.

'It was something about a pig, wasn't it, Trudi?' Karen prompted.

'Yes; and they dressed them up old-fashioned. Bet had to wear curlers and a head scarf. She wouldn't have done it if she'd known that first off. She would've died if anyone had seen her.'

'Wayne wouldn't have said no to curlers and a head scarf, would you?' Nick said.

'I wouldn't say no to a bikini for thirty quid.'

'Is there anything you'd say no to, Olivia?' Stephen asked.

'Not a lot. If I had the chance of some work in film I'd take it.'

'Who wouldn't, for thirty quid a day,' Wayne agreed.

'As a matter of fact, I'd hope to get more. You've described work as extras.' She explained, choosing the words carefully in order not to pull rank or put down Trudi's sister.

'It's the difference between professional and amateur,' Stephen concluded, proving as often happened that Olivia's tact was unnecessary.

'You must be rolling,' Wayne admired.

'I would be if I could earn that every day.'

'You have to look at it like this,' Karen interpreted. 'She might do a part then have nothing for weeks. Isn't that right, Olivia? So she has to stash some of it away.'

'And she hasn't actually got a part in a film at the moment,' Stephen pointed out and they all laughed.

'Anyway, I'm more interested in the theatre.'

'Pays better, does it?'

'Wayne, you are awful!'

'Not likely. I barely clear a hundred a week.'

'That's not much of a catch if you can't rely on it,' he commiserated. 'Have you ever thought of television? There must be money in that.'

Eager to establish her association with a star, Karen reported, 'She was on the telly last week, weren't you, Olivia? She told me.'

Wayne opened his mouth but before he could inquire the fee, Olivia said, 'That's why I'm here.'

None of them had seen 'Mystery of the Week', though after Olivia's description Nick told her he was sorry to have missed it, his regret expressed with a fervour that suggested his adoration of Meryl Streep was under siege. Neither could any of them remember when they had last seen Rita.

'Probably not since that night she got pissed,' Wayne tried to calculate. 'Have we? I can't be sure.'

'I don't think so,' Nick agreed.

'Mind you,' Trudi pointed out, 'she could be here all evening and you'd hardly notice. But that time was different.'

'It wasn't only different; it was unique! Most times you sit here spinning out half a shandy, but she was loaded. Drinks all round. No sooner through one than she was shouting for another lot. I was so sloshed I couldn't get up till Mum got back from work next day.'

'So what's new, Wayne?'

'Because I got sloshed. That's what's new.'

'Give over. Your stinking hangover is of no interest to Olivia.'

'It wasn't a stinking hangover. Painful, I grant, but I loved every minute of it. I lay there saying to myself: Enjoy it, man, let yourself enjoy it; it could be·years, or never, before you're laid out with another like this.'

'To hear him talk anybody 'ud think nobody else is skint. And it's Rita that Olivia wants to hear about,' Karen, mistress of ceremonies, reminded them.

'Are you really looking for her?' Nick asked.

She nodded, thinking: at the end of this, he's going to ask me out. And warmed by the thought, she discovered that the sickness of the bar had at last drained from her throat.

'I knew she was missing,' Trudi announced, 'because of that in the paper.'

'Both her neighbour and grandmother have mentioned that, but I haven't seen the report.'

'Has she a grandma as well?' Karen asked.

'As well as who? Most people have, or have had.'

'As well as her mum, of course. You *know*, Wayne. And she was enough.'

'She means a real cow,' Trudi interpreted.

Disapproving, Stephen glanced at Olivia and blushed. 'Rita never called her that.'

'Well, she wouldn't, would she? She never stood up for herself.' But she did on the day she left home, Olivia thought. 'You wouldn't catch me putting up with what she did.'

'What sort of thing?'

Trudi shrugged. 'Oh, you know – questions every five minutes, being in when they said.' She floundered, aware that she was enumerating the sins of all parents.

Then recalling some peculiar to Rita's, she added more confidently: 'Her mum was in here once nosing about, asking where she lived. I didn't split on her; not that I knew anyway. And another thing – one night she locked Rita out.'

'That was her dad,' Nick corrected.

'Her stepdad.'

'He can't have been. They had the same name.'

'He was her stepdad, I tell you,' Karen insisted. 'Rita wrote another name once on a book in junior school; I can't remember what it was. The teacher said she had to write what her mother had put when she brought her in. I said to her, you do as you like, but she wouldn't.'

This appeared to confirm Trudi's description.

'It's strange what you learn,' Stephen reflected, twirling his glass. 'Rita never told me that.'

'Kept things to herself.'

'All the same.'

Arrested, their animation stilled, they looked at him. Then Karen glanced towards Wayne, leant across and whispered, 'I expect she would have told you, Steve, when – you know – she thought it mattered.'

Consolatory, the rest murmured agreement, recognizing an affection they had not previously noted though puzzled that the girl's secrecy, of no moment within their casual companionship, should give such pain. And Olivia thought: It is symptomatic of her temperament, that face sulking into the camera, the taciturn member of this group. It was Rita's right to conceal what she wished, yet that could cause distress, just as her leaving home – an unexpected bid for independence – had brought grief. In the interests of our own needs, how far are we justified in ignoring others? she wondered; and with a sudden remorse thought of her mother.

Conscious that he was required to relieve their silence, Stephen mumbled, 'Perhaps Rita doesn't want anyone to look for her.'

'Provided that she's safe. That's what I'm trying to find out.'

'Anything could have happened to her,' Trudi stated, not entirely without relish.

Karen tutted, derisive. 'Such as?'

'It was in the *Evening Chronicle*,' the other defended.

'I wish I'd seen this.' She would have done had she been interested enough in the town to buy the local paper. Perhaps Mrs Winterton would have a copy. 'What did it say?'

'Something about violence not being ruled out. I didn't read it. My dad did, though, when we were having tea. They went on about the woman who had the house where she had a bedsit.'

'Mrs Drew.'

'That's right. She's done a bunk, too. They were asking her to come forward.'

'She'll be daft if she does.'

'But Wayne, they're *asking*!'

'So what? Just look at it her way.' He cleared his throat in preparation for showing them the way Elizabeth Drew could look at it. 'There's been violence, hasn't there? So . . .'

'Not necessarily. Trudi said it hasn't been ruled out. Why did they put that?' Nick asked.

'Rita's room was turned upside down,' Stephen told him.

'Right,' Wayne resumed quickly. 'There's been a fight. First person the fuzz can lay their hands on – he, or she, is for it. Mrs Drew's cleared out, so she's the first suspect.'

'That's ridiculous; I know. I've met her, when I used to visit Rita.'

'I'm not suggesting she was mixed up in it, necessarily. I'm just saying that if there's been a fight she'd be advised to scram, sharpish. She stay around, and the boys in blue will be on her for sure. All they're interested in is making a charge. Remember our Al? He got caught riding a bike without a licence when he was fifteen. After that, they never let up. Any complaint, first thing they did was grab Al: shop-window broken – pull in Al; a fight – fetch Al; kids smoking grass – our Al must have shoved them it. In the end our dad went down to the station and told them if it didn't stop he'd shop a few of them. Knew enough to get some of them inside for life. So if this Mrs Drew's got any sense she'll stay out of the way for a bit.'

'I take your point but I can't imagine a landlady thinking like that.' Yet the woman in the supermarket had feared police interference and had considered Elizabeth Drew wise to get away. 'Can you imagine it?' she appealed to Stephen.

'Not Mrs Drew.'

'You're assuming that the room was done over before Mrs Drew left,' Nick addressed Wayne.

'I've met a neighbour; she noticed that the milk hadn't been taken in and deduced that Mrs Drew left a short time before Rita since she would have remembered to cancel it.' Olivia decided not to introduce the red herring of the knocking men.

'She could be right, but the timing ought to be cleared up. If the room was turned over after Mrs Drew left, then she's in the clear. All the same, I don't agree that it would be intelligent for her to stay out of the way. That would make it look as if she knew something about it and you couldn't blame the police if they suspected she was implicated.'

'Nick's talking sense. But this could have occurred after they had both gone,' Stephen argued. 'It could have been a straightforward burglary. That's what it looked like on Pennine News.'

'I took it for granted that was what it was, at first,' Olivia agreed; 'but the programme wasn't explicit. It didn't say that it was a break-in and apparently the newspaper doesn't suggest that as a possibility.'

'They must have eliminated that, then,' Wayne concluded. 'Maybe this Mrs Drew did it herself.'

'Leave off, Wayne! I've met her. She was slim, and young. I wouldn't say more than about twenty-two.'

'Looking like Olivia?' Nick admired.

'Only when Olivia's not talking. Mrs Drew has the same sort of features but they are less defined. She was – it's difficult to describe – pulled down, somehow, and quiet and shy.'

'You couldn't say that I'm any of those.'

They laughed. 'You wouldn't stick us for long if you were,' one expressed a group complacency and Olivia thought: Poor Rita!

Dismissing this view of Mrs Drew's personality, Trudi asked, urgent, 'Do you mean, Wayne, that she might have done Rita in?' and talking over Stephen's appalled objections, 'It said there might have been foul play.'

'*Might* have been. In other words, they know nothing and they're just providing some sensational reading for people like you,' Nick rebuked.

'Look, *I* didn't read it, did I? It was my dad. And people do get murdered, especially young women. That's not my fault. For all we know, that Mrs Drew might have clobbered her and stuck her in the canal.'

'Or it could have been her stepdad,' Karen suggested. 'For her money.'

Deflected, the other repeated, 'For her money?'

'Yeah. It's often money, isn't it? It 'ud be like this,' ignoring the incipient giggles. 'Rita's stepdad finds out that her proper dad has died and was loaded. He's left her everything, but it's to go to her mum if Rita pops off first. Now her stepdad knows he'll never get a handout from Rita because once he locked the door on her and he calculates that it's on the cards he'll kick the bucket before her. So, wanting to have a chance of a good binge while he's still capable, he gets in his car one night, forces himself into Rita's bedsit, gags her, breaks the place up to make it look like Mrs Drew done it, shoves Rita in the boot, drives to the canal and throws her in. You were right about the canal, Trudi. It's so mucky the Council 'ud be ashamed to have it dragged.'

Flushing, the other tried sarcasm to moderate the applause. 'You shouldn't be wasting time with us; you should be writing detective stories.'

'If I did, I wouldn't come to you for plots.'

'And I wouldn't read them.'

'No. You'd leave that to your dad, wouldn't you?'

'Look, he's not responsible for what goes in the paper. All he said was, if there's talk about foul play then there must be something in it. It was Wayne said maybe Mrs Drew did it herself.'

Their noise was attracting attention. Customers passing the doorway paused to listen, were stared out and then went on. While Olivia recalled Mrs Booth's account of the journalist's visit. He had learnt nothing from them to add to the one concrete fact that he already had: the state of Rita's room; but he had implied fears for her safety. From which it appeared he had fabricated a report to titillate the readers' armchair taste for blood. Again Olivia regretted that she had not bought the local paper. Since she was looking for a girl in one of the towns it covered, she should keep up with its news.

Wayne, either to circumvent mockery or to assert the truth, was insisting that his idea had been misinterpreted. 'I meant, did over Rita's place herself. That night Rita had all that lolly: perhaps she pinched it, then cleared out, and Mrs Drew was doing the place over to see if she could find anything to prove she had.'

'That's a terrible thing to say. Rita isn't a thief.'

'Look, Steve, I didn't say that to get at her but we can't afford to be soft about it. We're trying to find out where she's gone or what's happened to her and for starters we have to know why. It's the only way. If she did pinch the money, then she would have a reason, like wanting to do a bunk. It doesn't make her a thief, not in so many words.'

'All right, suppose we accept that,' Nick came in; 'it doesn't explain why Mrs Drew's gone off as well.'

'That could be just chance.' Speaking more loudly than was needed, Trudi redeemed previous blunders by this emphasis on logic. 'She might've gone away for something else, something that had nothing to do with Rita, whether she'd stole money or not.'

'That's right,' he approved. 'Every little thing's not forced to be connected. It's easy to go over the top. This isn't a book; it's something that happened here. Not every small detail has to add up. There are lots you have to throw out. You can't expect everything to have a heavy significance, like,' he cast around for an example, 'like Rita telling me that last time she was here that she was exhausted since she'd been up most of the night.'

'Did she say why?'

'There you are! I told you Olivia would make a good private dick,' Karen complimented her protégée.

'Not directly. I got the impression that it wasn't by choice, though; more like something had been going on and she'd been dragged in. There can't be anything in that, Olivia, surely?'

'Probably not.' But in some measure this corroborated the neighbour's story. Though prurient, busy with scandal, she could not be entirely ignored. 'Can we go back to that evening Rita got drunk? Let's forget about the money for a moment and concentrate on her. For example, her mood.'

'She was all right. Anybody would be, wouldn't they, with a purseful like that? Not mean with it, either.'

'I don't think she was all right,' Stephen said.

Karen agreed. 'Wayne reckons that if anybody is throwing their money about they're having a good time.'

'Well, wasn't she? There was nothing stopping her. She was here with us, standing the drinks, enjoying herself for once. It was like a party, nicer because it wasn't expected.'

'On Monday when Karen and I ran into each other, she told me that Rita had been upset.'

The other nodded. 'It seemed to me she was trying to shut something off. It wasn't natural, her letting herself go like that. What do you think, Trudi?'

'I thought it was creepy at first, but then I didn't notice much after a bit.' They giggled. 'I remember, though, going down to the lav and she came with me. I stood by the basin and waited while she went in first. I think that's right, but I wouldn't swear to it; I was already half cut. Then she came out and she hadn't been able to do up her zip – she was wearing denims – so I had a go. It took me hours, or felt like it, because the teeth were caught in her pants and I said something like, "Anybody coming in now, Rita, would get the wrong idea." It was the daft sort of thing you say, you know – mumbling on to help the time pass, not trying to get a laugh. But it did. It practically laid her out. She was so creased up, I couldn't go on fiddling with the zip. Only it wasn't nice laughing. It was more like hysterics and I did wonder whether I ought to give her a slap on the face. I didn't because I didn't like to and because she was crying as well, with the laughs, until gradually it got worse and she was just crying. When she stopped I wet a paper towel and dabbed at her face and lent her my powder. I had to put that on for her as well. When we got back I realized that I hadn't used the loo.'

'She must have been more drunk than I realized,' Nick commented.

'I don't think she was, then. It was creepy. I didn't like it.'

'Soon drowned your sorrows,' Wayne laughed.

But the rest were puzzled, their expressions sombre, and as the barman in the adjacent room called for last orders they raised their glasses and sipped the last drops.

'She'd hurt her wrist,' Karen recalled suddenly. 'That 'ud be why you had to help her with the zip. When we were going out she tripped up the step. I grabbed her and she let out such a yell! "My wrist got twisted," she said because I asked. "I'm not generally that clumsy." Afterwards it came to me that she must have been referring to that glass she knocked over. She must have been using her left hand.'

'She didn't mention any injury,' Stephen muttered, 'though I took her home. As far as the gate.'

While Olivia, listening to the ambiguity of 'got twisted', connected it with Nick's deduction that there had been an incident when Rita was 'dragged in'. Suddenly the talk round her seemed irrelevant. 'I must be going,' she said.

'Keep in touch,' Karen grinned. 'You know where to find us.'

'I'll come with you. There's something . . .'

Disappointed that Stephen's offer had preceded his, Nick asked, 'Are you on the phone? So we can give you a ring if there's anything else.'

'And you give us a buzz if you're on to anything,' Wayne said. 'You can count us in.'

Their voices clacked round her. Their upturned faces were featureless discs receding before the image of a hand gripping, screwing a young girl's arm. She reached out, urgent to save. 'I'll give Steve my number,' she promised them.

'I didn't like to introduce this in front of them, knowing what they would make of it,' Stephen began when they were outside; 'but I've got a key to Mrs Drew's house.

Rita give it to me that night, saying that any time I wished I could let myself in. I refused it because I couldn't imagine such an occasion but she wouldn't listen. She was so determined I should have it, I took it in the end just to satisfy her. Frankly I found it rather ironical to be given a key to a house I no longer visited. Probably the only occasion in my life it'll happen, too; and useless.'

'You could quote it in the future as customary procedure.'

'Some hope! But I'm telling you because, if you ever want to have a look round, that's possible.' He stopped under a lamp, found a diary and scrawled a telephone number. 'Here,' tearing out the page, 'and shall I take yours? Nick thought that advisable,' he reminded her, shyness requiring another's authority to make the request.

She dictated her number but did not tell him that it was monitored. She had no desire to cause Stephen to worry for her.

They walked on, talking about what had been said, but afterwards she could remember nothing of this conversation, gentle and almost elegiac in the amber light, because of Josh.

He had come upon her as she walked towards the lavatory, Stephen having gone ahead to wait in the street, and barring her way had snarled, 'Don't think you can get away with it, you bitch. I've about had a bellyful and I'm not standing for any more.'

Forced against the wall, she saw a hand swing then drop as heels clattered on slate slabs.

'Night, Josh,' the bartender's wife dismissed him. 'See you tomorrow. After you, love,' holding open the door for Olivia.

Cramming damp paper towels into a plastic bag, she asked, pretending casualness, 'Are you all right, love? You look a bit peaky.'

'It's nothing. I need to get to bed.'

'There isn't much that doesn't cure. But if that Josh said anything to you, don't you take no notice. He's not my cup of tea, I admit, but there are circumstances. His wife's forever leaving him. He'll fetch her back, then she'll go off again. Sometimes I think you can't really blame her, but it was her married him and she ought to stick to it. She owes him that. A man loses his self-respect when he can't keep hold of his wife.'

And when does a woman lose hers? Olivia thought.

Chapter Seven

With sixteen members in the agency and seven at present in work, the rota changed each fortnight and Olivia was on duty Thursday that week. The morning was lambent with colour, encouraging economy on bus fares and prompting a sense of release. Pausing to buy apples at an open market, Olivia was salved by the dreamless light and the sun's unguent on her flesh. The hours ahead at typewriter and telephone would be busy but peaceful, and the thought of them relieved the crush of the man's chest and suppressed the threat of his fist; suppling her movements and brightening her face. Neither was any of this diminished when Dora Booth joined her by the stall.

'You're up in good time,' she greeted.

'It's my turn at the office.' She explained. 'We've taken some space in Crimple Mill.'

'That's a fair walk. Nice early on, mind you, but wearisome after a day in the sheds. I was there, start of the war, then it went in for munitions. A fine let-down, that, after weaving.'

'You'd hardly guess at either, now. It's been divided into what are called compact units to rent. In other words, microscopic, but we don't need much space. On the first floor there's the main office of a travel agency, a couple who make soft toys, a restaurant, a woman who designs posters, and us.'

Mrs Booth sneered. 'Come to a pretty pass, hasn't it, when a mill that used to turn out thousands of bolts a week is filled with folk doing nothing useful.'

'I hadn't considered that,' she admitted, though she would have expressed the change in political terms.

'You haven't seen as many years as me.'

The stallholder proffered the apples and waited for payment. Olivia searched for the correct change, hoping that Mrs Booth would accept her concentration as a signal to part. But was disappointed.

'I've been thinking about you. There's something that should have been said,' she told Olivia abruptly. 'I didn't know he hadn't, till you'd gone, second time. It's not my business, looked at any road up, but I said to Charlotte, she's owed it; the young woman should know why he was after seeing her. You were round in the afternoon, Monday, weren't you? And that man from the *Evening Chronicle* came in the morning. It was because of that.'

'Mr Dale wished to see me because a journalist had visited you?'

'That's right. He's got more up on top than Charlotte, though I'm her mother that says it, and he had his suspicions what might come of it, so he wanted to tell you there was nothing personal.'

'How could there be anything personal – anything related to me? We hadn't even met!'

'They'd seen you on the telly.'

'But representing someone else. Mr and Mrs Dale knew nothing about me, *myself*.' And no more about Elizabeth Drew. 'I haven't seen the report but I know that violence was mentioned. They could hardly suggest that I was responsible for that, if there were any.' She giggled; their confusion was so ridiculous.

'That's finished, then. You don't sound to have been put to any inconvenience.' However she did not move away.

'I must get on. I'd like the chance to open the post before the telephone starts ringing,' smiling to herself because today, in the office, the handset would not slip in her palm. She could not convince herself that the exchange's interception was foolproof.

'Yes; it's a fair walk,' the other repeated. Then thrusting her basket against Olivia's legs, 'If you do come across Rita, you tell her that her grandma's found out. It's taken a bit of time but she knows now and she'll be round her quick if she doesn't shift herself, the sly little madam. You tell her it's the last thing I'd have imagined coming from her. I've never been so disgusted, but I'll undertake not to bring her mum into it if she comes and tells me.'

Pinned against the market stall, disconcerted as she'd been at their previous meeting by a swift change of tone, Olivia saw that the annoyance and disgust were less important than the emotion they concealed. For the woman was no longer spry, a sexagenarian in energetic health; she was old and ill, her cheeks rusted and flaking, dry as if the juice of her life had drained off.

'Yes, I'll tell her, if I find her,' she agreed, pushed the basket aside and walked quickly up the street.

'She's round the twist,' she reminded herself; 'absolutely barmy,' trying to forget the desolation in the woman's face. 'They all are. Like her daughter Charlotte's, her speech is maniacal. They string words together in an intelligible sequence but the sense is malformed. It means nothing. They talk in riddles as if trying not to admit to themselves what it is they are saying. You could call it the sub-text, except there's no text for this to be sub!'

Enlivened by this notion, she stepped into the pavement's sunny border and strode among early shoppers whose expressions were matched to the routine business pursued. Terrors, follies, passions were undisclosed and, choosing not to doubt the crowd's public face, Olivia accepted its ordinariness with relief, turning her memory from the one that remained by the stall. 'I'll think about it later,' she promised herself. 'There's no time for that today. Which I hope will give me plenty to do but which will certainly be uncomplicated. A rest from the Dales.'

She raised her face to the light, invited back her former contentment and, ignoring litter, dust and spent buildings, she willed herself into a holiday mood as she walked through a car-park and along decaying streets towards Crimple Mill.

The first three hours were as occupied as she had hoped – hoped because activity increased the chance of engagements. Already ringing as she entered the office, the telephone was not an enemy but an ally humming goodwill. She wrote down the details of this availability check, telephoned the actor, declined with stagey sighs his equally stagey invitation to join him in bed, and reported back to the casting assistant. She followed up two inquiries from a maker of commercials and another from Northern Video Productions who were looking for a plump, unexceptional-looking (!) actress in her thirties to lend credibility to a nursery-nurse training film. She read the previous day's entries in the log book and chased a television director through a phalanx of minions to announce that the agency had just the man for a part and solicit an interview. She scanned the sheets from the Script Breakdown Service that had arrived that morning, underlined forthcoming productions with parts suitable for colleagues, and began on introductory letters. Copying out a theatre's address, she noticed that BBC 2 was planning to dramatize *Moll Flanders* and, to anticipate their search for a cast, she telephoned the library to ask them to reserve the book. Returning to the letters, she discovered they had run out of photographs of one of their members so she switched on the answering machine, locked up and ran out to order another set of prints. Ten minutes later, back in the office, she found a request on the machine to phone Alnwick. She did so. They were offering Earl a part, and as soon as the line was clear again she was pressing out his number, delighted to be the one to give him the news. But there was no answer and feeling like a child trusted with a secret but bursting to tell, she left the desk, filled the kettle at the tap in the corridor and brewed herself tea.

She opened the letters delivered in the second post and was puzzling over a cheque for their 'Mystery of the Week' engagement from which it appeared that Alan had been paid more than herself, when she was interrupted.

'Look what I found lurking on the stairs,' Earl greeted, dragging in Raymond. 'With felonious intent.'

'I have to live up to my reputation. I started painting one of my outsides this morning, then the customer went shopping and put all the windows on the latch, so I've knocked off for a beer.'

'We're not licensed,' she told him.

'I know. That'll have to be remedied. I shall bring it up at the next meeting. Normally when I'm on shift I fetch in a couple of cans. I'll not stay long. How's tricks?'

'I'll not take my coat off; I'm not stopping,' Earl mimicked the accent.

'He's got a job.'

From the evidence of the next minutes, an onlooker would have deduced that Olivia had offered it. She was embraced, kissed, danced and whirled in the air. 'A good thing this doesn't happen every day. I'm getting past it,' Raymond wheezed as he dropped her to the floor. Then, 'Let me be the first to congratulate you, Earl. You deserve it,' and resorting to the formality of his generation, he grabbed the other's hand.

'Now look, you've embarrassed him. He's blushing under the coat.'

Again they were laughing; and as they discussed the company's season, the tour of theatres and halls scattered over the lovely Northumberland fells, the plans to attend performances, they were clamorous, exultant, partners in triumph. This party mood seduced them to optimism about Olivia's forthcoming audition and it informed their comments on her search for Rita Dale.

'Now don't you neglect the learning for that test,' Raymond advised.

'I don't have to learn anything specially for it, just polish up my regular pieces.'

'We'll have to coach Raymond in a few. All he's experienced so far is interviews. He hasn't suffered an audition.'

'It's my face they want.'

'Lucky that's the limit of their desires, Ray, because we certainly should have trouble persuading them you haven't got defective vision.'

'You know about that little misunderstanding, Olivia? I'd got this notion he'd be like a young lad I used to play with down our street – he'll be a grown man now – and I was looking out for him. It's easy for an idea to get fixed. And what I'm saying is, you ought not to get wrapped up in looking for that girl,' he continued without a pause to indicate a change of subject. 'It's a job for the Constabulary. Earl remarked that you were seeing some of her mates. What did they have to say about it?'

'They really went to town on it, when they could keep to the point.' She recounted their conversation.

'That's codswallop! Murder!'

'The stepfather theory wasn't serious, Raymond.'

'I'm pleased to hear one of them had some sense. If that had been on the cards, they wouldn't have let it on to the telly without more caution. Believe me, all that's happened is that young lass has nipped off, probably pinching something on the way out. Nothing very remarkable.'

Olivia did not rouse herself to invite an explanation for the wrecked room, nor did she mention Rita's sprained wrist, her crying in the lavatory, her reference to a sleepless night. Warmed by the sun's stroke through the polished glass and sleeked by Earl's good fortune, she felt lazy and disinclined to resume the questions of the last three days.

And when Earl said, 'That sounds plausible enough, Olivia,' she did not remind him that plausibility was concerned with appearances, not truth.

'You don't have to prove her dad wrong,' he insisted.

It was a second before she understood. There had been so many accounts, hints and guesses since their hamburger on Tuesday evening that he was out of date. 'No; I can leave her mother to do that. But I should like to know why she went. Karen said she thought Rita was happy until recently. In spite of the goings-on at the house, described by the neighbour.'

'So there's a knocking shop on Hackney Street!' Raymond gasped through hoots when she had finished. 'Next time you've got a tale like that would you mind giving me warning. It's enough to make a chap swallow his false teeth. I must say they've kept it secret. There isn't a body I know has got wind of it. Not even Arthur, and he has all the news *before* it's happened; goes by the look in the eye. I can't wait to see his face when I tell him.'

He rose, leant against the filing cabinet as if it were a bar and, pitching his voice to a circumspect confidence, addressed Earl. 'Here, Arthur, I've got something to tell you. You're not going to like it, I can assure you of that, being as it casts doubt on your standing as the man with the news.'

'I'm big enough to take it.'

'It's not the beer belly that's in question, Arthur, but the heart. I would have said, the mind, but we have to be realistic. It's like this, Arthur. I was up at a house on Hackney Street yesterday, plying my trade with brush and distemper – I still call it that, you know, though it's really that newfangled emulsion – and this old biddy comes with a shovel and clocks me one on the head. "What's that for?" I asked, being of a curious nature and glad I was wearing my helmet, it having a visor, you see, which protects the eyes from the paint. "For keeping us up all night with your knocking," she answers. "Don't think I'm deceived by you painting that gate. I saw you last night as I righted the curtain . . ." '

'And vowed I would give you a thump on your pate,' Earl chanted.

'Do me a favour, will you, Arthur: keep off the poetry and stick to writing jokes. England's Glory number three hundred and sixty-eight, and we don't have to quote it, very near raised a laugh. You go on like that, by the time you reach four figures I reckon you'll be challenging this biddy in the Back Streets Comedy Contest. Except to qualify you have to be round the bend, and you may be on the gullible side, Arthur, but you're not half-baked. I can see you're gagging, so I'll put you out of your misery. Wait for it, Arthur. Take a good grip of that bar. I didn't know it any more than you at the time, but I was painting the red-light district. A bit small, as it turned out, because there's only the one house, but there's room for expansion. Not over this neighbour's fence, though. She's not in favour. So she bangs on the wall. All night they're rolling in, men still in their muck. But not in our class, Arthur. If we were gasmen lodging in Hackney Street and called out, we'd wash us in the Men's before we went back, wouldn't we? Or if we'd done overtime in Hudson's, we'd wipe the grease off before we came in. Or if your missis had fallen out with you – a risk, Arthur, unless you improve on those jokes – and she'd set up in Hackney Street and you reckoned another bloke was there licking the cream, you'd down a few one night and go round with your mates to see him off, wouldn't you? No, looking at you, Arthur, I can see you wouldn't, but there's many that would. And another thing that wouldn't worry you would be her next door

– that is, if you were a gasman or down at the yard – because you wouldn't have time to notice some nosy parker with nothing better to do than stand at the curtains, and with an imagination that 'ud do credit to her hubby's comics. But I can guarantee you one thing, Arthur, if you were a young lass living in that house – you have to force yourself to get inside that – you'd get fed up with it all, now and again, and if your stepdad turned up, as some have the habit when they calculate their daughters are presentable young women and well out of nappies, you'd smile sweetly, take his bribe for affection and blow it in the pub. And you'd do the same if your landlady had a bloke who, to get you out of the way for a couple of hours, handed over a wad. And now, folks, we'll finish with a singalong with Ray, that all-time favourite, "Sonny Boy". A-one, a-two, a-three!'

They had polished off the first verse and were into a deep-throated rendering of the chorus when the telephone sounded.

'I hope that I haven't interrupted a rehearsal, my dear,' Mrs Winterton said, hearing the lingering strains, 'though I was never fond of Al Jolson. Would he have been so successful, do you think, had he been a Negro instead of a white blacked up? Anyway, I'm phoning to tell you that I shall not return from my nephew's this evening but should be back by tomorrow night. So don't forget to lock up if you go out. Have you read what I left you?'

'I didn't see anything.'

'I put it by the phone. Perhaps other things have collected on top of it.'

'I wouldn't be surprised. What is it?'

'Last Monday's *Evening Chronicle*. There's a report on page three that you might like to con. I'm afraid I didn't notice it until I was looking for paper when emptying ashes out of the boiler. I thought you might be interested. And I spoke to the woman at the exchange about those silly calls.'

'Yes. Thank you.'

'I forgot that you would be at the agency today so I telephoned home first. It was a curious feeling being required to quote the number I was phoning when it happened to be my own! Then the request for your name was unexpected, so I stumbled over that. You will appreciate my fears about my sister Dorothy. However, the arrangement was necessary. I must leave you now, but don't grow anxious. I'll be home tomorrow.'

Replacing the handset, Olivia wondered why she should grow anxious.

'That would seem like a natural break,' Earl said. 'Mustn't hold up the good work any longer. Keep cheerful, lovie.' He put his arms around her. 'You pay attention to what our Ray says; he's been around for centuries – that shop-soiled face proves it. He'd make a better sleuth-hound than either of us.' By including himself he reaffirmed his willingness to help her, but with their raucous parody of the song still in her ears and with her wrist circled by his hand, polished aubergine lightening to rose in the palm, her task seemed no longer important.

'Do you really mean better, or a detective with more style? I think Raymond belongs in the Inspector Clouseau category.'

'A brilliant piece of casting! We must remember that, if anything similar comes up. He has a perfect record, having managed to shake hands with the wrong man. You may yet get another job, Raymond! See you later.'

'Was he addressing you or me?' she asked when he had left.

'Both. That's if you're in agreement. Him getting a part calls for a celebration. I'll introduce you to my local; it's the Pig and Whistle. I expect you'll have heard of it. If you board the number eighty at the clock round seven, I'll meet you at the terminus, then I'll fetch you back.

The missis can come, too; it's about time she met a few of you. Sometimes the way she looks I reckon she thinks this agency is another one of my stories.'

'And isn't it? But thanks, it's a lovely idea. I'll buy a sandwich round the corner and join you straight from here.'

'No need for that. I'll stand you a chicken in a basket if you're feeling peckish. Not one of my more sophisticated jokes, that, but it'll pass on a good night. Chicken, you see, Olivia, and peck-ish.'

'I didn't want to egg you on.'

'Not bad, if they got it. When I'm running short of material, I'll give you a ring. I'll be off, then. You know, whoever painted this place out didn't do such a bad job,' he remarked as, standing by the door, he scrutinized the office. 'I'm referring to the workmanship, not the colours.'

They were yellow and purple, fanning like spotlights down the walls and providing bold frames for notices and theatre posters. 'Earl did it.'

'I might have known. It's arty. He's a talented young man.' Raymond hesitated. 'Speaking in confidence you understand, Olivia, I'd like to tell you something. I've kicked around a bit and I'll be forty-five next March, but Earl's been an eye-opener to me. I'm ashamed to admit it because it doesn't reflect well but till I joined here I'd always been hard on his sort. (I'm not talking about his colour.) I took the view of my mates and them in the Clubs. I'm not giving excuses, just saying that I never thought; it was automatic to sneer. Perhaps that was because if we didn't we were feared that we might be taken for the same. I don't know. But I don't see it that way now I've met him, and I want you to know that I'm grateful. There's room for improvement in all of us and I'd not like to think I was too blind to see it or be too stuck to make the change. And there's one thing I'm certain of, something I'll never do again, I can guarantee that. I'll never take them off in the Clubs – you know, pansy, getting an easy laugh. I blush now to think on. I never thought I was being more than just mucky, exciting sniggers at the lengths they go to, doing what they do.'

His final phrase seemed to echo another, but she could not place it immediately and Raymond having confessed to a prejudice was now waiting for her answer, his look nervous.

'That's all right, Ray,' she said inadequately. 'You needn't have told me.'

'I'm one of this outfit now, aren't I? I wanted you to know. Put the record straight.'

'In the circumstances it cannot be entirely that.'

Their seriousness broken, they laughed together. 'There'll always be a word sticking up ready for someone to trip over,' he observed. 'Now don't forget the number eighty leaves from the clock at seven, give or take a few minutes.'

'I'll be on it. And Ray,' she halted his opening the door, 'thanks for the deduction. After the last three days I needed to hear some sense. What you worked out could be a lot nearer the truth than other suggestions.'

'Well, I'm the man on the spot. I know how things happen round here.'

'Anyway, it was good of you to help. I imagine that act would go like a bomb in the Clubs.'

'Bless you, girl, the lads wouldn't like that. Too subtle by far. I can see when it comes to some things your education's not all that it should be. I'll take you round a few. What they want is something broader and jokes they're easy with. Like: "Ta ta for now, then. Be good. But if you can't be good, be careful; and if you can't be careful, buy a pram." '

Refreshed by this interval of company, Olivia finished the letters, went out for a sandwich and paid the telephone bill. Recording this, she was reminded of the cheque from the television company and, after examining the invoice again, decided to inquire why there was a difference in the fees.

'I'm wondering whether there has been a mistake,' she explained to the casting assistant. 'I understood it was an eighty-pound minimum with overtime as a percentage of that. Could you tell me at what point overtime starts? I did the same number of hours as Alan Featherstone but my payment is less.'

'I'm sorry; I should have detailed the fee breakdown. Sloppy of me. I assumed you would recognize the reason. It's quite correct. Mr Featherstone has received the agreed rate for the programme plus an additional fee for the short piece of dialogue which wasn't scripted.'

'Thank you for clearing that up. Alan will be delighted.' She wanted to ask, what unscripted dialogue? But if the company were lavishing cash on film that didn't go out she felt under no obligation to argue.

'To be frank, we didn't intend to use the lines, so you might say that Mr Featherstone is lucky.'

Another riddle-monger! She seemed to attract them. 'You didn't intend to use the lines?'

'Good heavens, no! That was a mistake. The editor had to dash off immediately, so he left a message. Unfortunately it wasn't picked up. Mr Featherstone was asked to improvise a few lines to round off, some appropriate comments to give the reaction of the ordinary man in the street. Anything more might have compromised the director. As it is, that's exactly what has happened. There's been the devil to pay and I'm thankful that I'm well out of it. To be fair, I expect that Mr Featherstone must have thought the camera had stopped rolling after his first remarks, though I consider even those to be questionable. Certainly, though, it was meant to cut all of them. Instead of which, the whole two minutes went out.'

'Thank you for the explanation. I'm sure Alan will be

as sorry as you that things went wrong.' But not enough to contemplate reimbursement. 'Do keep in touch. We're in the middle of designing new CVs to bring us up to date and shall be sending out copies as soon as they're ready.'

So Alan's lines must have come at the end; and the director must be over-reacting to feel compromised by a few lines so mumbled that they couldn't be heard. Except that the director had struck her as very laid back and Alan never mumbled; one of his weaknesses was an incapacity to throw anything away. Then she recalled how she and Judy had mimicked him, had begun to fool about as the credits came up. Perhaps his voice had been over those. She would have to look at the recording again. Since in Rita's room the director had achieved shots that were nearly pornographic, it would be interesting to see what overstepped his tolerance in speech. She could not imagine how this would impugn his discretion or why it was so important. She would watch the recording again, dissociate herself from her own part in it, listen carefully through to the finish, and consider objectively the final effect of a film which did not incriminate her.

But as she made herself a cup of tea before leaving the office, she was surprised to hear the rattle of the spoon against the side of the beaker and though to steady it demanded an effort, she allowed herself to wonder only why she should be so exhausted after a single day's work.

Chapter Eight

Waving goodbye to Raymond, she watched his car slide round the corner before pushing her key into the lock. It had been a jolly evening and her tiredness was healthy as if she had spent a day outdoors. Her body was lithe; skin tingled. Astride the mat in the hall she performed a few exercises, laughing at herself, 'You're drunk.'

But she wasn't; she was happy and she wanted this to continue, was anxious to prevent its passing away from her before it was fully enjoyed. And urgent, she returned to the door, to make into reality the sensation of her hair settling back against her cheeks after wind-blown miles she had not walked, for the only way to do this was to go out again, out of the passage which constricted her, its walls leaning in, its linoleum curling under the brand of the street lamp, its stale air shrinking from the wide night.

The impulse was arrested; the happiness died. She pushed herself away from the door and walked towards the entrance to the basement, admitting that the desire for freedom had been an instinct to escape which she must control, admitting it was panic that contracted the hall, that there was a reason for the draughts, and asking herself what could have stopped her ears against the crunch of glass when she entered the house. Possessed by the certainty, she did not search elsewhere and went down the steps, but laboriously, placing a foot beside the other on each tread before descending to the next in order to delay the moment when she must reach her room.

She let the door bang back and stood on the threshold. She did not go in. It was not hers any more. Her tenancy had been gentle. There was no sign of that now. It was a place gaping and bruised. Undefended, it had cracked open and spilled under the force of another's tearing hand.

Slowly, her legs heavy, she shuffled away from it, took hold of the handrail and pulled herself up the steps. Thinking, 'I can sleep in the kitchen. There's a sofa. I shan't be cold. It's covered by a rug. I can get under that. Nobody will notice.' But at the top of the steps her head screwed round without her volition and her eyes, dragged along the phosphorus shaft, observed its brilliance unhindered by dusty glass, then the empty pane in the door. Remembering, she told herself, 'The person won't come back. Lightning never strikes in the same place twice.' It was a phrase of her mother's and she would have denounced its use but her palate was dry.

In the kitchen she opened a tap and started at the juddering pipes; as she raised a cup, the sound of water slopping on to the draining board lifted through the house. She felt watched, listened to; that the spirit of the intruder was no longer confined to the ruin at the bottom of the steps; and choking on shallow breaths, her flesh rising to cold points, she leant against the sink, shocked by her fear, shocked too by the discovery that against this malignancy she was insufficient and that she must call upon help.

'I'll telephone Earl,' she whispered to herself as she tiptoed into the hall. The thought comforted her. The feel of his arms hooping her to him, the stroke of his fingers in her hair, his permission for tears, cajoled her.

She dialled a number. 'Judy?' she asked.

'Who else? You're lucky. I've only just got in. I'm knackered. The bloody lights fused half an hour before the call and I mislaid three props. Alan tells me you've got an audition. That's brilliant.'

'Judy, will you come?'

'Come? When? I'm likely to be working on Sunday if the first night's anything to go on.'

She had forgotten. 'How was it?'

'Hairy! The director was seen leaving at the interval. You having a party?'

'This isn't a party.'

'Olivia, are you all right?'

'I don't know.'

'You don't sound it.'

'It was silly to phone. You're so far away.'

'I'm here at the end of this line.'

She could not answer. Words stopped at the futility of the hope.

'Olivia? What is it?'

'I shouldn't have phoned. I'm sorry. Being foolish. There's not really anything you can do.'

'Christ! Hang on. Let me think. The last train and coach will have gone, but there's the van and it's not loaded up. Even so, I couldn't be with you in less than an hour and a half. That any good?'

'Oh, Judy . . .'

'Save that. No problems. Except that I'm famished; I haven't eaten since one. So while you wait you can do something useful and throw a few things together.'

'I can't. I can't go into my room.'

'What?'

'It's been turned over. Somebody's broken in.'

There was a hiss of sieved breath then. 'Say an hour and a quarter. It may be no more than fifty miles. Have you telephoned the police?'

'No.'

'Then do that, and don't move anything before they arrive.'

'I shan't. I can't touch it.'

*

'No, I haven't touched anything. I can't,' she repeated, leading him into the kitchen.

'You're a sensible young woman.' He laid down his cap and took out a notebook. 'What time did you get back?'

'I didn't look. It can be only a few minutes ago.'

'Between ten-thirty and eleven sound all right? Any sign of anything at all out of the way when you came in?'

'Only the glass.'

'I meant in the street. But yes, there's no doubt how entry was effected. Better than a notice, Welcome. Leaded lights are easy enough, but a bit of clear glass puttied into the frame! They didn't even need a cutter and could see in to check before they began. I'm sorry, Miss; I know this isn't the right moment for criticism but I do wish people would pay more attention to what we say. A door like that wants something more than a rim-lock on it. All they had to do was get a hand in, see, and turn the knob. But you'll have noticed.'

'Yes.'

'An interest of mine, anti-theft devices. You'll have heard of the Mulholland Bolt? You haven't? Mine. Quite a simple invention. You could have done with one on that door. They're in all the ironmongers and I'm hoping one day they'll get into Woolworths.'

'This isn't my house.'

'But you'll pass on the word? I'll want the name of the owner. The Duty Sergeant said you reported that she's not at home, but before that, let's take a look at the damage.'

'The room's in the basement.'

'That's right,' consulting his notes. 'You must tell me if anything's missing.'

'Could I do that tomorrow?'

He stared at her. 'You've taken this badly, haven't you, Miss? That's not unnatural. Folk do. But it'll wear off, once everything's set to rights,' he consoled, avuncular. 'I reckon tomorrow will suffice. After all, it's late. So I'll go down and examine then you can come into the station in the morning and we'll put in a report. Now you just get that kettle on and make yourself a cup of tea while I go down and see what's what.'

Returning, he tutted, filled the kettle and put it over the gas. 'Here, let's be having that rug that's under you,' he said and draped it round her shoulders. 'You're a right one, you are, sitting there shivering when there's means to be warm. Haven't you heard of First Aid? I hope I'm never knocked down when there's only you passing.'

So he prattled in the manner of a nursemaid distracting a child while he opened cupboards, found Mrs Winterton's tea caddy, sugar bowl and tin of dried milk. 'There's no fresh, so we'll make do with this,' he told her. 'It belongs to the owner, doesn't it? She'll not mind us cadging in an emergency. What's she called?' and, attempting discretion, placed his book on the draining board out of her sight and scribbled down the name. 'It's not the tenant we have to concern ourselves with in the event of a break-in, you see. The owner's the one. It's a question of house insurance, so it's him we have to trace. You'll not believe what a job that can be at times. We're lucky here, your landlady living on the spot. Pity she wasn't at home tonight.

'I'll let the tea stand a few minutes; you'll benefit more from it strong. Then you'll be able to go downstairs and get into bed. Tidying'll keep till the morning. There's nothing broken, Miss, and no other abuse so it's not so bad as it looks at first sight. They'd be after immediate cash because the video-recorder's still there.

'Now what about that for a cup of tea? Strong enough to stand your spoon up in it. I don't fancy one myself, thanks; we've got a new coffee percolator down at the station and I'll help myself to a cup when I get back.

116

There are a number of things I have to mention before I go, Miss. I sent a call out to our Scenes of Crime Officer and he was free to come straight away but, as I expected, there aren't any fingerprints. As far as gloves are concerned, you could say that nowadays burglars are all gents. Kevin washed the dusting powder off when he'd finished; he's a nice lad, is Kev. So we haven't added to the mess. And another thing: since it's too late to get some more glass in, I've fixed a chain though I'm one hundred per cent certain that they'll not be back. You fasten that chain behind me. You must have been wondering what I was up to, hammering and making such a din.'

'No,' she said truthfully because she had not heard.

'Talk about breaking and entering,' Judy said, standing beside her. 'Well, I've entered without breaking in. Gave me quite a buzz. I suppose the chain was some copper's attempt at defence; no good, though, left hanging. Is there any tea left? Heavens, it's stewed. Is that why you haven't drunk it? I must say this isn't much of a welcome. I was expecting some supper.'

And then Judy's arms were round her and a hand was stroking her arm and there were murmurs that did not upbraid the retch of tears.

When she was quieter Judy helped her lie down and covered her with the rug. 'I'll go and clear up.' And Olivia slept.

Sounds woke her, a slithering then a low curse, and finding herself, by the cushions and the patch of window, in the wrong place, her memory hurled back. Sweat slimed her groins and her throat clicked in an attempt to cry out.

'It's OK. Only me,' Judy interpreted. 'I came to see how you are. I've fried eggs and bacon. Four o'clock is rather early for breakfast but the canteen's preparing for the morning shift. I hope you're hungry,' and she switched on the light.

At the top of the stairs Olivia said, 'Smells good,' but hesitated.

'My cooking may be out of this world, ma'am, but my cleaning is miraculous.'

'Is that so?'

'Straight up.'

So she went down the steps and entered the room which was restored now and tranquil. It was hers again. Its blemishes and shortcomings, inherent; its deformities had not been induced. And now her weeping was quieter, an expression of gratitude, while Judy fussed at the stove.

'I've sorted most things out. Those I couldn't find a home for I've stacked behind the settee,' she told Olivia while they ate. 'You'll know if anything's been taken; obviously I can't tell that. But your cheque book's still here and some money in an envelope, so he probably got scared and cleared out. He was a cheeky devil, coming in the front door, but he must have felt quite exposed here at the front.'

'You would expect him to pocket the money, though.' Revived by sleep, her sight not scratched by evidence of his passage, she could look round the mended room and consider what had occurred.

'Not necessarily. He may have intended to take the video-recorder. He'd been playing it, unless you'd left it on. No, I didn't expect you would. I thought he might have been after that sort of thing so I went upstairs to check, but nothing's disturbed in the rest of the house.'

'Mrs Winterton doesn't approve of newfangled machinery.'

'I realized that. I didn't like snooping about but I couldn't help noticing the mangle in the scullery and the meat safe where most of us would have put a fridge.'

'I like it.'

'Yeah. It's cute.'

'So you think he was interested in the video-recorder?'

'Seems like it. Pretty typical, as far as I've gathered. Anyway, something, some noise, stopped him. A good thing it did before you arrived back. I sometimes imagine what I'd do if I were to come across a burglar. I always manage to sock him one before he does me. Which reminds me. I heard from Alma this week. She's touring in *Trafford Tanzi*, lead part.'

'That's marvellous.'

'Isn't it? But also risky. She's thinking of claiming danger money. She had a lot of coaching, of course; they all did. But during rehearsals the chap playing her husband threw her and broke a couple of ribs. It was bloody painful but she says she could put up with that. What she couldn't come to terms with was his clumsiness. This Fandangle Cob only got the part because he's done some wrestling and he was so enthusiastic he kept forgetting it wasn't a proper ring, though even there the bouts are faked. She's furious. You know what Alma's like. She can't forgive him for being so unprofessional and says she's thankful they weren't in a thriller in which he had to bump her off, otherwise she'd be communicating by a medium. But she's determined to pay him back. Now she's playing the scenes with him for real and guarantees he'll have at least two broken ribs by the end of the tour.'

They laughed. 'So much for Alma's professionalism.'

'That's what I thought.'

'I would have benefited from some coaching in wrestling this week,' and she told Judy about the man in Greasy Len's. 'There was another man, too, called Josh,' and to recount his molesting her, she had to explain her reason for being at the Gate and describe her search.

When she was half-way through, Judy called for an interval while she made coffee: 'Gallons of black.'

'I shouldn't be telling you this now. You ought to be going home. I'm being selfish.'

'That's right. And I'm loving every minute of it. Have you considered reading it on the BBC? It surpasses any story at bedtime I've heard.'

'Do you listen to that?'

'Only as therapy, when I'm sick of stage management. I think, there but for the grace of God I might be intoning down a mike as a substitute for cocoa and Mogadon.'

'Or Radio One.'

'Or sex.'

'That's subversive.'

'Depends how you look at it. In overpopulated countries it's compulsory.'

'Sex?'

'No, you fat head; a "Book at Bedtime".'

Having begun her account it was impossible to abbreviate it, and by the time Olivia had finished the light from the street lamps had been replaced by a whitening sky.

'It's a really peculiar situation,' Judy agreed, 'and I think you've done very well to find out what you have. I want to think about it. I honestly can't be constructive till I've had some sleep. We need to weigh up all the things that people have said, try one story against another and see if there are any relations, whether any of the pieces fit. But a couple of things do strike me. One is that, being simply you, a member of the public and not the fuzz, you've been able to investigate only so far.

'Take what the neighbour said – and Raymond's interpretation may be close to the mark – you can't follow it up and go round searching for those men, to check. You've no way of testing the accuracy of anyone's statement nor can you insist on systematic recollection. You have to rely on accounts that may be riddled with private motives. That group in the pub might have felt guilty because they knew so little about Rita and they

120

might have been over-compensating for that, or just happy to have a go at giving you help: for example, when she knocked over a glass it could have been the drink, not a strained wrist. You're subject to the whim of others and the level they are prepared to confide. You've been told that Mrs Dale is ashamed that Rita left home and assume that she's searching for her because, like Charles, she must still be alive. (It's a wonder you haven't had nightmares after Mrs Booth's unhinged confession; I shall have.) But after what she said to you, it seems to me that there's more to it than that. The woman's as mad as her mother. She's not just looking for Rita. She wants revenge. What was it she said?'

'In the end folk get their deserts.'

'Deserts for what, in this case?'

'I've no idea. Though, apparently, it isn't anything that I would ever do in spite of looking like her.'

'Rita's landlady?'

'That's right. Elizabeth Drew.'

Judy fluffed up the cushion at her elbow and replaced it with busy neatness. Then she switched off the light and walked to the window. 'There's the other thing that struck me, Olivia, only I'm not sure this is the right moment to discuss it. Neither of us can be objective after what we've seen tonight.' It was the first time she had admitted shock and, her body slack with fatigue, she leant her forehead against the glass as if controlling nausea.

'I'm sorry, Judy. I shouldn't have phoned.'

'Don't be stupid. If you hadn't I should have felt slighted.' She hesitated. 'Look, Olivia, I'm in no state to work this out and I don't want you to think that I'm deprecating your interest in Rita Dale, but I'm more concerned about something else. We shouldn't ignore the fact that ever since you started looking for her there have been offensive incidents of some kind or another focused upon you.'

'I've thought about that, but they are coincidences. On Monday night that bloke was abusive because Earl's black, and the barman's wife explained the man at the Gate – Josh.'

'Other people's reasons, Olivia. That doesn't make them right. I'm not convinced. It's a deception to argue coincidence. Too much has happened. In five days! You yourself are dissatisfied with Mrs Winterton's rationalization of the telephone calls – you confess to being convinced, intuitively, that they are meant for you – and then there's tonight. Olivia, I don't like it, but I have to go. This play can't get by without stage management; it's got little else.' But she did not laugh and, her face to the glass, she squinted up the well which was always in shadow. 'So I can't stay with you. That's why I want you to pack a case and come and doss down with me.'

Astonished, Olivia exclaimed fatuously, 'You're not serious?'

'I am.'

Turning, she presented her face. The skin was mottled, pocked by dilated pores, but not only through weariness; it was not only weariness that inflamed the eyes within puckering lids and dragged the expression. It was fear. And Olivia thought, I had no right to impose it; even friendship is not justified in exacting so much.

She said, 'No, Judy; you've done enough. There are limits.'

'You don't believe that. There aren't.'

'Oh, Judy.' It was hard to answer. 'Please don't be hurt; I'm not fobbing you off. But I can't accept. That would be running away.' She had argued coincidence; now she was admitting that was improbable but Judy did not rebuke.

'I've never been an admirer of gratuitous bravery. Stay at my place till things cool down.'

'I can't know when that will be.'

'Still, a few days away would be some respite.'

'Don't, Judy. I should be sorry, I know.'

'In that case . . .' She left the window. 'Now I must go.'

'You're exhausted. You mustn't drive back before you've had a nap. I feel shattered, and I had three hours' sleep upstairs.'

'I'll see how I feel after another cup of coffee.' Which Olivia made.

Having drunk, they sat in silence. Like two who had partaken in a vigil, their responses spent, they contemplated without vigour the emotions of the night and were blunt to the prod of dawn.

At last Olivia spoke. 'You have the bed.'

'I think there's a sleeping bag in the van. That'll do.'

'No. Don't argue. I've a sleeping bag somewhere.'

'OK. If I've gone before you wake, take as read my best of luck for the audition on Saturday.'

'Thanks. I meant to write but didn't have time. How did you know?'

'Alan told me.'

'So you're in contact again?'

'No. The telephone conversation when he told me about your audition was the death-rattle of a mouldering relationship.'

'And you didn't say! We've spent the whole night talking about me, about my affairs, and you kept quiet about this!' She was alert again, woken by shame. 'But you have to go to sleep.'

'I don't think I shall anyway. I'm done in, but through the sleep barrier. We finished, really, last week-end, but being Alan he had to have it in duplicate. I've known for weeks that it was inevitable, but I kept deceiving myself. I loved him. Truly; I did. Though there were things about him I couldn't take.'

'But they didn't matter. You said that he'd relax when he'd got work.'

'I'm not referring to his posing and egotism. What

stuck in my craw was his collector's mentality. He'd staple a reserve ticket on anything and he tried fixing one on me. I wouldn't have objected quite so decidedly had I been consulted; I'm not promiscuous. But when the ticket comes to be regarded as a receipt of purchase and no one else has permission to view the goods, then I'm for out. The imagery's deliberate; that's how he saw me though he called it "adoring" and "cherishing" — using words like that. So when he was thwarted, when he finally assimilated that his name wasn't the only one on the ticket, naturally it was my fault. There could be no other explanation.'

Olivia nodded. 'I can guess. He spoke to me on the phone on Tuesday.'

'God! It was awful. He was petulant at first: "You think more of Olivia." He couldn't understand why, if he were my feller, I could want to have friends. He wasn't only objecting to other men. In fact I think he could have pretended to tolerate them; it was the idea of close friendships with women that he found, incredibly, disgusting. By women, of course, he meant you. When I refused to be coerced he became vicious. Playing second fiddle on account of a woman wasn't his idea of a good time. His words.'

Above them in the street a milk-float rattled. Soon there would be the newspaper boy, the postman, the electrician next door revving up his van; all premature. The night had not yet ended.

'If that's how he thinks, Judy, you'll be pleased it's over, eventually.'

'I already am. I couldn't believe what I was hearing, and it all came so pat; almost as if he were reciting a part. He must have been storing it up for weeks. I didn't argue. I had no wish for a reconciliation and in any case I was too shattered by what had gone before. I had told him something, you see; something that happened a month or so ago. I had expected him to understand and

124

sympathize, though the expectation was really a need. His reaction was horrible: accusing, blaming me for what I had done. That started the row and he went on to you.'

Hunched in her chair, a finger smoothing a seam of her denims, she assembled the memories. Olivia waited.

'On Saturday evening as we came down here we were talking about that kerb crawler. I hope you haven't been bothered again?'

'No; that was the only time.' Before Judy's seamed face the lie was justified.

'I pointed out that we automatically assumed the person to be a man and you asked if I'd met any women kerb crawlers. Immediately after that we walked into here; I commented on it and your question was lost. I wanted to answer it but we had too many other things to talk about. Just before we watched the recording of "Mystery of the Week" I introduced the subject again but the moment wasn't appropriate, particularly for something so grim. Perhaps, had I confided in you, there would have been less urgency to tell Alan.'

'I'm sorry.'

'No. I'm not sorry. His attitude showed him up. I haven't met any women kerb crawlers, you see, Olivia, but I've been taken for one.'

Outside, a car slowed at the corner then accelerated. They flinched.

'I was driving the theatre van piled up with stuff and I passed a woman at a bus-stop. There was no shelter; it was bucketing down with rain and I knew that she had at least twenty minutes to wait. So I stopped and backed up. "Want a lift?" I shouted, leaning across and fiddling with the door, then inanely because she wasn't rushing to accept, "It'll be a squeeze but worth it." She put her hand to her stomach as if she were about to throw up and sidled behind the board displaying the timetable, and I was so astonished I just sat at the wheel, staring.

125

It was unbelievable. She was wearing a beige coat and the rain had soaked through, making a great rust-coloured stain across her shoulders and there was another across the top of her thighs. She had a plastic rain hat shaped like a sou'wester and water was running off the brim on to her face. She kept twitching her cheeks to flick it away and licking her top lip to stem the drops, but I suddenly realized that it wasn't rain on her face but tears. When I comprehended this I wanted to say something to her but I couldn't think of anything and then she said – whispered, really, but I read from her lips – "Please go away." '

'That's terrible.'

In the morning light Judy's face was colourless; a thin glitter snailed down a cheek.

'But you must have misinterpreted,' Olivia reasoned, stretching towards her. 'Probably she was distressed about something else and didn't want an observer.'

'No; it was me. And there was nothing I could say. I drove off.'

'It's appalling to be faced with that. And then having to go without correcting her.'

'It's more appalling if for some reason she expected it. I went because I was thinking of her.'

Olivia argued no more. They sat together reflecting while the morning sounds thickened and the room round them assumed the shape of day.

Then gently, removing the plimsolls speckled with paint and trying not to interrupt the oncoming sleep, Olivia eased her into bed and thanked her for what she had done.

'No probs,' she murmured. 'Felt I was back on the job. Because . . . funny thing . . . not like clearing up a room done over . . . more like a stage set. Weird.'

She had gone when Olivia woke, roused by the lunch-time scuttle of children. She had made the bed, just as she had tidied up the rest twelve hours earlier, obliterating all signs of the intruder's presence. But there was one sign she had been unable to remove though she had prevented its discovery in the brittle dawn hours. When Olivia rolled up her sleeping bag she flicked aside the cushion which Judy had so meticulously arranged. It tumbled over and lay like a small fat animal on its back, showing its belly. Out of which innards squeezed where a knife had plunged.

Picking up the cushion, pushing back the flocks and smoothing her fingers along the wound, she felt sweat spring as a point explored her own flesh and, seeing once again objects which revolved, writhed, twisted dizzily at the turn of a camera, Olivia watched their secret begin to uncoil, spread out and promise a comprehensible shape.

Chapter Nine

She was a long time before she found the fragment of paper, not in her handbag but in the pocket of her blouson where she had pushed it on Wednesday night. Upstairs, having dialled the number, she listened to the repeated signals and became apprehensive that her purpose would be frustrated by his not being there. His co-operation was essential.

'I hope you haven't been waiting long. I had the record player on rather loud,' he apologized. Though physically he had the same sex as Alan there was no other resemblance; they were at opposite ends of the continuum. On another occasion recognizing this she would have rejoiced but now she was merely thankful.

'Steve, have you still got that key of Rita's?' It was an unnecessary question but, not yet prepared for what she might find there, she could not request entrance outright.

'You mean you'd like to get in?' he said it for her. 'Certainly. No trouble. Have you had an idea?'

'I just thought it might be helpful to have a look,' she evaded. Then, sorry because he deserved more, 'I'm not suggesting that we may discover where she has gone, only that we may pick up hints about what happened.'

'That's possible. We may get a lead.' His answer was too prompt, to conceal disappointment, but the attempt was brief. 'It may be too much to hope we find a letter with a forwarding address,' and simulated a laugh.

'Yes. That would be too convenient.'

'When do you want to go? I'm free any time.'

On the point of replying, 'Immediately', she was halted by a flickering recollection, a duty already redundant but which she must perform. 'There's something I have to attend to.' She did not know how many hours to allow. 'Could you manage six?'

'Of course. Would you prefer to meet at the house or in town, say outside the station?'

'I'll see you at the house.' But her eyes on her goal, she sensed windows curtained against her and though it was summer there was ambushing darkness between the lamps, and she could not walk down that street alone. 'No, Steve, on second thoughts I'd rather not meet there. Let's make it outside the station.'

'Fine. Till six, then.'

'Thanks.'

She replaced the handset and stood puzzling over what she must do, but the telephone claimed her attention.

There was a gush of questions: 'How long's this been going on? Have you been receiving abusive calls? That operator made me feel as if I were first suspect,' and her explanations. Followed by: 'Your rail ticket arrived this morning. Rather than put it in the post since you might not receive it before you leave tomorrow, I gave it to Ray to drop in. He said he'd be passing. I'd hate to question his reliability but he was up to his eyes in Snow Cem at the time, metaphorically speaking. Is the ticket with you?'

The concern was irrelevant. Tomorrow was meaningless. The future was bounded by a room beyond Elizabeth Drew's door. Without bothering to check, she answered, 'It's here. Thanks for the trouble.'

'All part of the service. I must return to the monthly accounts. It's as well one of us isn't just a pretty face. Funny how at drama school they never said I'd need my O-level maths. Best of luck with the Piccolo. Do us proud, love.'

The draught was as chill as moonlight and walking to the door she examined the hole. Perhaps with cardboard and sellotape she could make a temporary repair. There was a precedent in a window upstairs, so this mimicked normality would prevent alarm when Mrs Winterton returned. Olivia wished the old woman to learn about the episode from her, calmly and simply, not from deduction.

Activity was a beneficial distraction. Looking round Mrs Winterton's kitchen she found an empty carton under the sink and, surprisingly, in a drawer a roll of sellotape mossy with fluff. From a newspaper under the telephone she cut out a rectangle, tailored it to the buckled lead and transferred the pattern to the side of the box. The next stage was laborious; cardboard admits a steel point less readily than does the fabric of a cushion and, when it had finally punctured it, the bread saw left whiskery serrations along the edge. She plucked and picked until it was smoother, prised open the lead flaps and slotted the piece in. It fitted so well there was no need for sellotape and she smiled, admiring her handi-work, pleased too because it suggested an advance, even a small victory. No one could see into the hall now; the spy-hole was shuttered.

Tidying up, she stroked flat the newspaper she had cut at and, looking out, framed in the space she had created, was Rita Dale's face. It was older than it had been on the television and did not scowl at the photographer but it was still private and unsmiling, the eyes pursed with distrust.

'I shan't hurt you,' Olivia told her. 'I'm not crazy. I shan't lock you out, or make you clean his boots, or womb you up.'

When she had thrown the hacked cardboard into the bin and returned the saw, she laid a page over Rita's face and folded the newspaper. Promising that she would read the report over lunch, she pretended that the postponement was not caused by what it might contain but by her next task.

'May I speak to the operator who intercepts our calls?' she asked and dictated the number.

'We all do, whoever's on shift.'

'Can you tell me anything about them?'

'What do you want to know?'

It was an unanswerable demand. Until she was offered some substance she had nothing on which to base questions. 'I thought you might have an idea . . .' She floundered.

'Would you like to speak to Customer Relations?'

'I don't think so, thanks.'

'Well, I can tell you that we don't make a report and we're not private dicks, so we don't ask the caller's name or trace the number. That's not possible, anyway.'

'I see.'

'There's been only one this morning since I came on at eight, and that seemed genuine.'

'Yes.' She could not bring herself to ask whether there had been calls on Wednesday evening or Thursday when the house had been empty for over twelve hours. All she knew was that none had got past the operator during the previous night. 'Do you think this . . . persecution . . . has stopped?'

'Your guess is as good as mine, but it could have. It often does after several days; the caller is frightened off.'

'That's what I understood; this has never happened to me before.' She recollected her mother's story, the mention that once the calls had been intercepted Gillian and her husband had been no more disturbed. By a disappointed woman formerly loved by Alex. And making the connection, Olivia thought, horrified, Could my tormentor be Alan? He would believe himself to have as much reason as did the one whom Gillian had succeeded. But he could not be responsible, she told herself, relieved; because Judy was with him on Saturday night and most of Sunday. Even so, remembering his malevolence, she was visited by a new apprehension.

The operator was saying, her tone more sympathetic, 'It's not nice, I know, picking up the phone and hearing all the filth and sewage some of them pour out. We get it here from time to time, especially at night.'

'My caller doesn't speak.'

'One of those, is he? They're worse than the foul-mouthed brigade, in my opinion. If you're sharp enough you can answer back, give them some of their own medicine, but the silent ones give me the shakes. It's like he's got you on a string, playing cat and mouse. And, of course, if he can quote the subscriber's name when we ask, he's put through like everyone else. But obviously yours doesn't know your name, which is cheering.'

'Mine is not the name in the directory. But I'm certain he knows where I live.' Had he trailed her in his car, observed her through the bathroom's unscreened glass or, concealed by shadows, watched the throb of the house through the clear panes in the front door? 'When he had found the house, it would be relatively simple to trace the owner, then look up the telephone number in the book.'

'As far as I know, generally all they do is hit on a number, but you know the circumstances. Look, I shouldn't be doing this but there's a note Tony left when he went off shift. If I can find it. Right. It says, "Caller rang 756433 at twenty-two fifteen. Said we could lay off." The cheeky devil.'

A quarter past ten last night. While another was in her room? Or were caller and invader the same person who had concluded his evening with a message to the operator after he had finished his ravaging work? She shivered. 'Won't you be carrying on, then?'

'Because some unidentified pervert gives us permission to stop? Not on yours. It might well be a ruse –

you can't put anything past that type – and in any case the service is for a fortnight, free. If you'd like us to discontinue it you'll have to speak to the supervisor.'

'I'll tell Mrs Winterton. Thank you for being so helpful.'

'You're welcome. Bye.'

Encouraged by the operator's good sense, Olivia went down to the basement thinking, If it is a ruse it won't be successful. She said it wouldn't affect what she did. She will make sure he doesn't get through to me. And he won't try any other way. He will stay anonymous. He and his coward breed come by stealth: along a silent telephone wire, or with quiet engine stalking your back, or creeping furtively upon a deserted house. He and his kind do not come in the light.

Thus finally she conquered the fears which since waking she had striven to control; for as her eyes flinched at the sight of the cushion sliced by an unknown hand, her neck had pricked at the memory of a faceless threat behind a car wheel and her ears had listened again for the voiceless presence at the end of the wire. Now, more peaceful, she embraced the afternoon hours, looking neither at the night that had passed nor towards the one that jutted ahead; and with a sense of release she savoured each moment and what it brought.

She watched the slivers of cheese curl and pile into a soft drift against the grater; she examined the vegetables' convectional patterns in the pan of boiling soup; opening a bag of fruit, she gazed at the smudged stipple on the skin of a pear. Thoughts were shapeless; she let them glide by and did not attempt to give them form.

Later as she sat in the bath, her legs brown and skin taut, she received a stranger novelty. Usually she regarded with a mild disappointment some of her features, others with a guilty pride, but now they excited a childlike attention. Her soaping hands massaged the line of a thigh and the dip of breasts, explored the secret

133

whorls of an ear, and found them all mysterious, the well-spring of awe. She did not seek to explain this, nor did she reason why, cocooned by a silk foam, her body became a pupa, a chrysalis, which she contemplated as a thing autonomous and detached from herself. For she was an actress, content to bide her time until the metamorphosis was complete.

So when she dressed in clean underwear, fetched the yellow sweat-shirt airing by the boiler and pulled that over a blouse, she did not question for what she was preparing. Unhurried, she was not flustered when at last she remembered that the appointment that had eluded her was at the police station, calculating that she had time for that before she met Steve. When, leaving the house, she found an envelope on the mat containing a ticket and a pencilled message, 'Sock it to them, love Raymond' she was indifferent and unaffected by nerves. And when she placed the envelope in her bag she was not startled to discover that, poking out of the usual litter, were the newspaper and the video cassette.

'You look pale,' Stephen greeted. 'Are you OK?'

'No less than I ever am. I had a late night.'

'It wasn't meant as a criticism. Only, it's very noticeable. You look bleached out.'

'No doubt there'll be a regeneration.'

He smiled. 'A straightforward revival will be enough.'

She did not argue.

They walked through the town. Stephen talking. 'I've been thinking a lot about Wednesday night. It was interesting that they all had something to say once they were invited to think. I had trouble getting their talk into some sort of order, trying to separate the wheat from the chaff, mainly because I couldn't be certain which was one and which was the other. It's a question of likelihood. I mean, the idea about murder was silly; obviously Mrs

Drew did nothing violent, but those fantasies were enough to remind you that someone else might.'

She did not remind him that someone had. Nor did she point out that there were kinds of violence other than physical assault. She remembered that there had been bags stacked on the pavement, securing departure, and in the kitchen behind the secretive 'best' room, the strike of a young girl's bayonet tongue; and, blenching, she saw a lawn on which were rucksack and boxes and heard her own voice shouting farewells above the idling of a theatre van.

'However, you have to keep in mind that some things they said may have no bearing on the situation at all,' Stephen continued. 'As Nick insisted, every little detail's not forced to be connected and I expect that story of Trudi's is one of them – how Rita went hysterical at her joke when she was helping with her zip. What you have to remember there, because it may be significant, is that Rita couldn't use her hand; the way she laughed then cried is unimportant. Yet that's the bit that nags. I can't get it out of my mind; it haunts me. It won't go away. It's as if it were trying to tell me something that I should pay attention to. But that's illogical.'

'I don't think so,' but she could go no further. As he spoke, she too was haunted; by a face. But it did not laugh, ironic, at a jokey remark. It shuddered, unable to receive an uncalculated generosity, its flesh bloated by tears under a film of rain. Tears which, later, Rita had shared.

'Some suggestions were outrageous, of course, such as Rita's stealing money. It's unfair to offer that as the reason for her suddenly having it because we can't imagine any other.'

She did not tell him that Raymond had suggested a bribe. Ahead of them she could see two gaps between the houses. The second, unblocked by television vehicles, was her street.

'You have to be careful that an idea doesn't become fixed, particularly when you can't prove it. I thought she was upset the night she got drunk, and so did Karen and Trudi, but we could easily be reading that into the situation to find a reason why she's disappeared. Really, her behaviour wasn't so different from normal. When Karen said she thought that Rita was trying to shut something off she was describing Rita, full stop. I ought to know.' He paused, dismayed by the bitterness. Defensive, he added, 'I mean, she never said anything to me about a strained wrist, though I saw her home. But you have to admit,' struggling to be just, 'that could be Karen's imagination; I doubt if she were in a state to remember what anyone said. However, her claim that Rita had a stepfather must be right.'

That had been the first time Stephen had learnt of him. Hearing his voice twang and the street now upon her, Olivia found his hand, glad of their reciprocal need. In this manner they walked together towards Elizabeth Drew's house.

They were in without fuss and there was no director, no woman with a clipboard, no young girl dashing to powder her face, but her stomach was snatched as it had been then, as it always was before walking on to a set. Though this was not a set; it was not built to create an illusion of reality; it was the hall of a small terrace-house, unassuming and plain. The first time she had entered she had leant against the door, panting after her flight from Alan's harsh face as he had asked her about Judy's next visit. Then, she had sensed a menace to something she treasured but could not identify. Now, again she felt panic; and, looking round this hall so similar to the one where she lived, she wished she had never left that other and that this evening and night would be a continuation of her own private day. Because, though there was no Alan waiting by the gate and this narrow space was empty of cables and camera, the hall still had the capacity to present a crisis. Today, however, this danger she felt was not confined to her own life; it embraced those that had existed inside this door. Folded within the yellow sweat-shirt and cotton trousers, the pupa stirred.

'That's Rita's room,' Stephen told her, pointing.

She delayed with: 'Shall we look upstairs first?' and saw his relief.

The stairs were uncarpeted, the treads covered with strips of linoleum nailed into place. Matting, its edges bound with plastic tape, led them along the landing and into the bathroom from which, as from Mrs Winterton's, could be seen the backs of houses along the parallel street. After this, the likeness ceased for the bath was modern and undistinguished, no cobwebs rigged the ceiling, no insects dried on the sill and there was no dust to skitter and roll in the draught. Nothing hinted a young girl's use or why it had ended. Not knowing for what they were searching, they pushed open the next door into the bedroom over the kitchen, small as Mrs Booth's but not a monument, simply a dump for discarded possessions; and though it had been sometime tenanted, it was not by a ghost. For in a space made between suitcases, cracked lampshades and vacuum cleaner without a bag, was a child's cot. Yellow flannelette was tucked round the mattress and a cellular blanket lay folded at one end. Starched and ironed, a linen picture book invited and a soft toy gazed through the bars, expectant.

'She hadn't any children,' Stephen remarked.

'Do you think this was . . . in hope?' After Charlie, anything was possible.

'No, I don't. I'm not writing that off,' he assured her hastily, 'but considering other evidence. What is called hard facts. I heard a baby once. Rita said it belonged to a guest.'

As they opened the next door, metal coat hangers

rattled on a hook, drawing to their attention the absence of wardrobe or cupboard for clothes. The only furniture was a bed, a chair, a dresser and a carry-cot resting on a tin trunk once an emblem of domestic service and in keeping with this room whose square of carpet was thin and faded and whose curtains hung in meagre folds. Attempts had been made to soften this austerity. A pot of ferns had been set on the dresser; a Van Gogh print, unframed, had been tacked to the wall; a misty demi-john holding a miniature garden had been placed in the hearth; and though the bed had no coverlet, it had been provided with deep rose blankets which looked friendly and warm.

Except for the addition of a small table, the second bedroom was a copy of the other even to the cot.

'She seems to have a lot of guests,' Olivia said. 'This place is a hotel.'

'More like a hostel. Still, who needs more than the basics when you visit? And it's all meticulously clean.'

They went downstairs. 'Now for it,' he said.

She could contrive no further excuse. Holding herself taut against the view she dreaded, she noticed that his hand shook as he turned the knob. But it was not as they had expected and, poised in the doorway, they heard the whistle of expired breath and felt the tension slip off.

'Someone's tidied up.' Then apologizing for the superfluous observation, 'I was ready for something else.'

'You can say that again.' She meant, say the first sentence again, because words made this normality permanent; they insisted that her vision of the room dissolving once more into chaos was a mirage.

'The television people must have done it.'

'That's unlikely. It could have been the owner. I gather it's the owner the police always inform when there's been a burglary – if the tenant's absent, I suppose.' She did not explain how she knew this for she had not told him about the previous night. Her account would have prompted his sympathy and returned her to yesterday's concerns; she did not want that. 'This house is rented from a Mr Catchpole – the neighbour told me. That must be why the police haven't searched for Rita. Or Mrs Drew. There was no need. They simply contacted Mr Catchpole; the neighbour said they had brought him round. Presumably he allowed the television company in and then cleaned up later. That was thoughtful.'

'Yes. It must have been an unpleasant job. I wouldn't have liked doing it. I'd have hated folding things up, putting them back in the drawers.'

'Perhaps his wife helped him. Notice that we're assuming that the owner is male! She may be a woman.'

'Would that make this easier?'

'Probably not.' She thought of Judy. 'But a woman is more accustomed to intimate ministerings. In families it's generally she who nurses the sick.'

'Which must be rotten if by nature you're squeamish. This one couldn't decide where all Rita's stuff went, though. She's left a few things out.'

A pair of striped ankle socks lay knotted in a corner; a record sleeve was propped against a leg of a chair, the record still on the turntable. In the hearth stood a box full of a jumble of make-up, curling rollers, transistor batteries, a hoard of ringed beer mats, a Snoopy outfit and two felt-tipped pens.

'She may have left them like this on purpose, I suppose, to give the place a more natural look, so that it appeared that no one had ever disturbed it,' he suggested.

'And does it look natural – normal?' The evidence made the question unnecessary but to inquire had become a habit.

He laughed. 'Heavens, no! Rita couldn't keep a room like this. It was always a tip. In fact when I think about it, the person who broke in must have had most of his work done for him. I'm sorry. That's facetious, a reaction after what might have been.'

She nodded. 'Her grandmother would agree.'

'And I shouldn't criticize,' he went on, contrite. 'I'm not that tidy myself. She might have kept her things better most of the time and I saw them at their worst. I didn't come often and didn't stay long. I was merely picking her up before we went out. I've thought about that. I was never in for more than a few minutes and I'm not a great observer, so that must be why I was confused by the programme. When I felt that the room didn't seem right it must have been that I'd never looked at it properly, never examined it closely. My visual memory must be poor.'

'It may not be a fault of your memory at all but the camera angles. Seeing an area from a different viewpoint you can often not recognize what is really familiar.'

'I expect you're right,' he answered, but he was not wholly convinced.

They stood together in the middle of the room, their eyes passing over the stacked magazines, the market stall ornaments, the plimsolls scabby with mud, the fat cushion whose holed fur had been hidden against the duvet by a considerate hand.

'I'm pleased that someone has put her things away, that they haven't been left out, even though there was no one to see. Like corpses after an attack. But it doesn't help us to find her,' he mourned, dejected.

'No.' She did not tell him that the frustration did not matter now, that it was hardly more than a disappointment to be got through until a movement at the edge of her mind took a precise form.

'We oughtn't to be here. It's her place.'

Acquiescent, she turned to follow him and saw paper lift and skitter across the chest of drawers as he passed.

She stopped its fall but before she had pinned it securely under a magazine she had seen the logo and name.

'Do you ever visit the pawnbroker, Steve?'

'Come off it. What have I got to pawn?'

And what had Rita? They had come to examine a dismantled room and to look for clues that might lead them to its tenant; now that it was set to rights and again private, it accused them of intrusion.

'There's a pawn ticket here.'

'That's her business,' he disapproved.

But for the moment her condition of the past week and its preoccupation were reasserted and though guilty at the prying, she lifted the receipt. Aloud, propitiating forgiveness, she read: 'One hunter watch, gold . . . £42; one cigarette case, silver . . . £3; one pair of plus-fours, 33″ leg . . . £1; one leather belt with ornate buckle . . . £1; one lace christening robe . . . £2; one white shawl . . . £1.'

There was a long silence.

At last, 'I wish you hadn't read that.'

'So do I, now.'

'It explains the night in the pub, but she didn't spend all that amounts to, thank God. Poor girl, she must have been desperate to pawn all that. She was ripped off, too. Three pounds for a silver cigarette case!'

'No; its only value is the weight of the metal. We had a neighbour once who ran a jeweller's shop and gave loans on the side. He would have been interested only in the watch. I imagine that this fellow was, too, but since she left it, he must have agreed to take the case and clothes as a personal favour. He certainly would have no outlet for the clothes.'

'They weren't worth pawning.'

'She wasn't concerned with their value,' Olivia murmured.

You tell her it's the last thing I'd have imagined coming from her, she had said; but it was not her granddaughter's conduct that had aged her. It was the despoiling of the spirit who had kept her young, forever reaching towards the reunion with one who had been granted the fairy touch and who would dazzle her confined life with joy.

'How do you mean, not concerned with their value? She bothered to pawn them.'

'She may not have intended to. They may have been the result of an impulse.' She hoped they were.

'I don't see why. She must have thought carefully about what she was doing. It's a strange collection. Plusfours! However did she come to possess a pair of those?'

'It would be the watch she went for. After that, the choice would be random.' Opening the trunk, grabbing, squeezing the plunder into her bag, fearful lest at any moment she would hear the key in the lock, the steps ascending the stairs.

'Went for?' she heard Stephen say and then, 'I see.'

She looked across at him and comprehended the disillusionment in his face. 'I assumed you understood, Steve,' she apologized.

'Where from?' he asked bleakly.

'Her grandmother. They belonged to her great-uncle who was killed in the last war.'

'That's obscene.'

She could think of nothing to console him except: 'No doubt she means to recover them as soon as she can.'

'That makes no difference.' He was picking at the door jamb like a child who pretends an intense absorption in order to appear unaffected by punishment. 'I said to you that one has to be careful that an idea doesn't become fixed. Talk about, physician heal thyself! I was totally blinkered; I automatically rejected Wayne's suggestion. He had nothing to base it on, of course. That is, as far as I know. Because, really I don't know her any better than he does. I can see that now. Olivia, I didn't know her at all.'

142

'I think that's how she wanted it.'

'Yes.' He moved into the passage. 'Do you mind if we go?'

'All right.' To extenuate their flight she said as she joined him, 'I expect we've seen everything of interest. This back room must be Mrs Drew's?'

'It's the sitting-room. She lived downstairs,' nodding towards the door at the head of the cellar.

'Lived?' She recalled the spartan bedrooms blank of a permanent occupier and their deduction that these rooms were intended for guests. She had forgotten Elizabeth Drew, had not wondered where she slept. 'She has made the basement into a sort of bed-sit?'

Indifferent, he answered, 'I suppose she must have. She was always down there when Rita shouted to say she was going out. She never left without doing that. She insisted, though she wasn't obliged. She was the lodger and looking after herself; she didn't have to keep her landlady informed.'

This is the house, Olivia recited to herself; this is the hall; her room is at the bottom of a flight of stone steps. Her arms were heavy; legs were cumbersome; the mind echoed with the rustle of a pupa that stretched.

'You go,' her voice said. 'I haven't finished. There's something I must see. No, please; you've had enough. Please don't wait. I'll give you a ring. You've been splendid,' and she watched fingers touch his cheek and felt it dimple under lips.

There was a handrail fixed to the wall and she used it to guide herself. It was thick and rigid and held her as she lurched. At the bottom, the window showed stalks of dandelions whose seed clocks dispersing whiskered the panes and freckled the light. More was not needed. On the other side of the door her eyes were not stopped by the shadows lying in bars nor did they blink at the stab of what they found. Because she had looked on it before, though she had not guessed its riddle. Now this room would surrender it. For she was almost ready; it would soon be completed. The spun filaments were unfurling to release a new creature, delicate yet sure.

But first she must repair this ruin. She pulled off the yellow sweat-shirt, rolled up the sleeves of her blouse. And the only surprise she felt as she began on her task was that she had been so obtuse. She believed she had achieved detachment, for the cycle of hours of the one she had looked for had not taken over her own; but softly, imperceptibly, another had filled the place. Without her knowledge, she had been led by this other, and she had connived with her selflessness. Olivia now knew that it was the wrong woman whom she had sought.

Chapter Ten

Diligent as the policeman, she first examined the window and found, ghostly under the grey dusting powder, the scores of a chisel round the latch. Two nails had been driven through the frame to keep the sash immovable but that was the limit of the owner's concern. He did not conform to the generous person they had made him to explain Rita's unsmashed room. With the window secure behind her, she began on the drawers.

The task was as uncongenial as Stephen had imagined but she performed it conscientiously and without haste, keeping her hands steady and swallowing down the tart sickness as she folded the ripped underwear, stroked up the crunched jewellery into an envelope, threw away flattened tampons and replaced in its splintered box a twisted and split Dutch cap. And gradually her occupation was no longer a task but an unqualified service, a ceremony of healing. Each piece was taken up, smoothed into wholeness, cherished, found a place, as she did for the absent woman what Judy had done for her.

When she had finished the twilight had piled dense in the corners but a street lamp umbered its centre to translucent brown. In which light she prepared herself for a discovery that, after talking with the casting assistant, she had planned but shunned, and she could not control her revulsion as she took the cassette from her bag. The last time it was used had been by the one who entered Mrs Winterton's basement, by the one who had left it switched on, who playing it over had checked that the devastation he was engaged upon corresponded with this on the film, with the devastation she had just repaired. Contriving a scene that had puzzled Judy: like a stage set.

Olivia inserted the cassette and while it wound back she looked at the room she had re-created. The room that belonged to Elizabeth Drew. Though she could not assess that everything was positioned correctly, she was satisfied. Kicked furniture had been polished; earth spilt from overturned plants had been swept up and patted round the roots; the lanced cushion had been dressed with sticky tape. It was appropriate, waiting. Knowing that the cocoon's silk was ready to give up a pupa transformed. So, with a fearful exhilaration that screwed the muscles of her stomach, she saw as she bent to start the film, a moth twirl through the lamp beam and come to rest on the bright screen.

A street of stone terrace-houses was slotted into the frame and one grew larger, pushing out the street. Her eyes were taken up the path and invited to peer into the cellar well which held the window behind her, then they were brought to a woman who came out of the door, closed it and ran to the gate. Watching critically, she thought, They did well to find an actress so like me, but surely I don't go around banging gates. Immediately there was a cut to a Telecom engineer's raised head, then herself hurrying away. Like someone whose mission was over; who had undertaken a job, done it competently then left. 'But it didn't stop there,' she murmured and rose to run the tape back to the scene the other had watched.

She looked at Rita's face with interest, younger in this photograph but no less guarded than the one she knew, and she followed the objects of her room as they were spun by the camera's lash; but reconstructed violence no longer disturbed her. Instead, she was shocked by the presenter's words. They linked the 'scene you have just witnessed' with Rita and implied that it was her room that had been shown. Agitated, she jumped from her chair, stopped the cassette and rushed upstairs, panic-stricken lest the girl's room, too, had been attacked, jostled by the necessity to put it right, compelled by the instinct to protect as urgent as it had been when she first made the girl's acquaintance and which had grown more insistent during the last few days.

Inside the door she stood panting, feeling foolish, irritated at being so easily misled. For anyone who knew the rooms could distinguish this from the one in the television programme. There, the ceiling was low, the light stooped in cautiously from the garden above; here, deep cornices raised the height of the walls and a bay window greeted the sun. She would have enjoyed living in it herself and, switching on the light, she surveyed what she had surrendered: the bed, wider than her own; the chest of drawers she had placed there instead of the cheap cupboard downstairs; the wardrobe more grand than her jumble sale tallboy; the armchair more luxurious than her dilapidated sofa empty of springs. Collected from second-hand shops or dumped by more affluent friends, this furniture was not expensive, neither was it particularly tasteful, but it was the best in the house and from it a stranger would deduce that this was her room. There was little wonder that the basement had been thought, by landlord, police, television people, to house her lodger. She had made the choice deliberately, giving Rita the less shabby, spoiling the girl to compensate for a relinquished home. From whose obsessive neatness she generally rebelled but on this occasion she had adopted her mother's example of sedulous cleaning. Had in one respect gone further, she thought, her mind shying away from the knowledge of what Rita had done, and to calm it with order she removed the record from the turntable, patted it into the sleeve and flicked out a screw of paper trapped down

147

the chair's arm. Straightening the creases, she saw that it was a rough draft of the girl's letter whose copy she had read some weeks before, that had been in an envelope together with the two bent fragments that just now she had tried to forget. Again, to shut off that memory, she sought distraction and feeling her way to the basement, she returned to the programme on the cassette.

After, diminished by distance, she had been lost at the end of the street, the camera switched again to a Telecom engineer who walked round the van to his mate and lit a cigarette. He took a puff, spoke to the other, then the camera moved back to the house, over which shot came sentences she had not heard before: 'Did you see that, Dave? She was leaving in a hurry. Makes you wonder what's been going on. Looks black for somebody.' There was a slight pause as the 'Pennine News' credits came up and music began, but through this came clearly though fragmented, further words: 'I wouldn't mind if one I knew shifted as quick . . . but when a couple of women get together, there's no room for a man . . . playing second fiddle on account of a woman isn't my idea of a good time.'

For a few seconds the words hung slack in the air, then they twanged taut and she was off the settee, kneeling in front of the set, playing the scene over and over again, trying to distort the speech to an acceptable shape, to impose an innocent meaning, to make it conform to her disbelief. But she could not and finally she depressed the button and crawled into the diluted light under the window, away from the darkness of the set. She had heard from someone that the actor had been asked to improvise. In such a programme that was inexcusable. He should not have been invited to comment on the way she had left, suggesting that some heated quarrel had caused the haste which the Telecom engineer claimed to have seen. But that was less important than the effect of his last words. Someone had told her that it had not been intended to keep his remarks in the programme, had confessed that they ought not to have gone out, but apology was useless. Because, she recalled, he had been asked to give the reaction of the 'ordinary man in the street'. Did this represent the view of the ordinary man in the street? For this actor, assured that most of his audience would approve, had expressed his resentment against any woman who might share the affection of the one he wished to possess. There on the screen she had been associated with a competition for affection; she had been accused as if personally she had come between this man and his girl, and she felt bruised and swollen by the punch of his spite.

Some of his words seemed familiar; his statement that playing second fiddle on account of a woman wasn't his idea of a good time, she thought she had heard somewhere before, and it sounded not impromptu but studied, almost as if he were reciting a part.

She wondered how other people would react to them but comforted herself that their effect would be transient and would be quickly absorbed beneath the wash of other sensations. They could influence few in their attitude to her. Then a memory shivered; she made a connection and again she was up, had switched on the light and was hunting for a handbag, was tipping out its contents and salvaging a newspaper she had seen when she had removed the cassette.

Once more Rita's face regarded her, this time out of a snipped frame, and thinking that this might block out other details in the picture, she was visited by the hope that when she lifted it something of the girl's closed nature would be uncovered – a passion, a recreation, even a pet – but there was nothing. The other still eluded her.

Speculation on the disappearance of seventeen-year-old Rita continued over the weekend as no more news came in, she read.

After nights without sleep, Rita's parents were in a state of collapse as they spoke to our reporter in their house in Cattlegate which was unusually quiet this Monday morning.

'She seems to have vanished off the face of the earth,' said Mr Dale her father, a shop manager. 'It is terrible for parents at a time like this when you don't know what has happened. I wish anyone who knows anything at all would speak up.'

They are particularly anxious to contact a Mrs Elizabeth Drew who Rita was living with at the time of her disappearance. As shown on Saturday night's Pennine News' 'Mystery of the Week' which first uncovered the incident, Drew, who is believed to be separated from her husband, was seen leaving her home in Hackney Street in a great hurry two weeks ago according to a Telecom employee working in the area.

'Her room being turned upside down in that way makes you think there had been some foul play,' Mrs Dale agreed, and violence has not been ruled out. 'I can't understand why this woman hasn't come forward,' she added.

It is several months since the brunette Rita went to live with Drew but Mrs Dale could not confirm whether there had been the normal rent-paying arrangement. However, she confirmed that Rita Dale was an impressionable young girl.

'We're staying by that telephone night and day till we hear something,' Mr Dale said. 'We're both worried stiff.'

It was the usual worthless report and her impulse was to stamp it into the waste-paper basket and apply a match but, arrested by the extravagance of her disgust, she read it again. The effect of 'Mystery of the Week' had lasted longer than she had predicted, she admitted to herself. The journalist had relied on it and gone much further than the programme's 'It is thought that the scene you have just witnessed may be connected with Rita's disappearance.' He had linked it with herself. Naturally he had not done this outright; the hint was sly. But by stating that she had left 'in a great hurry', then by mentioning in the next sentence the possibility of foul play and following that with a reference to her continued absence, he had led readers to a comfortable assurance of her guilt. 'There must be something in it,' someone had said.

That was not all. Examining the passage a second time and interpreting it out of feelings made raw by the workman's words, she identified that 'something'. For the strange interest in rent-paying arrangements was not as casual as it seemed; it was calculated to raise the suspicion that the lodgings she had provided might have been free as a result of some kind of intimate relationship: 'when a couple of women get together'. Which Rita had succumbed to, because she was young and 'impressionable'. The journalist made the arrangement a certainty with that insidious word.

She put aside the newspaper and for many minutes she sat, her hands gripped in her lap, while she waited for her pulse to quieten. It was not the insinuation itself that rocked her; love has many forms of expression and is not to be judged by outsiders' rules. What appalled her was the prurience fingering greasily a relationship that was private and delicate and offering it to the coarse public gaze. Infected by jealousy, the actor who was the Telecom man had played his part better than he had imagined. His words had been picked up by the journalist who had therefore added lechery to the suggestion of foul play. Though less conspicuously sensational, the report followed the style of many newspapers and endorsed their reputation. It was a small, cunning essay on their main ingredients: violence and sex.

She hoped that Rita had not seen it, though she did not think she would have noticed all that was there. Whatever her talents might be, they were not literary. Pulling the crumpled sheet from her pocket, she considered it again. The corrections made it harder to decipher than the neat copy but if she were to fetch that she could not avoid seeing what had been placed with it in the envelope. So she read this first attempt, saddened that Rita had felt she must copy it out, an action which showed once again how defensive she was, and without trust. However, she winced at the 'Dear Mrs Drew', Rita's spontaneous address; the 'Dear Elizabeth' in the transcript had been a second thought.

Dad came after you went to the shops and I said I'd go with him. I know you have your~~e~~ own opinion, but I do'nt mind him and Il'l say not to come after, I'ave had enough with Mum. You ~~was was saying~~ said we would be better of fliting at the present, so ~~its~~ its' alright going with my Dad. He says I can stop if I like his hous and his ~~wife/s~~ wifes name is Phylis.

I saw Steve the night after that man had pushed himself across the step and I gave him the key like you said. I didn't tell him it was to keep an eye on the house. I did'n/t see why he was being brought into it. I expect it'll stop again. You said it has stopped before for a bit when you ~~are'nt~~ ar'not at home.

I have not been to tell Mrs, Bellamy like you asked what with Dad coming first of and wanting to go as soon as I have packed. He saies I'm to write this while he gose to the garage to fill up and nip in to see a mate.

You can have my room back if that is convenient. I don't want the things I have left because my Dad says his going to buy me a lot of new. So good-bye now, with thanks.

     Yours Faithfully,
     Rita C. Dale.

It was not a letter to return to. There was nothing in it to muse upon or enjoy and she folded it quickly, wondering whether Rita would have said more than, 'So good-bye now, with thanks,' if she could have scraped together the words; then told herself firmly, no. In any case, more would have exceeded their agreement. Within her own terms the girl had been a considerate lodger; for example, she had always let her know when she was going out, which forestalled worries. That was her way of expressing appreciation and it had to suffice. When she had taken Rita on she had not wanted thanks or the obliged gratitude of a dependant. She had done it because, seeing the girl, she had felt driven.

152

About to replace the letter in her pocket, she saw on the reverse side a postscript which Rita had not transferred to the neat copy. Perhaps that had been prevented by her father's return. Even so, the haste to be gone which this betrayed was painful.

PS. Do/n't you worry about my wrist. Its nearly better but you should'nt have let that man get of so easily pushing in and then carrying on and shouting all that about me and you. I dont care what he saies about your visitors, he can say what he likes about them but not about me/ and you. Your not to think I ~~mindded~~ those women com/ing, they ~~didn't d'not~~ did not bother me much and I'm going with my Dad because I want and not ~~throw~~ thorough them or those men. I never said but I think it was those wommens' fault, they only got what they could expect because if they had put there foot down they would/n't have had the trouble.

Yes, she had felt driven. Rita's appearance, so withdrawn and vulnerable, had urged her predisposition to shelter. It was the strongest emotion she had. Shuddering, remembering what lay in the envelope, she admitted how deceived she had been.

The letter had done one small service; it had reminded her of the others and since she was here, she would go upstairs and check. She never knew when they might come. Sometimes she thought her house was like a hotel; no, more like a hostel, she corrected and smiled.

She smiled at the rooms, too. They were always ready and though she could not afford to furnish them more comfortably they were peaceful. That was all that was required. They provided a brief rest. She noticed that the leaves of a fern were brittle and she took the pot into the bathroom and watered it under the tap. She had been away longer than she realized; she could not remember how long. The occasions of flight merged. She had once told Mrs Bellamy – or it might have been one of the others – that she herself was lucky; she could get right away. But when ructions came, they hadn't a chance;

they could go no distance nor manage a permanent change. Economics and fear tied them. They could dare only a few days. They could seek no other protection for if they reported it, were seen anywhere near the police station, they would be punished before anything could be done. Last time after Mrs Bellamy had been here – or it might have been one of the others – he had struck so hard at her feeble threat of Authority that he had broken her spectacles. So now she avoided policemen; she could not risk his thinking she had been talking to one. She had been safe up here, though, and so were the others. That was why she put them upstairs. They were out of reach when the knocking started. She wondered what the neighbours made of it; and hadn't someone once suggested that it was her own husband knocking, coming to challenge a man who had replaced him? She wished it were as simple as that. But so far she had succeeded in dealing with it, except the night when Rita had let one in. She felt guilty about that because she had been hurt. Until then she had prevented the girl's being involved and hoped it was not the reason why, later, she had come home drunk.

She was growing tired; the day was nearly over but before she left she would find herself something to eat.

The shelves in the kitchen were divided into sections marked by sticky labels. Printed on these in the girl's handwriting were their names: Elizabeth and Rita. This precaution could appear to indicate scrupulous house-keeping but in fact was a separation typical of the girl. To share would have compromised her position as lodger and might lead to friendship. Rita didn't want that. So she had resented being included in the man's accusations, not caring, of course, whether or not they were accurate about the other woman but insisting in her letter only that he should have been corrected about Elizabeth's relationship with herself. After that, it must have been a shock to hear her friend's joke as she helped with the zip – someone had told her that the girl had been practically hysterical. Sadly she wondered whether Rita's tears were a terrible private regret that she could not behave more naturally.

But, looking at the labels which emphasized the division of food that she herself had shopped for, she felt the rebuff and was stung by its unkindness. In defiance she took a packet of cream crackers from Rita's shelf, spread three biscuits with margarine, added slices of cheese and took them on a plate down to her room.

Sitting beside the television, its screen now blank of images, she was able to reflect more calmly on the effect of a few improvised words. Which had provoked false conjectures about her and had planted inaccurate deductions concerning her private life which distorted her generosity. But perhaps it was not so surprising. Delusion occurred without the prompting of any device. A man could approach another on a station believing that he had been the boy with whom he had played in his street. Thinking of this, she saw the moth glide to the lamp and heard its wings tapping inside the shade. Soon, satiated with light, it would fold and rest. And suddenly she felt anxious, not for herself but for the one who had taken her place. She was weary, but she must last a short time longer; there were things that must be said before she went away.

'I couldn't know that they would try to reconstruct it,' she apologized, 'or that you would play my part. Would you have done so had you suspected what might come of it? Had imagined that a young man's jealousy would swell the hatred beyond the screen's frame? For it already fermented. I have been abused, struck, up there in the hall. This would increase, rush to a climax, and I would go away. The break-in was a climax; it was a warning. I didn't clear up; I couldn't; I walked out of the house immediately; I didn't even cancel the milk. I was free to go because Rita had done so already; she was out of danger. She had written her letter.

'But going, I left them with you. You who resemble me in features and have, like me, this urge to protect. Though you thought it was Rita you were protecting when in fact you had offered yourself as a substitute for me. An understudy, you would say, required suddenly to step under the lights. And so they transferred their attention to an actress. Because many would make no distinction; I do not have to remind you that people often cannot distinguish between actors and the characters they portray. If those who harassed you had stopped to think, they would have remembered that I was reported to have gone away, but I doubt if that knowledge would have deterred them. Even those who may have sensed that it was not I they pursued would find you an equally satisfactory prey, because you were implicated, having represented me on the programme. So they applied to you everything that had been hinted about me.

'For the men who harassed were not necessarily all like Josh who had a personal grudge and believed he was speaking to me when he said that he wasn't "standing for any more". (A man loses his self-respect when he can't keep hold of his wife.) No. That piece of film and the report in the newspaper gave licence to men besides those who had reason to seek revenge.

'There was an occasion in a hamburger restaurant when a man accosted you. He could have been one of those who knock, the one who telephones, a kerb crawler or a man innocent of such abuse, just eating a meal by himself; but surely he had read the report. Incited by that, he attacked you not because of your young man's colour, as was suggested, but because of his homosexuality. The deduction is feasible. You almost guessed this yourself when your friend Raymond apologized for his previous attitude to men like Earl, for Raymond's words "doing what they do" echoed the ferocious challenge of the man in Greasy Len's.'

She paused. 'I know this grieves you. I understand why you are ashamed. For you once confessed to Judy that you could not rid yourself of disgust when you thought of Earl with men, and now you ask yourself whether that is any different from Alan's revulsion for you. But your response to Earl's sexuality does not prove that you are no better than Alan or the man in the hamburger restaurant. You do not share their blame because you do not allow your feelings to alter your behaviour. You must not be so severe with yourself. It is hard to be entirely free of prejudices. They will leap up without our volition, but you have discovered what it is like to be the victim of one this week.

'There may be others, too, who would like to insult you. Mrs Dale is jealous of me; at least, I'm sure she must be because she thinks I have taken Rita from her. Miserable at her daughter's leaving home, she was gratified to be offered a culprit for her loss, particularly if that culprit were presented as disreputable, inferior to herself. Thus she was shocked by the journalist's description of me as "that type" but she did not object to it as did her mother. The old lady told you that Mrs Dale had allowed the man to put ideas into her head and words into her mouth. Since it was less humiliating to believe that someone had influenced Rita to leave her, she quickly adopted his suggestion that the girl was impressionable, though you remember that she was still testing the novelty of his word on her tongue.

'After this, the stepfather was clever enough to anticipate how the interview might be reported, and feared that this might recoil on you. Inviting you to visit them he tried to warn you – you mentioned to Earl that you thought he was holding something back – but finally he hadn't the courage. Then that morning in the market you rejected Mrs Booth's attempt to enlighten you.

'You have told me that the mother hoped I'd get my deserts. Well, she may be satisfied if she ever learns that others have taken their revenge.'

Her energy had almost gone. She was played out. But something remained which their minds cringed from and they had pushed it away, telling themselves that it was not their concern; they were not its target. It was meant for two others. That argument was an evasion, however. If they looked upon the thing together its horror might be exorcized.

So they watched as one lifted the envelope which had also contained the copied letter and neither turned away her eyes when the two bruised fragments fluttered out. Each had an edge which was uneven, chopped by blunt scissors that had cut through a word written by a ballpoint pen. She slid the two pieces together and read out: 'Dead' and the date which was the same as the one at the head of the letter. Then they watched as the pieces were turned over. The face had once smiled but now, sliced through, its halves had the rictus of a skull; hacked off, a leg hung from the bumper of an Army truck; the word scored into the back had raised weals across the broad khaki chest. Before the blades had gone through, the picture had been cancelled with deep lines connecting the opposite corners.

Together they stared. The young woman who had committed this act had lodged with one of them; she had been searched for by the other and occupied her thoughts; and each reflected as Stephen had done that she was still a stranger.

The remains of the photograph had been laid on the floor. Once it had been whole, lovingly treasured in an album or put out 'to air'; and faded, it had a dark border where light had been stopped by a frame. Now dismembered, cloven, his laughter sheared, the soldier looked up at them, his eyes still unclosed, and a ceremony seemed necessary. She bent down and gently, keeping the two pieces together, she revolved them until the harsh diagonal strokes took the shape of a cross.

Now it was over. She could go. She found her handbag, rolled down the sleeves of her blouse and pulled on the yellow sweat-shirt. Then she turned off the light. Upstairs she found that in all the rooms the lamps were on and rebuking herself for such absent-mindedness she switched them out. No curtains had been drawn; the house must have been like a beacon, but tonight it had fetched no one. Olivia smiled to herself. It was as it had been before.

Leaving the bedrooms she thought of Elizabeth preparing them for the others; she thought, too, of Judy restoring her own shattered place and was content that the one below, here in the basement, was again tranquil. So, reaching the hall, standing by the door as she had done that day of the filming, she did not experience apprehension and dread. Because she now knew that it was generosity and affection for which she had trembled, and that they were less fragile than she had feared. They had not cracked under the club of violence and abuse.

She went through the door and closed it carefully behind her, making sure that the catch slipped into place. She walked down the short path and passed through the gate. This time she was not moving to a director's instructions. This time she was free; herself.

She had finished the job, had completed what she had set out to do. But it wasn't like coming out of the theatre after you have given a good performance, when you are high. This was not elation she felt but sadness. It wasn't as you feel after a good performance when the energy is still pumping and you know it will continue for hours. It wasn't at all like coming off stage. Because she felt so tired and completely used up; her lent life had been ephemeral and now her body was a husk and she must wait for that which had gone from her to be replaced.

So it was some time before Olivia heard the footsteps behind her. At first, absorbed in this private renewal, she took no notice, expecting them to pass. But they remained and gradually she acknowledged that she was being followed. In front of her the street was empty and neutral, holed by darkness between the infrequent lamps; behind her, matched to her strides, was this threat. For a moment she considered rushing up a path, banging on a door and shouting for admittance, but she could not do it. Even had there been lights in a house, that might not have been possible, and to fetch someone from bed, noisily importuning assistance and thrusting her crisis into this sleeping normality, was beyond her. She had no idea of the hour.

She walked more quickly but the distance between them lengthened for only a minute; the steps jerked rapidly before becoming even again as they adapted to her speed. Then there was a slight catch in the rhythm and suddenly they were walking in unison, their legs swinging to the same beat, and there were no longer two patterns of echoes but one, fixed, undeviating, relentless; the pursuer concealed by the sound of the pursued. At which, sweat gathered and breath was erratic. Passing through the arc of a street lamp she cried out as a squat shadow edged under her; it grew and she saw it was her own. No other came alongside it, a measure of the space left her which she must preserve. But the light

160

weakened and her frail tape was sucked into the night which reared before the next faraway lamp.

Then she was running and the feet behind her were not in time with hers now, they drummed out a new pace and she must not be overtaken by them and what they brought: a hydra head, one face masked by the windscreen of a car; one featureless and mute at the end of a phone; one thrust over a table spitting grease; one driven into her cheek turned from the smell of drink; one hissing venom; one fat with salacious gossip; one above the dungarees of a workman releasing hate. She must keep ahead of them but she was tiring, her body was old, its spirit had not yet returned. If she could reach the next lamp she would stop and face this thing that hunted her but it was closer, drilling her ears with obscenities and abuse, strident, without a pause.

Until at the thin edge of the light its ferocity slackened and her hearing became tuned to cadences, plaintive, which told her of those who sit lonely amid others' laughter, of men whose language is fists humiliated by jeers at the empty house, of those so unsure they dread inclusive affection, of all the desperate unloved whose caress is the fear they have dialled. But as together, prey and predator, they reached the light's core, these wraiths dissolved into breaths which sobbed pleas for her charity, which choked on the vista of paced streets empty of a figure yearned for, which surrendered all claims if only she would give assurance of life; while a hand reached out, touched her shoulder gently, pleadingly, and a name was called, the one she had recently shared.

And swinging round, Olivia saw, covered with tears so heavy that they could have been taken for rain, the face of Charlotte Dale.

Chapter Eleven

'How did you fare with the audition?' Mrs Winterton greeted. 'On Friday I was home and in bed before you came in and you were out again before I descended for breakfast yesterday, so I couldn't wish you luck. Last night I'm afraid I was the one keeping late hours. Well, tell me; don't hold me in theatrical suspense.'

Olivia grinned. 'You're doing that yourself. I don't know whether they want me, of course. They decide next week. But the audition went quite well, though it was one of those exploratory affairs when they give only half an ear to your prepared pieces because they're more interested to discover how you would fit their style – hence the assistant director leaps up and you're asked to improvise with him.'

'Really? What was the task?'

'My behaviour when pestered by a chap on a station. I had to push him on to the line eventually. The play they are opening the season with is *Masterpieces*.'

'I don't know it. I confess that the theatre stops for me with George Bernard Shaw.'

'There's been quite a lot written since then.'

'So I understand. Did you acquit yourself well?'

'As a matter of fact I was rather pleased with what I managed.'

'That's splendid. Perhaps the events of the past week have borne fruit. Yes, I mean that precisely.' She paused; her eyes held Olivia's. 'This morning I had a long telephone conversation with your charming friend, Judy. It seems that I have not been supervising you very well.

Would you want that? You must ring her back, please. Then you must join me for a cup of tea and tell me all about the burglary.'

It was characteristic of her, Olivia approved, that she had not rushed into that first.

'A policeman paid me a social visit yesterday. The originator of the Mulholland Bolt, I understand. I was flattered. Besides yourself, Olivia, my path is rarely crossed by the great. Though I have one small objection: that you did not leave me a note informing me of what had occurred. As I believe I stated on another occasion, you must not think it your duty to shield an old woman from the terrors of this world. And should you aspire to do so, a square of cardboard in a door is hardly adequate. However, I forgive you. Meanwhile I think we should apply our minds to more serious kinds of protection. You make that telephone call, then we can discuss them.'

'How was it?' Judy demanded.

'Not bad. I was exhausted when I arrived, but recovered. You know, the usual adrenalin. How's the play going?'

'Picking up. The producer has let it be known that for the time being his suicide is postponed. Are you still affected, then, by the break-in?'

'No, by the day after. It's too long a story for now, Judy, but I'm sure they're both safe.'

'Both?'

'Yes. Not only Rita but Elizabeth. I'm reasonably certain that there were attacks on her similar to those on me. She runs a sort of unofficial refuge, which can have no chance of remaining a secret in this town, so the husbands know about it. I've been in the house and I found a letter. It was opened, from Rita, and explained that she'd gone off with her real father. So Elizabeth must have left after that. It was the wisest course since the heat was on.'

163

'I hope it's off you.'

'So do I, but if it isn't, at least there'll be no surprises; and I could probably evade it – try a new colour rinse, throw away this sweat-shirt, find a different image. Elizabeth's is too much of a strain.'

'Don't be facetious, Olivia.'

'I'm not being, entirely. Obviously I should be safe if I didn't have such a provocative double.'

'A false nose and whiskers wouldn't be enough to put off those who've already identified you and know where you're living.'

'You mean the telephone freak?' Two days ago she had assured Judy that the kerb crawler had not reappeared. 'I think he's probably given up. I haven't received a call since Wednesday.' Thanks to the exchange.

'Sounds promising; but I was also referring to the burglar.'

'Yes. I don't think that one will break in again. It was very bright of you, Judy, to suspect that wasn't a spontaneous mess; it was made, as far as possible, on the model of the programme. As a punishment – for either me or Elizabeth. Probably the person wasn't sure which. The room on "Mystery of the Week" was hers, you see, not Rita's. Steve always thought there was something strange about that part of the film. It didn't match the room he remembered.'

'But you shouldn't assume that you're out of danger,' Judy persisted. 'I'm not thinking only of the break-in.'

'I may not be, but the harassment seems to be cyclical. There was a reference to it in Rita's letter, something like: "it stopped before for a bit", as if there are calmer patches between crises. Please don't worry. Look, the problem will be solved if the Piccolo offers me the part. Otherwise, I'll sort something out. I have the impression that Mrs Winterton is about to propose measures to suit a state of emergency – what *did* you say to her? – and I can always call upon Steve or Earl. Except that neither has much credibility as a bodyguard. It's Elizabeth that needs protection, Judy, and I shall keep an eye on her house and visit her when she returns.'

'Will you? I can appreciate the reason, yet what a bizarre meeting!' Reunion, Olivia silently corrected. 'But I suppose you won't be in any greater danger than you have been in this week. Which reminds me of that man in Greasy Len's. I can't understand why he was so outraged at your being with a chap who was black.'

'I don't think it was Earl's colour that was the problem. There had been a newspaper report following the film.' About to describe the few seconds they had missed, she paused. She could not repeat those improvised lines of a man Judy had once loved. She could not let the other know that one cause of her being victimized this past week was their friendship. She said, 'I didn't see the report until Friday. It was nasty. It helped to create an atmosphere, an environment, which encouraged what happened. It was based on delusions and prejudice. Whose target was me.'

'Oh, my dear. Look, why don't you trundle over and tell me at leisure? See the play, too. You can stay as long as you wish.'

'I'd love to, and I'll come very soon; but not now. I've already arranged to visit Mum and Dad. Tomorrow. After I've taken some things out of pawn.' To redeem them would require all the fee for 'Mystery of the Week'. Such a use seemed appropriate.

'Heavens. "That it should come to this!" Whatever could you pawn?'

'Nothing; but someone else managed it. And I intend to return the loot to its owner before I go home.'

REMEMBRANCE OF THE SUN
Kate Gilmore

In a country embittered by the Shah's oppressive regime, romance must take second place to revolution, and Shaheen is prepared to sacrifice his musical talents, his plans for a college education in America, his love for Jill, and, if necessary, his life. Set in the turmoil of Iran before the revolution, this is at once a touching romance and a fascinating account of two young people from very different backgrounds torn between love and political ideals.

I CAN'T STAND LOSING
Gene Kemp

Patrick Gates is trying very hard to be positive but living at 17 Constance Place makes it pretty difficult. The Gates family are, in Patrick's own words, a bunch of no-hopers, excepting himself and Mum who somehow keep them all going. Then comes the memorable day when Mum packs her bags and says she's off to Greenham Common ...

MADAME DOUBTFIRE
Anne Fine

Lydia, Christopher and Natalie are used to domestic turmoil and have been torn between their warring parents ever since the divorce. But all that changes when their mother takes on a most unusual cleaning lady. Despite her extraordinary appearance, Madame Doubtfire turns out to be a talented and efficient housekeeper and for a short time at least the arrangement is a resounding success. But as the children soon discover, there's more to Madame Doubtfire than domestic talents ...

THE UNDERGROUND CONSPIRACY
Catherine Storr

What Jass does in her spare time is not terribly wrong, but neither is it strictly legal. So she doesn't want anybody else butting in on her secret – least of all an unknown cousin who has come to stay. But when Jass's secret 'game' leads to serious, frightening trouble, she's only too pleased to have Colly to confide in.

BIANCA
Joan Phipson

The first time they see her, Emily and Hubert catch no more than a glimpse of the girl's terrified face as she and her rowing boat loom briefly out of the mist, before it disappears back across the water. But it's a face which haunts them both and they quickly become deeply involved with this strange girl and her mysterious past.

RUBY
Rosa Guy

Ruby is lonely, desperately lonely. Friendless and despised at school and oppressed at home, she feels worthless and unloved. Then she meets Daphne, beautiful, strong, ambitious Daphne and they become friends. Their relationship gives Ruby a taste for life and the strength she needs to stand up to her tyrannical father.

Ma Mountain

PAULINE LEWIS

Scripture Union

© Pauline Lewis 1997
First published 1997

Scripture Union, 207–209 Queensway, Bletchley,
Milton Keynes, MK2 2EB, England.

ISBN 1 85999 080 0

British Library Cataloguing-in-Publication Data.
A catalogue record of this book is available from the British
Library.

Printed and bound in Great Britain by Cox & Wyman Ltd,
Reading.

*To those families who have left houses and lands
for Christ's sake and the gospel's, especially
those I knew in Papua New Guinea*

Chapter one

Matthew loved the mountains. He sat on the veranda, staring across at the steep wooded slopes, but this morning he wasn't even aware of their beauty. All he could feel was a dull ache inside. Suddenly his pen dropped from his hand, and to his dismay a large tear landed in the middle of the letter he was writing. That was the last thing he wanted to do, to cry.

Oh no, he groaned inwardly, seeing his mother coming. She was uncreasing her back as she walked across from the cook house, making out she was glad of a break from bending over a smoky fire.

"Hey! I like your artwork," she exclaimed, looking over her son's shoulder. "Is this the plane we came in when we flew up from the coast?"

"Oh, Mum, you are hopeless!" Grateful for the interruption, Matthew spoke teasingly. "This is supposed to be the small mission plane that will be coming here – once the airstrip is finished," he added, in a tone that implied, if it ever is.

"Are you writing to Tim?"

He made no objection when she began to read over his shoulder. He would have done if they had been back home, but somehow things were different up here. It was just the three of them, on this remote mountain. They couldn't afford to have secrets from each other. Just a few of the men of this mountain tribe were able to communicate in pidgin, the trade language, and they were only just beginning to learn the "true talk" as they called the local language.

"Dear Tim," she read. "This is a picture of the plane that will be coming here to bring us supplies, once the airstrip is open. Then we will get mail every week, and bread and meat and other stores." The writing was smudged after that, and she didn't attempt to read any further.

"You'll have to tell him that our roof leaks."

Matthew was aware that his mother knew what had happened. He appreciated her tact.

"I'll get the kettle on. Dad will be back in a minute, shouting for a cup of tea."

"I'll fetch you some firewood." There was a pile ready chopped under the house. Mum could have got it but Matthew was glad to have something to do.

He felt better as they squatted companionably by the open hearth, trying to coax a blaze and at the same time avoiding the pain of getting smoke in his eyes. Until his mother started him off again, that was.

"Are you going to finish off Tim's letter, or shall we get on with some lessons after this?" Jenny asked, harmlessly enough, she thought.

Matthew didn't want to hurt his mother. He knew she was trying to help, but he felt angry, really angry! It all came bursting out.

"What's the point of anything, Mum? Letters or lessons, it doesn't make any difference! We don't

6

know how long it will be before we can find someone to carry the mail down all that way. We couldn't read most of the last load that was brought up, because the man fell in the river. If we find someone who says they will go, there is no way of knowing that it will reach the government station safely."

The fire leapt up into a blaze and the kettle was soon singing. They filled a flask and escaped out again into the sunshine.

Matthew thought he had got away with his outburst, but as they sat there on the verandah his mother began to reason with him.

"I know it's tough, Matt," she began, "but it's only until the airstrip is open. Then we'll have regular supplies, and Dad will be able to do all sorts of improvements to the house. They'll send up metal sheeting for the roof. I'll have a proper stove and a water tank, and we'll be able to have the two-way radio. You'll be able to tune in for School of the Air then..." Jenny trailed off as Matthew turned away so that she couldn't see his face. He was angry with himself for being such a baby, and angry with the whole world for placing him in this embarrassing position.

Words began to splutter out. "When the airstrip is open! When! When! Everything is going to be wonderful when the airstrip is open! They told us it would be open in a month. We've been up here three months already and how much progress has been made? I don't believe it's ever going to be finished. I... " He knew it would hurt his mother, but somehow the words came out. "I wish I had stayed at home with Gran and Gramps."

The little wood-framed house shook as

Matthew's dad leapt up the steps to join them.

Now I'm in for it, thought Matthew, ready for any excuse to be sorry for himself, but he managed a watery smile when Jim exclaimed, "What's up with our mish kid?"

It was Gramps who had first realised the significance of his initials: Matthew Kenny, MK, Missionary Kid. He'd felt pretty pleased about it at the time. He supposed he had better try to live up to it. Picking up the mug of tea his mother had poured for him, he snuggled in between his parents.

He felt the strength of his father's arm on his shoulder, as they looked out across the mountain peaks that were spreading around them. There were still wisps of the morning clouds drifting below.

"We may feel like we are at the end of the earth," Jim commented, after they had sat in silence for a while, "but it's so beautiful here. And there are all these other mountains and so many tribes that could be reached, if only we can have a church here on this mountain."

Matthew felt him withdraw his arm as he clasped his mug with both hands and again relapsed into silence. At last he spoke.

"Matthew is right, Jen." He was looking over his head to his mother. "The work isn't going ahead as it should. I've just been over to the strip and you can't see any progress from last time I was there. Our Max is not a happy man. I don't like the atmosphere there at all. This is really something we need to pray about."

Pray! Pray! Matthew had been taught to pray almost before he could speak. It wasn't that he didn't know that there was a God who listened to his children, but he was glad when his mother came out with what he was thinking.

"Jim! We do pray. We've been praying every day, and you know that our friends at home are praying too."

His dad was silent for a while, but Matthew didn't miss the wink as, handing his wife his empty mug, he suggested that Mattthew might be excused his lessons that morning.

"I've got to visit old Kaki," he explained. "It would be nice to have my son's company. You have him most of the time."

Matthew was about to leap joyfully from the steps of the veranda, but his mother gripped him firmly by the arm.

"Walking boots, Matt! Your sandals won't last long once you get into the mud."

It felt good to be striding along the bush paths, trying to keep up with his father. He was too busy skirting his way around the circular vegetable plots that the highland people made, balancing on the logs that had been thrown across the bogs, and clambering over rough hewn stiles, to worry about the airstrip and contact with the outside world.

They reached firmer ground and, as Jim dropped back to walk beside him, Matthew was expecting a lecture. But Dad could be pretty tactful. They were usually the best of friends.

"You're getting to be a real explorer, Matt," he began. "There aren't many boys that have done a trek like ours when we came up here. Three whole days climbing mountains, and wading through bogs—"

"Yeah! It was the vine bridges. They were the really scary part. Oh, I hope the photos come out."

They were back on dangerous ground now. These photos would be in their long-awaited mail. He knew his father was trying to steer the conversation back to safer territory when he went on, "Poor old Mum. It was a good job you had the courage to go over, or I don't think we would ever have got her across. She wasn't going to stay on one side with you on the other."

"It was scary, though. The water all swirling and gurgling underneath, and the bridge swinging and swaying."

There was no more talking for a while for, after crossing another stile, they were scrambling up a sharp scree. Matthew was using all his energy to try to keep up. He was glad when, panting for breath, his father flung himself on a fallen log. He flopped down beside him. He knew a sermon was coming, but at least he could get his breath.

"You know, Matt," Jim went on, "It isn't only when we are having adventures that we need special help. It's when nothing exciting is happening that we need the most courage."

"Like today, when it seems that the airstrip is never going to be finished?" Matthew leaned companionably against his father to show that he got the message. They sat quietly for a while, watching a tiny bronze lizard that scampered across the rocks, lifted its head in wonder at these two monsters, and then was gone.

"I suppose you're right, Dad," said Matthew at last. "On the trek up, I was thinking about all the stories I would have to tell the kids at home, and how they would envy me. But when you are doing your school lessons all on your own, and no cricket, and no one to play with... it... it's a bit tough, isn't it, Dad?"

He jumped up, hauling his dad to his feet, to show that he was ready to go on.

They clambered on for a bit, Matthew trailing behind again, and then Jim turned. "That must be Kaki's house, over there." Matthew smiled at the way his father pointed with his nose, as the natives did. "But you know, there's no need for you to say that you have no one to play with." He glanced behind at the bunch of brown-skinned boys who watched them expectantly. One or two had followed them as they left the mission house, and by now there was quite a gathering.

He recognised Kepa, Masala's son. He liked him. With big brown eyes and a cheeky smile, somehow he knew he was safe with him. They were all smaller than him, anyway. Maybe he could show them a thing or two. He didn't specially want to go with his father to sit in the smoky darkness of a native house anyway, but he wouldn't sound too willing.

"They can't even speak properly," he complained.

"Hang on now!" Jim protested. "We're the ones who can't talk properly. We have come to live in their territory now, and they speak the language of this place. Try to understand them, Matthew. I know we have come to teach them, but they have got lots to teach us too. Don't forget that."

He felt self-conscious just standing there as his father walked away, so he pulled out his pen-knife, and began to whittle a stick. He didn't want to appear too willing to make friends, after all.

The children gathered around him now. They were gabbling away, but one word was often repeated. "Look!" Yes, that was what they were saying, "Look!" They were showing him their bows. One of them ran and searched for the right branch, and showed him how to shape it.

By the time Jim had returned, Matthew had made his own bow and was having a lesson in archery. He was so absorbed in this new skill that he had forgotten about the smell of their unwashed bodies, most of them clad in nothing more than a belt and a bunch of leaves to cover their buttocks.

"Wow! Look at our mish kid now," his father teased. "You'll soon be a highland warrior. Are you coming with me, or shall I tell the boys to bring you back?"

"Yeah, you go on, Dad. I'll be all right."

He could see that his parents were pleased when he eventually turned up, his bow slung over his shoulder and his companions chattering around him. No sign of his morning blues now.

The next morning the Kenny family were eating their porridge huddled around the fire in the cook house, but as soon as the sun had melted away the damp mists that wrapped the village, the children were there.

"Mattio! Mattio! Come! Come and play," they called in their own language.

"I come," he responded.

"Why, Matthew! You're learning faster than I am," his mother remarked. "You'll soon be talking like one of them."

Matthew didn't want to sound too keen to

affirm this new-found friendship. "Silly things!" he remarked. "They can't even say my name properly."

"Why, no, Matt," Jim told him. "That is a sign that they have accepted you as a friend, when they put 'o' at the end of your name. That sounds good – Mattio. You have been accepted."

"Half an hour, Matt, and then it will be time for lessons," Jenny called after him as he grabbed his bow and ran off, but it was much more than an hour before he returned.

He was grateful that his parents were seated around the table with Masala when he slipped in, though he had been surprised to see him there. He had thought he was working on the airstrip, but no. They were absorbed in a language lesson. He got no more than a frown from his mother as he took his books onto the veranda. The lecture would be saved for later. He knew he should be trying to make up for lost time but somehow he couldn't concentrate. He opened his books and chewed his pencil but got no further.

He was relieved when at last his father went off with Masala and his mother came out with her stool and sat beside him. He waited for her to tell him off, but in the end he had to break the silence.

"I thought Masala couldn't come for language lessons because of the work on the strip," he ventured at last.

"Oh Matt!" she confided, "There's trouble brewing. That's why Masala was here today. He isn't going to help at the strip any more and if he doesn't, of course none of his clan will. Your dad is ever so worried. He's saying that he shouldn't have brought us up here with him – as if he could have survived on his own," she added.

"Anyway, what happened to you? You have usually been so punctual since Gramps gave you your watch."

"Oh Mum!" Matthew groaned and slumped forward, his head on his hands.

"What is it, Matthew?" She pulled her stool nearer in concern.

"Well," he began at last, "you know that I don't understand much of what they are saying. But we came across this group of the older boys, and they didn't even notice us. They were so busy talking, as though it was something very important. They were talking about the white man—"

"Dad?" his mother interrupted, and he could see the colour drain from her face.

He reached out his hand to reassure her. "No, I don't think so, Mum. I think they were talking about Mr Bull, Max, who is in charge of the work on the airstrip. Mum— " He paused. It was hard to find the right words to tell her. "I learned the word kill, when they wanted me to shoot at a bird with my bow and arrow, and Mum, I'm sure that the men are planning to kill Mr Bull!"

Chapter two

Matthew had his school books spread out on the table before him, but he couldn't concentrate. He had thought his mother would have told him to stop imagining things when he had told her what the young men had been plotting, but instead he found that she too was worried. His dad had gone off to try to talk to Masala's clan.

He watched his mum now as she walked back from their temporary cook house. Her tumbling curls were dragged back into a pony tail and she was walking like Gran did sometimes, as if her legs didn't want to go.

"Mum!" he called. It was comforting to feel her hand on his shoulder.

"It's tough when you are just waiting," she remarked. "Why don't we leave your lessons until Dad gets back and we hear some news? I don't feel much like language study myself. What about a game of chess?"

Grateful, Matthew ran off to get his pocket set that had been a parting gift. "I'll beat you, you know," he teased as they seated themselves, their legs dangling over the edge of the veranda. They would see Jim coming from there.

"Do you think he will be long?" Matt asked, as

he set up the board.

"I'm afraid so," Jenny replied. "You know these people. They never decide anything in a hurry. They love talking and everyone in the clan must have their say before they decide anything. Conversation is their art, you know. Dad won't be able to hurry them. Here – am I supposed to go first?"

Matthew picked up a pawn in order to reply to his mother's move, but his thoughts were away on the other side of the mountain with his dad.

"They wouldn't really kill Mr Bull though, would they, Mum?" The thought sent a shiver down his back. If they killed Mr Bull, then what if his father upset them, even without meaning to? Their family might be next.

"We certainly hope not, for then there would be endless trouble. The government would send troops up and that would be the end of our work. They would never allow us to stay after that."

"Masala's clan wouldn't kill him," Jenny went on. "We feel sure of that. He is truly a Christian. It was through him we were asked to come here, you know. But the others – I don't know. It is whether Masala will be able to persuade them."

"Are you going to move, Mum, or not?" Matthew wanted to change the subject, but then it was he who brought it up again.

"Why do they hate him so – Mr Bull? And couldn't Dad help him to get away? Hey! Don't cheat, Mum! You can't make a knight go that way!"

Jenny laughed. "I can't play chess and answer you at the same time. We would have done better with ludo. Now then, one question at a time. Why do they hate him? Well – you've seen him with them. He came up here thinking he was Pharoah or something, and could force the people to do whatever he wanted. The money was good and maybe he thought it would all be a big adventure. But it took longer than he thought and you know how difficult these people can be. And I suppose he got fed up with living in a tent and with all the trouble of getting mail and supplies."

"Homesick, like us," Matthew interrupted.

"Yes, like us," Jenny agreed, "only we know that God wants us here and that makes all the difference."

His mother seemed so confident, so sure in her faith. He used to think that no one loved the Lord Jesus as much as he did; that he would always, always trust him. But now, up here, everything seemed different. It wasn't so easy to feel sure about things any more. He wished it was.

She went on talking about Mr Bull. "He tried to bully the men; even threatened them with a gun. But the worst thing of all in their eyes was that he made Okono look small, in front of the women and children as well as the men, and to them that was unforgivable, because of course Okono is one of their leaders. You know what they say: Mr Bull gave him shame."

"Was that when they went on strike?"

"Yes. They say they don't want aeroplanes coming because it might bring more men with whips and guns."

Matthew's head was in his hands. This could mean danger for them all. Yet deep in his heart he couldn't help the guilty hope that this trouble could be the means of them all going back home.

Jenny gently prized the pawn from his hand and put the board away. Matthew didn't complain.

"I am coming O! I am coming O!"

"Oh, here she comes, Mum. It is your mate, old Kokamu." He felt a measure of relief as he watched the wrinkled old figure. With spindly legs and a staff in her hand, she came striding over the rough terrain.

The old woman held out her hands, grimed from her labours in her garden, and pressed Jenny closely to her. Matthew made sure that he was out of reach.

"Well, well! There's a picture of contentment," Jim exclaimed, when he returned to find the two women bent over Matthew's Bible picture book, with Matthew standing, helping his mother out with some of the words, as they explained the stories to the old woman. An hour had passed without them realising it.

His fair skin was flushed and beginning to burn from his morning out in the sun. "You two – sisters!" he explained, pointing from Kokamu to his wife, but the old lady was indignant.

"I am her mother," she insisted, holding her wrinkled skin against the smooth flesh of the young woman. Matthew hopped around with glee.

"Wait until I tell Gran," he accused, exploding with mirth, but then he felt his dad's arm on his shoulder, gently leading him away.

Uh, uh, he thought. I've said the wrong thing again. If I had some of my mates here, they would sure appreciate the joke.

But his dad explained. "It's a wonderful thing, Matthew, that these people are willing to accept us

18

as their own family. You know, a lot of these people wouldn't believe that the white man was really flesh and blood as they are. Some of them told their children that at night we turn into snakes and swim in the river."

Jenny, overhearing, joined in. "That's right. We shouldn't laugh at dear old Kokamu. Didn't Jesus say, 'He who does the will of God is my mother and brother and sister'?"

She waited until their visitor had gone before she brought out their lunch.

"Rice again," Matthew grumbled.

"I'm sorry, folks," Jenny apologised. "Once the airstrip is open we will be able to have—" and then she clapped her hands to her mouth. "Should I say, if?" she added feebly. "Come on, Jim, you had better tell us the worst."

"It's good news and bad," Jim began. Matthew listened breathlessly. Maybe he might think their bad news good. He was all mixed up.

"They have agreed that it would be very foolish to harm Max Bull," his Dad went on, "and Max is more than willing to make his escape; but the thing is, he'll need a guide to take him back down to the government station."

"Couldn't he go on his own?" Matthew asked.

It was unusual for his father to raise his voice to him, but he did now.

"Matthew! You *must* learn this and never ever forget it." He spoke slowly and with great emphasis. "It isn't safe for any of us to try to go through the bush on our own. People have tried it and have never been seen again. The highlanders know how to find their way, but even for a European who is a skilled tracker, it is very risky. So I couldn't go with him, even if I wanted to. And I don't really want to either, or the locals would think I was siding with him." He spoke in a quieter tone, Matthew noted thankfully.

"Besides," he added, after a while, "although these people have promised not to harm him, some of the other clans might make trouble so he really needs someone who could give him some protection."

"There are wild pigs too," Jenny added.

"Wouldn't Masala take him?" Matthew asked, almost afraid to speak in case he said the wrong thing again.

"It would be wonderful if he would, but it isn't easy for him, because it was his brother that was shamed. This will prove that he is a real Christian, if he is able to forgive Max and help him. If he would go, then I know that some of the others would go too."

"Did you *have* to be a missionary, Dad?" Matthew was feeling fed up, his sense of adventure definitely wearing thin. Once again night had crept up on them unaware, casting its dark mantle over the mountains, and Jim was filling the hurricane lamp that was all they had to light them through the long evening. He used to enjoy a game of Scrabble, but night after night it could be a bit much.

"I did," Jim replied, "but if anyone is to blame, it's your mum. She knew she had to be a missionary long before I did."

"If we are blaming anyone, we had better go back to Gran. She was the one who always told me about missionaries for my bedtime stories," Jenny laughed. "But you know how it happened,

Matt. We thought we were settled in New Zealand, and then Dad was made redundant, so he offered to come up and help out with a building project."

"Yes, and you thought it was unfair, because you were the one who had always wanted to be a missionary," Matthew chimed in, laughing.

"Hey! You were as bad," Jenny teased. "You didn't want to miss out on the adventures."

"Well, then we heard about Masala, and how he had walked right across the range to ask for someone to come and teach his tribe. And I knew then that God wanted me to come."

"Us," interrupted Jenny. "Oh, go on Jim, tell Matthew. Hold on, I'll pour the cocoa and then we'll be ready."

From far away across the mountain they could hear the throbbing of the kundu drums. Jenny came and threw a blanket around their shoulders. Nights were cold and they were looking forward to when they could have a stove in the house. There was a feeling of foreboding hanging over them all.

Matthew already knew the story, but he enjoyed hearing it again. He didn't need telling twice when it was time to get into bed. It felt good to have his mother come and zip him into his sleeping bag.

"You see, Matthew," she said gently, as she stood for a moment by his bed, "you need to be very sure that you are where God wants you to be because sometimes it is very exciting – if you like excitement – and an adventure, but there are times when it is just tough."

"Like now, when Mr Bull seems to have messed everything up and it looks as if we will never have

21

the airstrip?" Matthew asked, sleepily.

He lay there, listening to the throbbing of the drums. Life could be very confusing. His parents were so sure that they were meant to be up here, but then, what about him? Should he be up here on this mountain? Had he come just because he thought it would be an adventure? Did he have to tag along because he was a kid? Did he matter to God? How could he work it all out?

As he lay on his back he held each of his fingers in turn as he remembered his very special text, "I – will – never – leave – you." His Sunday School teacher had taught him to say it that way, the day he had gone to her and told her that he had wanted to be sure that he was a Christian. It had been special to him when they had first known they were coming here, and as he repeated it now his worries seemed to slip away and he was asleep.

Suddenly Matthew was wide awake again. What could it be? He lay there, afraid to move, his ears straining, searching the quietness of the night. It was as though a tremor had shaken the house.

Matthew raised his head to listen, but then he heard his dad go to the door. He could hear the murmur of voices. His head flopped back on the pillow and the next moment he was asleep.

Chapter three

"Jacket on, Matt!" Jenny called as he was whooping down the steps next morning for a game with his friends before lessons. Feeling a nip in the air, he returned, not unwillingly, but snatching his coat from its peg he stopped, open mouthed. The mail-bag! It was gone!

"Mum?" Could he believe his eyes?

"Masala came for it late last night, after you were asleep," his mother told him.

It was then that he remembered how he had woken up, thinking that there was an earthquake. So it was dear old Masala!

"So, had he agreed to take Mr Bull down the mountain? It was a full moon. They aren't scared to travel at night then, are they?"

"They had already set out when Max thought about our mail and asked Masala to run back to get it. It was awfully good of him."

"Oh! Yippee! Yippee!" Matthew was dancing around his mother. "We'll be getting mail. How long will it take, Mum? When will Masala be back?"

Just then he felt a hand on his shoulder. He hadn't heard his dad come in. "Hold on now, Matt."

Oh dear, what now?

"Well, Masala may not go all the way. He might go so far and then ask someone else to guide Max. But our mail will get out all right."

"Oh, I'm sure the government officer will do his best to find someone to bring it up." His mother was trying to sound bright. "I've sent a list of supplies we need. Max will tell them the position."

Matthew sat down, deflated. Waiting was so hard. "But won't they send someone else up to finish the airstrip?" he asked. "They could send the mail with him."

His mother made her way to the outhouse and started to blow up the fire. Good old Mum, trying to comfort her family with the inevitable cup of tea. She knew that none of them was going to feel much like work.

His father sat against the wall, head in hands. "I'm afraid no one is likely to come after Max has given his report. Come to that, the surveying is all done. I could supervise the rest of the work. I've learned enough about it." It was as though he was talking to himself.

"You know," he went on, his words slow and heavy, "David Livingstone and Mary Slessor and people like that didn't have supply lines. They just made do with what there was locally."

"What are you saying, Jim?" Matthew sensed a tension in his mother's voice.

"That we should forget about the airstrip and make the best of things up here?" It was Matthew who put the words into his father's mouth. Suddenly they were both aware that his mother had collapsed on the floor, her face drawn and pale.

24

"Hey, Honey. It's that old fire. It's too much for you." His dad was anxious, clucking round her like a mother hen, but Jenny shook him off. "I'm all right," she insisted, once she had drunk the water they gave her. "Matthew, I thought you were going out to play. Your friends are over there waiting for you."

"I thought we were going to have a cup of—" his father began. Matthew stomped off unwillingly. He had understood, before his dad, that there was something Mum wanted to tell Dad, and she didn't want him to hear. But his mates were playing knuckle stones and calling him. He ran to join them.

"Mattio!" Jenny's cry came faintly to him. She was getting quite good at calling out like the highlanders.

"Have you finished with this magazine? Can I have some pages out of it, Mum?" Matthew asked as he ran back into the house. "I want to make some paper planes. It is really windy out. We could have no end of fun, and then I can explain to the kids about the big bird." Matthew began folding a loose sheet of paper when he was jolted back to reality.

"Oh, sorry, I forgot." His voice was heavy with sarcasm. "We are going to be tough pioneer missionaries, aren't we? No planes! No radios!" He flung the magazine down into the corner. Life had been tough before, but they had always known that things would soon be better; but for conditions like this to go on endlessly... Yes, Livingstone did it, but could he be a Livingstone? Could his mum and dad even?

His mother's hand was on his shoulder. He knew he deserved a lecture on sulking, but a glance at Jenny showed her not frowning but smiling, one of her special secret smiles that he associated with birthdays and Christmas and things like that. He turned expectantly.

"We've got something to tell you, Matt. Wait until Dad comes. He's just gone to see about some firewood. He won't be long." Matthew's mind began to spin. What could it be that he didn't already know? There had been no mail, or messenger.

Soon enough they were seated in their sunny spot on the veranda, Matthew in the middle as usual.

"Your mother has made me realise that it is very important for us to have the airstrip opened," Jim began, in his speechifying voice. Mother? Matthew's grey eyes were open wide. What could she know more than his dad? As Jim carried on with his address, Matthew had a strange feeling that he had rehearsed it.

"You see," Matthew heard him say, "God is going to answer your prayers for a little brother or sister, after all."

"Oh! Oh!" This took some thinking about. Matthew didn't know much about babies, but he *had* realised by now that they were not to be bought from the hospital, as he used to insist. And it was true; he had prayed. He had so wanted a baby brother to play with when he was small, but this was hardly a suitable answer. A baby, up here? Besides, he was too grown up to have a kid brother now. He felt a groan deep inside him, but all he said was, "That's nice."

"Where are you going, Matt?" Jenny called as he stumbled into the house. "Lessons." He knew he was hurting her. He watched through the open door as she walked a little way with his father. He could see his arm go round to comfort her; they were comforting each other.

It wasn't that he didn't want the baby, but, well, the idea took some getting used to. Besides, in not much more than a year he would be staying at home with Gramps and Gran so that he could go to high school, and his parents would be up here. They would have the baby and they wouldn't even miss him.

Deep in his heart Matthew knew that this was not true. Of course they wouldn't stop loving him, but still he felt hurt and rejected.

"I'm going over to look at the airstrip," Jim called later that day. "Anybody coming with me?" Matthew usually jumped at the chance of a walk with his father, but suddenly he was absorbed in a picture he was colouring.

"Matt, aren't you going with Dad?" Jenny called. "I've started this baking." "I'm busy," he lied, scribbling so furiously that he broke his pencil.

His mum's soft arms were around his neck. "Go with your dad, Matt," she pleaded. "It's hard enough up here without us hurting each other."

"Sorry, Mum," he mumbled and, pulling on his walking boots, he ran after his father's retreating form.

Glancing back, Jim slowed his pace until he knew that his son was nearly up to him and then strode on again. These narrow mountain tracks meant walking in single file, but at last they mounted the crest that gave them a good view of what was to be the airstrip and sank down onto a convenient log.

His father sat silently for a while and when he did speak it was as to an equal. Matthew liked that. It was as if, with the thought of a baby coming, he could be counted as grown-up.

"You see, Matt, we can't possibly stay up here unless the planes are able to land, for your mother would never be able to make that long trek back to civilisation once the baby is on the way; and she'll need to see a doctor from time to time to make sure that everything is all right." Matthew knew he wasn't expected to reply.

"This is the last thing we thought of," Jim went on, as if he were talking to himself. "We used to pray about having another child but in the end we thought God must be saying no, so we gave up all thought of it. After all, we already had one very special son." Matthew felt a gentle dig in his ribs and contentment began to melt away the lump of hurt that had seemed to have settled on his chest.

"So we must believe that this baby is to be a very special gift for all of us – these highland people too."

"How for them?" Matthew asked. From where they were seated they could see the mountains unfolding below them. His mum and dad really cared about all the people who lived there.

"Well, they will really believe that we are human, like them, when they see your mum with a newborn baby. You know what they say: we are sitting with them. That means that we have come to stay; we belong."

"That is what you were talking about in church

last Sunday," Matthew rejoined.

"About how Jesus came and sat among us? Hey! I'm glad someone was listening to my sermon." Laughing, Jim jumped up and hauled Matthew to his feet.

"If you understood my poor effort in their language, perhaps they did too," Jim went on as they walked right down to the plateau.

"I know that word," Matthew explained. "It's what the boys say if we meet someone from another place. They tell them, I am sitting with them."

Matthew tried to look knowledgeable as they walked the length of what was to be the strip.

"There's a root here, Dad, that will have to be dug out."

"Right," agreed Jim. "And see over there? That still needs to be levelled, and those rocks will have to come out. If only we could get the men to put their backs into it and all work together, it wouldn't take more than a few weeks. But they've made up their minds that they don't want the strip and I don't know what to do about it."

They were still talking over the problem as they sat down to the meal Jenny had ready for them.

"The boys would help. They are strong," Matthew suggested. "I'll tell them all about the 'big bird', as they call it." He thought this was a great idea, but his father didn't agree.

"If the boys help, it would be giving the men 'shame' as they say, and this would be the same problem all over again. We've got to let them feel that this is for them."

"It's the same with education. We are pleased that the government hasn't started a school up here yet because it will give us a chance to teach the adults to read first. Then they won't feel left out."

"But then what are we going to do, Jim?" Matthew was glad that his mother had spoken up.

"Guess I'll have to do it myself. We've got to be able to have a plane come when you need it."

"You can't!" Jenny and Matthew spoke in unison. But Jim was determined.

"I suppose he thinks that it's better to do just a little bit than nothing at all," Jenny answered when Matthew complained. He had so much wanted to go with his dad, but it was Matthew and Co these days. Once he set his foot out of the door, there were his little brown-skinned friends wanting to join in whatever he did.

Poor old Dad. "I thought maybe the men would have changed their minds if they saw me working," Jim sighed, "But they seem to be adamant. They don't want the planes to come." He had been going to the strip for over a week and there was so little to show for all his effort.

"Listen!" Jenny exclaimed as she stepped onto the veranda to throw out some crumbs. "The people are calling out. I think someone is coming."

Matthew rushed out. Anything to shake off the depression that had settled on them. He couldn't believe his ears.

"Masala! It's Masala!" he whooped, doing a war-dance in his excitement.

"Steady on, old chap," Jim cautioned. "We don't know if he will have any mail with him—" but Matthew was gone, racing off down the path with the children from the village, who had heard the cry from far away.

Masala! Yes, it was Masala, but how different he looked. He was wearing a brightly coloured shirt and neat khaki shorts, and he was clean shaven; and yes – there was a heavy bag slung from his shoulder.

A few words of greeting to their friend, then the family gathered like vultures round the sack. Matthew took the tins of supplies that his mother handed to him and placed them inside, but it was the letters that they were all after. They sat out on the veranda until, the last light gone, they were forced to come inside and huddle round the lamp.

Matthew had a letter from his pal, Tim. "Our team won at cricket," he chortled.

"Hey! Listen to this," Jim exclaimed, almost knocking the lamp over in his excitement. "It's from Ralph, the mission pilot. Mark's Gospel is ready, and there's a package of primers for teaching literacy, all ready to come up to us. Hallelujah!" He was nearly dancing. "And—" pausing for effect.

"Go on!" they screamed, as excited as he was.

"There's a two-way radio all ready for us, so that we'll have contact with the other mission stations, as well as the pilots."

"Ooo, look!" Matthew had been busily opening another letter, addressed to him. "This is from my teacher. No, not my correspondence lessons, Mum. I haven't opened that yet. From up here. She is welcoming me to School of the Air."

But Jenny was gently prising the letters from their hands. "No more reading tonight," she insisted. "We are straining our eyes. The rest can wait until tomorrow."

"Oh Father," Jim prayed, as they prepared to go to bed, "you know how much we need the airstrip. Please will you help us, so that these people may learn to love your Word. Amen."

"And Lord, you know Dad has done his very best, and he can't do it on his own." Matthew didn't pray out loud. He just didn't know if or how God was going to answer their prayers, but they simply must have the airstrip.

Chapter four

Matthew was sitting with his mother watching the activity. When they had first arrived they could hardly see the men labouring on the strip, but now, quite suddenly, everything had become clear and bright.

"They are a bit like dreams."

"What are, Matthew?" Jenny asked.

"The clouds, Mum. They seem so real and firm, and yet once the sun gets up, they just whisper away."

Jenny laughed. "Well, let's hope that they will whisper away the day the plane is due, for if they don't, then it will be no mail for us. These single engine planes have no automatic pilot. They dare not fly in cloud."

They sat silently for a while, watching the men gathered from their various clans, their backs bowed in unison, their muscles rippling and a low musical chant rising from their throats.

How quickly a situation could change. One minute they were all wallowing in depression, his dad slogging his heart out on the strip and getting nowhere fast, and now this. At last you could see that it was an airstrip.

"It was a good job they liked Masala's new

clothes," remarked Jim who, seeing his family, had come to join them.

"Was that what made them change their minds?" Matthew asked.

"Yes, that and other things. Masala told them that if they were willing to work for the white man's money, then they could buy clothes like that, and that the government officer might help us to have a store up here – if the big bird, as they say, could fly in to bring in goods."

"Rain is coming! Rain is coming!" The call was echoed, and Matthew, joining in the exodus, scurried back across the rough terrain to reach his house before the storm clouds could soak them. He had the fire blown into a blaze and the kettle filled before his parents, breathless, flung themselves down beside him.

"How long before the plane will be able to come, Dad?" he asked.

"If they keep on working as they have done today, hopefully I should say another week."

"But how are we going to let the pilot know that it's ready?"

He heard the rasp as his father rubbed his stubbly chin, for now was his chance to grow a beard.

"He flies into the government station on a Friday," he began thoughtfully. "They will tell him the latest news, so then hopefully he will fly this way to make a reconnoitre."

"So, how will he know for sure that it's ready?" Jenny asked. She was anxious too. This was important. It did seem like a miracle that the men were getting the strip ready, but now, how to make contact with the pilot?

34

"Would he see if we wrote a message in very big letters and laid it on the ground?" asked Matthew. Realising this was not very practical, they all sat thinking, mugs in hands.

"I know!" he exclaimed at last. "You could make all the people stand, to spell out the letters. I've seen them do that in a television advert."

It had seemed a good idea when they had been sitting there by the fire, but now that it was to be put into practice Matthew felt a knotting in his stomach. The air strip was cleared and levelled. The sun had burned the last stray wisps of cloud off the side of the mountain, and the clansmen, wives and children too, squatted around, waiting and hoping for sight or sound of the plane. It was past midday, and soon the weather would be closing in. The children heard it first; far, far away, the faintest throbbing sound.

"It is coming o! It is coming o!" they shouted. Matthew was leaping and dancing too among the little brown-skinned bodies.

"Quick! Quick!" Jim called, and Masala joined him in marshalling the people into their places. Matthew was squeezed in among the throng that made the O of the great OK they were forming.

"Right now!" Jim commanded. "That's fine! Now! Don't anybody move."

Over the distant range a small moth-like creature appeared, gradually growing in size until the plane was zooming and circling above them. The people were chattering excitedly, but as quickly as it had appeared, after a dip of his wings, away it flew until once again it was hidden by the mountains.

"He's gone!" Their excitement had died away with the gradually diminishing view of the plane and now they were left with only dull disappointment.

Matthew felt a great anger rising in his heart. It wasn't fair. His dad had worked so hard, and prayed so hard too. Where was God? Wasn't he listening, or didn't he care?

But just then he saw Tundi run over from the other side of the strip and give something to Jim.

"Look! The big bird dropped it."

"He's sent us a message Jim." Jenny was shouting with excitement. "Look! The pilot must have thrown it out for us and we didn't see."

Matthew watched breathlessly as Jim carefully unwrapped the paper that had been placed inside a tube of bamboo. There was just one word: "Wednesday." That was all. But that was all they needed to know. Wednesday could not come soon enough. This was to be the big day of their lives.

"How do you know that the big bird is coming today?" Tundi asked. Seeing the family set out for the strip, first the children and then the adults had gathered with them.

"The pilot wrote it on the paper that he threw out to us," Matthew explained.

"Did he know what we meant then, when we all stood in our place on the strip?"

"Why, yes." Matthew was enjoying having all the answers. "You see, we made the letters – O K – he read them and understood."

"Hey! Interesting thing!" He shook his head in wonder. "They are signs, like when we go hunting. We see signs that birds and animals and people have made. They tell us what to do."

"That's right," exclaimed Jim, who had joined the conversation and now addressed those standing around. "Only people in other lands have worked out many different signs, so that they can not only send messages but tell stories too. We call this writing. It was writing that he threw down to us. The pilot is going to bring us books so that I can teach you all to read these signs and then you will be able to read God's book. There are many wonderful stories in it."

But he had lost his audience. Long before there was any sight of the plane, they had detected the distant throb of an engine. Theirs were the skilled ears of the hunter.

"It is coming o! It is coming o!" they shouted, Matthew whooping ahead with them, but then he was horrified as some of the children began to run onto the strip.

"Go! Go!" he yelled. His father was beside him, trying to shoo them off. Why hadn't they thought to tell them the importance of having the strip clear?

"Last time the plane came we asked them all to stand on the strip," Jenny explained to Matthew, as Jim frantically appealed to the men. At last they had made themselves clear, and now the people stood expectantly, lining the runway.

"Better tell them no running out until the propeller's stopped," Matthew prompted his father.

The tiny yellow insect they had seen buzzing in over the mountain had now grown into the big bird they were expecting. Matthew could see the pilot looking down and waving as he circled around and then he lined his plane up ready to

37

land, or so he thought. Down, down, down it zoomed. He heard the engine reducing its revs.

"Look! He is lowering the flaps," he called. Matthew knew a lot about planes. But now, instead of touching down as they expected, the plane flew in way above them, just to the side of the strip, seeming to make no effort to land. With a surge of power, it swept up again into the sky. Matthew watched, open-mouthed, with the rest of them.

"Ai! Ai! Ai!" the people wailed. "The big bird is going!" Some of them ran out again onto the strip. Jim was the first to realise what was happening. "Get back! Get back!" he shouted, above the roar of the engine. "It is coming in again."

Matthew felt his mother grasp hold of him and he returned her grip. They didn't know how to endure the tension. They had waited so long and they knew that they could only stay with these people if the pilot was able to make a good landing. Was the strip safe? Was it long enough? Right there on the plateau, if it was too short the plane would go crashing down the mountainside.

"Oh, Lord Jesus, help him," he heard his mother whisper. Her eyes were shut. She dare not look. It was a good job Matthew had his eyes wide open though, for he suddenly saw Leme, the deaf boy, start to wander across the strip, right in the path of the plane that was once again lined up to land. If he had paused to think he would probably not have had the courage to do what he did. Oblivious of the screams of the women, with one mad dash he leaped right in front of the plane and, dragging Leme down with him, flung himself onto his face.

He was only vaguely conscious of the engine

coughing once again into a full-throated roar. There was no time for praise or blame as he was dragged aside. Once again the plane was in the air, circling the strip.

They could hardly believe it when at last, almost on the brink of the drop that marked the end of the runway, the little yellow plane had rolled to a stop. The pilot was wiping the sweat from his brow as he jumped down to the ground.

"They told me it would be like landing on the top of a card table," he laughed. He was lean and bronzed with a rugged sort of face that crinkled easily into a smile.

Matthew stood back and watched as he was introduced to each in turn. He liked the way he made sure that he shook hands with the children too.

"Here! You take to Mr Kenny's house!" Jim translated for him, as the men placed the many boxes that he had unloaded onto their shoulders and set off across the mountain. Matthew knew that he had waited until the crowd had thinned before he introduced his family. Good old Dad.

"No, I'm not in a hurry to take off again," Ralph Emerson laughed. "That was quite an experience. My! You sure gave me a fright," he laughed, ruffling Matthew's hair. "You are a brave lad, but don't try running in front of a plane too many times, will you?" he teased. "You aren't a cat with nine lives."

"Come on, Mrs Kenny, I must keep an eye on the weather; I don't want the clouds closing in on me. My wife won't be very pleased if I can't get back; but I promised her that I would come and see your home, so that I can see what things I need to bring up for you."

Matthew liked Ralph. He was friendly and understanding.

"These are the literacy books Paul has sent you," he heard him tell his father, as Tundi dumped his load on the veranda.

"Great! I must get busy with those," Jim remarked. "Here, Matthew! Put them under your bed for now."

"And this is what you have been waiting for, your lifeline," Ralph told him, as Masala panted up with a heavy load. "Your two-way radio, and of course the battery charger."

"Mind you tune in for School of the Air, young Matthew. My daughter Paula is in your class. She's looking forward to hearing you call up. I might bring her with me on one of my flights, if you would like that."

As soon as they returned from escorting Ralph to the strip they got busy with the radio: their new toy, Jenny called it. They couldn't wait for six o'clock to come, when their mission was on the air and they could call up to some of their fellow missionaries.

"Next time he comes he is going to try to bring you a wood-burning stove that we can have in the house. And he is going to look out for a rain barrel, and a sink, and we'll fix up our own piped water," Jim told Jenny, above the static.

"What about light?" she asked, for it was almost dark, and they were only then turning to the load of mail that their postman had brought.

"Yes, we'll get it all fixed up," Jim laughed. "There is so much to do. I can start on enlarging the house, now that I have these extra tools. Hey,

40

Matthew! There are two packs of lessons for you, from your teacher."

But three days passed and the lessons were not even looked at, until Jenny declared that the holiday was over, and carpenter's mate or not, Matthew must settle down and do some school work, or he would be packed off back to his grandparents.

A month later, they were at the airstrip, awaiting the arrival of their little yellow messenger.

"I met Paul, the Bible translator, the other day, Jim. He wanted to know how your literacy classes were going," said Ralph. Jim hurriedly changed the subject, and started to organise the men to carry their loads back to the house.

"I'll send a message to Paul," he replied eventually, but Jenny looked at Matthew.

"Did the books come?" she whispered. "I haven't even seen them.

"They are still under my bed," was his reply.

That evening Matthew saw his father sitting quietly, his Bible in his hands. It was time for family prayers. They came and joined him, waiting for him to speak.

"I feel guilty," he confessed at last. "We have got our Bibles. We can read God's Word. And we came up here to bring God's Word to these people."

"I know," Jenny interrupted. "I'm just as much to blame. We have been so busy making our home nice that we have almost forgotten why we came."

Matthew had already dragged out the neglected box and now he placed one of the primers on the table.

"What are we going to do?" he asked. "Will you build a school?"

"I don't think it's the building that is most important," Jenny sighed. "The thing is, how are we going to convince these people that they *want* to learn to read? It isn't easy for older people to learn new skills."

"Another thing I feel guilty about," added Jim. "I am supposed to have made a survey of the tribes around here. Jenny, I'm sorry. I'll try to finish the kitchen, but then I think I must leave the work on the house for a week or two and go out on trek."

Matthew was excited now. This sounded like mish kid stuff.

"Oh Dad! Dad! Are we coming? Are we?"

Jim glanced at his wife. "No, Matt, I'm sorry. Not this time, I think."

Matthew understood. With the baby on the way, it wouldn't be wise for his mother to embark on too many adventures.

"But Dad! I can come? Can't I?" His father didn't answer. He didn't need to. Of course they couldn't leave his mother on her own.

Matthew would have loved to go, but as he lay on his bed that night he realised that even if he didn't go, with his dad away, maybe there would be adventures enough.

He felt his stomach begin to churn. He always felt safe with Dad around, but to be alone, just him and his mother... What would they do if there was any trouble?

Chapter five

"Tundi-o!" Matthew heard his mother call.

"I'll do that for you, Mum." Matthew was not always so ready to volunteer for household chores, but now he ran to fetch some wood to light the fire so that she could cook the tea.

But the wretched fire wouldn't light. Twenty minutes and half a box of matches later, he had produced nothing but smoke. His mother's hand was on his shoulder.

"Go and ask Tundi, Matt."

He hated having to admit defeat. He knew that Tundi was on the verandah, longing to be asked. Just a word and now, like lightning, he ran to his own house and came back, carefully shielding a burning ember. In next to no time the fire was blazing and Jenny's pots were boiling merrily.

"You know, Matthew, these children all know how to make a fire. Their lives depend on it. We have been brought up with electricity and gas, so it's much harder for us."

"There are lots of things that we know about and they don't," she went on. "That's why God has sent us here. But they have things to teach us too. Come on, we'd better clear away the dishes. It will soon be our time on the radio."

Matthew didn't answer.

"We mustn't miss that. Although Dad can't talk to us, he may be able to tune in to hear us, and he'll be wanting to know if we are all right." She was working hard to sound bright, but somehow he couldn't respond.

"Of course we are all right," he mumbled. He was missing his father dreadfully.

"That's us, Mum." Matthew nudged his mother, excited now as he recognised their call sign.

"Mike Kilo here," Jenny answered. "Roger! Everything is fine. Jim is still out on trek. Over."

"Let's hope Dad was able to hear us." There was a sigh in his mum's voice. He had better forget his grievance and try to cheer her up. He ran to fetch the Scrabble. It was going to be another long evening without his dad.

"Don't forget your School of the Air," Matthew heard his mother call, the next day.

"Course I haven't forgotten, Mum."

"Good morning, Mrs Barry," he answered when his call sign came. "Yes, thank you, we're fine. We're expecting Dad back on Friday. Over."

"Mike Kilo – can you repeat. I didn't copy. Over." The teacher's voice faded away and all they could hear was static. His mother was beside him now.

"The battery must be flat. Oh dear, I was hoping it wouldn't need charging before your dad got back. Well, we had better get it done before tonight. Run and see if you can find one of the men to come and carry it to the shed for us."

"Oh, don't worry, Mum. I'll manage." His father had shown him how to work the charger. But his mother's hand was on his shoulder.

44

"Matthew. It's too heavy for either of us." It was her best sergeant major voice. "Go and ask one of the men, please."

Unwillingly he went off, returning with one of Masala's brothers. To Matthew's annoyance, he seemed to know what to do.

When at last it burst into life, and then settled into its familiar chug chug, he returned to the house to find that his mother at least was comforted.

"Come on, Matt. Finish off your lessons and we'll walk over to see how old Kokamu is," she suggested brightly. "Let's take a notebook and pencil and see how many new words we can learn. Then maybe the battery will be charged enough by the time we get back, just enough to call in, and we'll put it on again tomorrow."

A couple of hours later, as they returned up the mountain side, there was no sound coming from the engine shed. Dismayed, they ran to look.

"Don't worry, Mum. I'll fix it. You go and get the tea," he insisted, as he ran back with a set of spanners. But Jenny was immovable.

"I'm sorry, Matt," she told him gently, "but you are only an apprentice and we can't afford to make a mistake. If we do something wrong we might wreck it for good. If we leave it, at least we know Dad'll be able to fix it when he gets back."

"But what about the sched tonight?" Matthew complained. "Dad will think we are in trouble."

"He may just think the weather is bad. We don't even know if he is able to hear us, anyway."

"But the pilot may have a message for us." Matthew was itching to have a go, but his mother was adamant.

The next day was Wednesday, mail day. Although the cloud was low, they had packed up some lunch and made the trip to the airstrip. Returning weary and disappointed, they heard voices calling out from far over the mountain.

"What is it? Surely it isn't your dad back already? Run and see," Jenny commanded one of the boys who had stayed with them.

"It is strangers, come to see you," he explained, when he returned.

When, breathless, they reached the house, there was a group of men they did not recognise. They looked fearsome in their great wigs and with their faces and bodies daubed with coloured clays, and undoubtedly they were angry about something. Matthew was changing his mind about adventures, but he must try to be strong, for he could feel his mother trembling as she gripped his hand.

"What are they saying, Mum?"

Jenny shook her head. The strangers were excited and neither of them could make out a word.

"Go and sit down, Mum!" He had seen the colour drain from her face. He led her through the group so that she could rest her weight on the edge of the veranda.

"Ungu is there," he whispered, spotting a familiar face among the crowd. Quickly, Jenny called him beside her.

"Please ask them to sit down, and then you tell me what they want." She knew that he would speak so that she could understand.

Matthew listened to their talk surging to and fro, until at last Ungu felt that he was confident to pass on what they were saying.

"They want you to send a message on your talking machine," he told Jenny.

"The radio! But it isn't working." His mother signalled to Matthew not to interrupt.

"Ask them why," she relayed to Ungu. "What is the message that they want us to send?"

Once again the talk flowed. They sounded so angry, but maybe it was just that they were excited.

"There are two clans fighting over some gardens down the valley. They want the government man to send some policemen to stop them. They say some people have been killed."

"Oh, Mum." He caught hold of her arm.

"It may not be as bad as it sounds," she whispered.

"But Mum," he insisted, "the radio isn't working."

"I know, Matt." She shut her eyes for a moment. Matthew knew that she was praying.

He watched then as she stood up, strong and confident now. She had certainly had some help from somewhere.

"Tell them our talking machine is sick," she told Ungu. "As soon as my husband returns, he will fix it and then we will send your message. But now we will ask some of the Christians here to go back with you and talk to these people. And those of us who stay here will pray that they will stop fighting and make peace."

Again the talk flowed, to and fro. For a moment he visualised these wild-looking men, bows at the ready, dancing round their little house, holding them hostage. Maybe his mother was having nightmares too, for he had to pull his hand away, she was squeezing it so hard. At last the men were gone.

Jenny pulled Matthew into the house and shut the door.

"These fights can so easily spread and become a tribal thing," she told him. "If only your dad were here."

"We must get the battery charger working, Mum," Matthew insisted. "You are always telling me that praying makes all the difference. OK. Let's pray, and I know I'll be able to do it."

He realised his mother had only agreed grudgingly, even though she knew that there is nothing impossible with God.

He tried to look confident as he checked the plugs and tightened screws, but in the end he was relieved when the fading light warned them that they must hurry back to the house to get the lamp lit.

"Listen, Mum! I think I can hear drums!'

His mother pulled the curtains across and made sure that the door was locked. He came and snuggled close against her, and felt her trembling. Oh, if only his father were with them.

Suddenly Jenny began to laugh.

"What is it, Mum?" Matthew asked, puzzled. He couldn't see anything to laugh at.

"Why, Matt. Don't you see? If Dad were here, we wouldn't be afraid, would we?"

"Well?"

"But the Lord Jesus is here, isn't he? He's promised never to leave us, and he's much stronger than your dad. So come on, let's cheer up. We will trust and not be afraid. Isn't that the text you had to learn for your Sunday School lesson?"

48

Matthew was first to wake next morning. Using the flask, he took his mother a cup of tea. As he sat on the edge of her bed they were suddenly conscious of a throb-throb-throb in the distance.

They looked at each other. "The battery charger!'

"Hey! Steady on, Mum," he cautioned, as his mother made to jump out of bed. Mornings were not her good time.

"I'll go," and he was off before she could stop him.

"It was Ungu," he explained, trying to sound casual, as he returned to find breakfast ready. "He tried some different petrol. He said there must have been water in the other lot. So it was no big thing."

"And we didn't think of it, did we?" Mum usually managed to put her finger on the spot. He felt a comforting arm around him. It was true. He was upset. This had been his big chance to prove himself a man, and someone else had stepped in and would get the glory.

"It would have been lovely if you could have fixed it, Matthew," Jenny said, as they sat down together. "I know how proud you would have been to tell your dad about it. But think about Ungu. You know, these people feel very inferior to us in so many ways. They don't know about books or planes or money, except what we are teaching them. It must have been lovely for him to think that he was able to help us, and do something we hadn't thought of."

"But what about me, then?" Somehow it all came blurting out. "You are all up here because Jesus has sent you... and, well, I'm not needed at all."

"Matthew – that's not true," Jenny replied. "Jesus wants you here just as much as any of us. You didn't have to come. You prayed about it just as we did. You could have stayed with Grandma and Gramps."

"Yes, but I don't do anything," Matthew mumbled.

"You do, of course you do," Jenny laughed. "You look after Dad and me, and make us happy. What would we do without you? And the people all love you – and that helps them to listen to the Bible lessons, because they are happy. You don't have to prove that you are needed by doing something important, you know. In any case, what would I do, when your dad is away, if you weren't here?"

Matthew let Jenny's words wash over him. He didn't know if they were true or not, but there was comfort in them.

"Come on," she coaxed. "We had better do some lessons, or Dad will think we have been truanting while he's away. He could be back tomorrow, if things go well."

"We'll be able to talk on the radio tonight, won't we?" Matthew asked. Whoever had fixed it, it was good to hear the familiar chug chug in the background.

"Yes, we'll leave the battery charging until evening, and then we can send out the message about the fight. We haven't heard any more news, so let's hope our men have been able to talk some sense into them, and that they have made peace."

Matthew tried to get on with his work, but whenever he heard voices raised he would rush outside to see. His mum was as anxious as he was.

50

"Oh, it's nothing Matt," Jenny would say. "Come on. Let's try to finish this page." But it was nearly dark when they heard a cry echoing from mountain to mountain. They could hear the excited chatter of the people as they ran to gather outside the church.

Oh, surely, surely it could not be more trouble?

Chapter six

Their anxiety had gradually melted away as they stood there together on the veranda of their house. Could it be? Was it?

"It is! It's Dad!" Matthew yelled, and with a whoop he was rushing down the path to give his father a bear-hug. As for Jenny, she was so relieved when she realised that the calling out had not meant more trouble that, once Jim was safely in the house, she burst into tears.

"Most wives cry if their husbands have to go away," he had joked, "not when they return! I won't leave you again." Matthew felt as though a weight had been lifted off his heart.

"Can I come with you, Dad? Can I?" asked Matthew the next morning. He was so glad to have his dad back, he felt as if he didn't want to let him out of his sight, but eventually he settled to his lessons.

"We should be able to send workers out to some of these districts, and it would be good if some of the hill people would come in for teaching." He listened to his mum and dad talking over a cup of tea.

"I've been praying so much about starting a Bible school," Jim went on, "but we can't do anything until we teach them to read. Oh, if only something would happen to make them want to learn."

"Jim! Ralph is on the radio," Matthew heard his mother call.

"Roger, Ralph," Jim responded. "We have an emergency. A man with a spinal injury, from across the range. Had an arrow in his back. I've told them to carry him here, to be flown out to hospital. Over."

"No, they haven't brought him yet," Jim answered, as a muffled response came from the pilot. "I'll call as soon as I hear news. Over."

"He'll take him then, Dad?" Matthew asked. His father had told them the story and they were all anxious.

"Yes. He's flying locally today and the weather is good – so let's hope they keep their word and bring the patient in."

Meanwhile Matthew had an idea.

"Dad," he asked, as they walked together over to their garden. "Do you remember how Gramps used to write me special letters, before I started school – and I wanted to be able to read them on my own?"

"That's right, Matt." Jim was quiet for a while, then he turned and gripped his son by the shoulders.

"Something specially for you," he said slowly. "That's right. That's what made you want to learn to read."

"Hey! Where are we going?" Matthew asked, for Jim had turned about and was pulling him back towards the house.

"Family conference," he explained, as they sat

down together on the veranda. "Go on, Matt. Tell Mum what you told me."

"When you were talking about having reading classes, I remembered what first really made me want to learn to read," Matthew explained, and he repeated what he had told his father.

"OK. Now, we are going to ask the Lord to help us, and then I want any ideas of what we can write that will be specially for these people, so that they will want to learn to read."

Jim's prayer was simple, thanking God for all that the Bible meant to them, and telling him how much they wanted these people to read it. Then they sat quietly, looking over the valley.

"Could we get someone from home to write special letters to them?" Matthew suggested.

"Hmm," was all Jim replied. He was chewing over that idea.

"We often get news over the radio – personal news I mean. You usually tell Masala or one of the men, and they pass it on. What about *you* writing it?" said Jenny.

"Hmm," said Jim again. More to think about.

"You could have a bulletin board," piped up Matthew. "That's what we had at school. All the important announcements were on that. It was the first thing we looked at as we went to our classes."

A long pause, and then, "Matt! I do believe you've got it!" Matthew suddenly found himself pulled to his feet and the three of them were whooping around like Red Indians.

"We'll put it outside the church each morning," Jim decided. "Jen, you're good at printing. You can write it out for us."

"Hey! hey! Steady on!" Jenny was laughing.

"We'll have to think this out – use simple words."

"But their spelling is simple. Once they've learned the letters, they'll be away."

"They know two letters, anyway," interposed Matthew. His parents looked at him, questioning.

"O and K." he explained. "Do you remember, they made the letters on the airstrip for the pilot to see?"

They had been conscious of voices calling in the distance, and now Masala appeared.

"They are bringing the sick man," he told them. "They'll be here before the rain comes." It was usually fine until midday, so that gave them some idea of when they would arrive.

"Roger," replied the pilot, when eventually Jenny was able to get through to him. "I'll try to make it by twelve. Let's hope the weather stays fine for us to get out again. Over."

"Tell me about this man, Dad," Matthew asked, as they sat by the airstrip waiting for them to arrive. "Was he wounded in this fight that they came and told us about?"

"I don't think so, Matt," Jim replied, "but they had stopped fighting by the time we arrived. It seems they think that every white man represents the government and so once they knew I was coming, they stopped. It was when I was looking at their wounded people that they told me about this other man, Kamenoo. He'd had an arrow in his back and hadn't been able to walk – for two dry seasons, they said. So I went to see. He was lying in one of their men's houses, on a wooden bed."

"Was it all dark and smoky in there?" Matthew asked. He had been glad enough to come out into the sunshine after just a few moments.

"It was. It must have been terrible, lying there all those months.

"Anyway," his father went on, "we had to talk for a long time before they agreed to carry him here, to be flown out to hospital. You could understand that he was afraid."

"Were you the first white man he had seen?"

"I guess so."

Jenny joined them, a flask in her hand. She had stayed behind to boil a kettle.

"I heard Ralph call up. He won't be long now," she told them.

"But the men haven't come. Oh dear, I hope we aren't bringing him here for nothing."

"It won't be for nothing," said Matthew. "He won't come without our mail."

"Mail isn't that important, Matt," Jenny reproved. "We could wait a few more days for that. An extra trip means extra expense, and every time Ralph lands here he is running a risk. Don't forget that our strip is very dangerous."

Matthew didn't argue, but he still hoped they would have some mail.

They stood anxiously, listening for the first faint hum of the plane. There was still no sign of the stretcher-bearers.

The children heard it first, and soon they were watching as the "big bird" circled round and then lowered its flaps, ready to make the run in. Once again they stood, their hearts seeming to miss a beat, praying for a safe landing.

The engine was switched off, and Jim was running up to apologise to the pilot as he leapt down from his cabin, when, "They are coming o! They are coming o!" came echoing over the mountains.

Ralph was being refreshed with a cup of tea when the strange party arrived. Jenny gasped when she saw the patient.

"Why look, Jim!" she exclaimed in indignation. "They are carrying him tied to that pole like a pig."

The pilot was shaking his head. "It will be a miracle if he survives after that. But I suppose it's a wonder that he is still alive at all, for all the help they give their sick. Come on. Let's get him to hospital as soon as we can."

He unrolled a stretcher, but there was a great deal of jabbering and arm-waving going on around the wounded man.

"What's the trouble now?" Ralph asked, glancing anxiously at the clouds.

"They need a 'watchman' as they call it, to go with him and look after him." Masala explained, "but they are all afraid to go in the plane."

"It's a big thing," Jenny sympathised. "I was scared, the first time I flew."

"Not only the first time," Jim laughed, giving her arm a squeeze.

"Well, come on," chivvied Ralph. "You know he can't go without a watchman. Would one of your local Christians go?" he asked Jim.

"That's too much to expect," he replied. "They don't know these people, and they might be away a long time.

As the talk flowed to and fro, Matthew walked with his mother away from the noise and the smell of unwashed bodies. She had turned a mild shade of green and didn't have to explain that it had all become too much for her. He was sitting with her on a mound nearby, when a boy from this other tribe came up to him.

"I will go with him," he said. "I will go in the big bird."

"Is he your father?" Jenny asked.

He shook his head. "I have no father."

"Aren't you afraid to go in the big bird?"

"I am afraid," he answered, "but I will go."

Matthew took him by the hand, and together they pressed through the crowd, which had been swelling all the time.

"No watchman – no hospital," Ralph was saying, and made as if he would climb into the cabin without his patient, but Matthew shouted to him.

"This boy will go," he told Ralph.

"OK. No time to argue. If we don't get him to hospital soon he won't be needing anyone to look after him. Load him in."

They watched as Jim carefully helped to lift the stretcher.

"Now you!" Matthew told him, and the boy leapt up lightly and squatted beside the patient. "I shall call you, Brave One," Matthew called up to him. "Brave One, we will meet again."

Matthew had a sense of joy in his heart, a feeling that something special had taken place in joining hands with this young highlander.

"Hey!" Ralph called, before he slammed the doors and was climbing into his own seat, "I nearly forgot. I've a special letter here for a young man. Here you are, Matthew."

Matthew had been so disappointed that there had been no mail bag, so he was puzzled that Ralph should now produce this letter. It wasn't until they had watched the plane disappear over the crest of a further mountain that he began to open it.

"Dear Matthew," he read, but he got no further, for rain was on the way, so he waited until they were seated round the fire at home before he got back to it.

"Why, it's from Paula, the pilot's daughter," he exclaimed, reading avidly. "Guess what? Next mail day, her dad has promised to bring her to see us, and she can stay a week if we will have her. Can we, Mum? Can we?"

"Can we?" Jenny exclaimed. "I'll say we can. That will be great. I'd say that is just what our mish kid needs to cheer him up, not to mention his mum and dad."

"Hey! Can I call out and tell the kids?" Matthew asked, but his father's hand was on his shoulder.

"Hold it, Matt," he exclaimed. "Couldn't this be something for our bulletin board?"

Jenny sent Matthew running to fetch pen and paper.

"Here! Come on! Let's sketch something out to show Masala, and then we'll tell him that only those who come to the reading class will know the news."

Jim ran and fetched the primers that had been sent up, so they could use some of the same words. Matthew was right in on this. He was better at the language than his parents, but then, of course, Masala was called to check it.

Two hours and several sheets of paper later, the bulletin was ready. Jim made a frame so that they could fasten it outside the church.

"Now then," Jenny sighed, "we'll put it up first

thing in the morning and then we'll just have to wait and see if it has the desired effect; whether we will be able to start our reading classes at last."

"Not wait and see, Jen," Jim added. "Watch and pray. We've done our best, but I believe God gave us the idea. Now we will see what he makes of it."

"He used our mish kid to help us think of it then, didn't he?" said Jenny, her arms around Matthew's shoulders. "And to provide the news," she went on. "Matthew Kenny, don't you ever say again that you are no use. You're part of this team, and what would we do without you?"

Could this really be true? And would this idea work? Would their bulletin board really make these people want to learn to read?

Chapter seven

"The plane will not come today." It was Matthew who first heard the cry as it was passed from one to another, until the news had spread throughout the clan.

"Mum! Dad!" he exclaimed, as he ran back to the house, "They're reading! They're really reading!"

He remembered the first morning when he and his father had crept out to fasten the board to the church door.

Watching from afar, they had seen a curious crowd gather. Then Masala, waiting for his opportunity, strode onto the scene to satisfy their curiosity. It is easy to read, he had told them, only you must come to be taught.

Jenny had been delighted when the women had decided that they wanted to learn too. She had started a class especially for them.

"One thing, we are never short of news," Jim laughed one morning as they had prepared a fresh bulletin. "What with news of Kamenoo's operation and his daily progress."

"It is wonderful that he'll be able to walk again," interrupted Jenny. "That is an answer to prayer."

"And Brave One," added Matthew. "He's going to school and the teachers are pleased with him. They are willing for him to stay on with them, even after Kamenoo returns, so he can have an education."

"I still marvel at the way he was willing to go like that," mused Jenny. "I've a feeling there's a story behind it. One day I'll ask your Brave One to tell me."

"Kamenoo won't be coming back yet," Jim went on. "Ralph was telling me that he'll have to stay within reach of a doctor for a few months in case anything goes wrong, so they'll be company for each other. Now then, are we ready for Masala to look at this before you do the final copy?"

"What about the white girl?" Masala asked, after he had checked through it, altering one or two words. Matthew felt a sudden lurch in his stomach. He was excited about her coming but somehow, with it just being the three of them for so long, the thought of a stranger joining them – well, he felt a bit nervous.

"We won't know until the pilot calls up," Jim explained. "It may be tomorrow."

"Don't say!" Matthew cautioned. "They must read for themselves!"

Masala laughed. He liked being in on the joke. "I promise."

"I hope she really will come," Jenny added, when he was gone. "That was the first news we wrote for them and three weeks have gone by. First she wasn't well, and then Ralph had an emergency and couldn't fit in our flight, and now the clouds—'

"Can I wear my best shirt, Mum? Can I?" Matthew pleaded. Paula was on her way at last and he wanted to impress her.

"Well, all right Matthew," his mother conceded, "but change as soon as we get back. I don't want to have to wash it again before Sunday."

Matthew watched the colour from the girl's face drain away as she was helped down from the plane. Some of the highlanders who had gathered were wearing their wigs; their axes were in their belts and many of them were carrying bows and arrows. One or two of the older ones still had bones through their noses. He supposed they were a bit fearsome, but all the same he was disappointed that she was not delighted by the welcome.

"Good morning, Mrs Kenny. It is very kind of you to have me to stay." How primly she spoke, and she seemed taken aback when his mother gave her a hug.

Matthew had expected some recognition. After all, she was supposed to be coming to visit him, but all she did was throw him a casual "Hello," and he found himself trailing behind as if he were unimportant as, having waved off her father, they returned to the house.

"Lemons! What a treat," Jenny exclaimed, opening the parcel that Mrs Emerson had sent up with her daughter. "We'll have pancakes for tea if you like. Can you toss a pancake, Paula?"

"This is the radio," Matthew offered, but all the response he got was, "I know all about that." If they had been back home he would have had so many games to try to catch her interest, but here life was limited.

"Why don't you take Paula to see the village, Matthew, while I am getting lunch?" Jenny suggested.

He had dutifully discarded his best shirt. It hadn't done much good.

"Yally o! Yally o!" exclaimed the children who had been hanging about hoping for another glimpse of the stranger.

"The white girl has come to sit with us," he informed them, secretly hoping that Paula would be impressed that he was able to talk in their language.

"Ei! Ei! She is big and strong," they exclaimed. "And her hair is like the sunshine," but Paula's only response was, "Don't you think it's rather bad manners to talk in front of me in a language I can't understand?"

"Oh Mum! She's so stuck up," he whispered, when at last he had a moment when Paula was out of hearing. "I can't do anything to please her."

"You pleased her when you dropped your pancake," Jenny laughed. "She was happy because she was good at that. You know, I think she finds it all a bit frightening up here, and she doesn't want anyone to know. This 'Miss High and Mighty' is all a big act. I'm sure that she's quite a nice girl underneath."

"Well, I sure hope that nice girl will come out soon," Matthew grumbled, "I'd rather have no company than this."

"Hush!" Jenny whispered, giving her son a comforting hug, as she saw Paula returning from the garden where Jim had gone to pull up some vegetables for tea.

"My father told me that there is a vine bridge

near here," Paula remarked, before they went to bed. "I'd like to see it and get some photos so that I can send them to my friends at home." She had won at Scrabble, so was in a better mood.

"If you wait till Saturday, perhaps we could all go," Jim suggested, but Matthew pleaded, "I could take her. I know the way.'

"Well, I suppose we could spare some of the lads to go. They would look after you."

The next morning the clouds were hanging low and the rain was likely to come early, so Matthew had a long morning at his lessons. He could have done without Paula taking it upon herself to guide him, in between writing her own letters.

The following day, however, the clouds were fast melting before the sun's brightness and off they set, with a stout stick each and a flask and sand-wiches in Matthew's backpack.

Andupi, one of the older boys, was their guide, and he was soon joined by a crowd of joyful piccaninnies who danced alongside and addressed the white girl hopefully. But Paula still seemed determined not to be friendly.

While they were still in open country, Matthew amused them with the game that his father would play, walking along, ignoring the children until they were crowding on his heels, and then turning round with a loud, "Boo!" and seeing them scatter with screams of delight.

But Paula was not amused.

"Why don't you tell them to go away," she said at last. "We don't want to be followed by a pack of screaming kids."

Matthew hesitated. These children were his

friends. But he was still hoping that he might impress Paula.

"Go home!" he ordered, reluctantly. "Yes, you too," he told Andupi. "I know the way. We'll be all right."

The young man stood for a moment, looking as if he would like to box Matthew's ears, but then, with a face like thunder, he turned away, annoyed that the missionary's son had given him shame, as they say.

"Come," he commanded the children who had been joyfully following, and led them back towards the village.

After all, I am not on my own, Matthew told himself as they reached the dense bush, trying to justify his action.

"We found some orchids not far from here once," he volunteered, as they slipped and slid endlessly downward toward the sound of the river.

"Orchids? You only get those in the very expensive florists," Paula replied, but then curiosity got the better of her.

"Are you sure they were orchids? Do you think we could find some?"

Leaving the path, they clambered over some rocks and then a little further to where a tiny streamlet was cascading down a bank. It was damp and humid in this hidden valley.

They wandered along until Paula exclaimed, "There! Look!" High above them, they saw a cluster of the delicate pink blooms. Together they delighted in their find.

"Do you think we could take one back to put in our garden? My mum would be so happy."

"Here! Let's eat our sandwiches, and then we

can put it in this plastic bag. We'll pack plenty of moss around it. Do you want to get a photo of them first?"

Matthew wished that Andupi had been with them. He would have dug out the plant with his bush knife, roots and all, with no difficulty. It was after quite a struggle with his scout knife, and with Paula impatiently giving advice, that the plant was packed away and they set off back to the main track. The undergrowth was dense, the rocks slippery and there was so much moisture dripping off the trees that Matthew began to wonder whether the rain had come early. He paused to look at his watch.

"Oh Paula!" he gasped. "It's half past eleven. We will never get to the bridge and home again before the rain comes. We'd better turn back and come again tomorrow."

For once Paula did not disagree. Her legs were all scratched. She had mud up to her knees and was gasping for breath.

"OK," she agreed. "Let's go home."

But which way was home? Matthew could not seem to recognise the familiar path that they had left. They could hear the river roaring away in the distance somewhere below them, and they knew that they must keep that behind them, but – which way?

Just then Paula gave a little cry. Matthew turned to take her hand to haul her up the steep bank, but it slipped from his grasp and he watched in dismay as she tumbled down and landed in a crumpled heap.

He wanted to cry. If only he hadn't listened to Paula and sent Andupi and the children away.

They were his friends. He needed them, and they were always so willing to help. He leapt down beside the girl.

"Can you stand, Paula? What have you done?"

"I don't know," she sobbed. "I may have broken my ankle. Oh, Matthew. I'm so sorry I told you to send the children away."

"My fault too," Matthew sniffed. "I knew I shouldn't have done it. I'll call out. Maybe some-one will hear us."

"Oo – oo – oo!" he called, from the top of a rock, but he could not make his voice carry as the mountain people could. Dispirited, he slipped back beside Paula. "Don't ever, ever go off on your own," his father had told him. "Don't you know that people have been lost up here, and never found again?" What were they going to do?

Chapter eight

How long would it be before his parents realised that anything was wrong? Matthew wondered. They had been settling down to write letters, as the children left.

They had been disappointed that he and Paula had not got on. Matthew had overheard them one morning. Lessons over, his mother had sent them to work in the garden, but inevitably they had started some silly argument and, taking a huff, he had returned to the house.

"They're like a couple of dogs, stiff-legged, sniffing at each other, and ready to snap at the least provocation," he had heard his mother saying, "and they are both lonely children, in such need of friends."

Matthew was ashamed to show his face after that, and had crept away in case they realised he had been eavesdropping. He resolved to make more of an effort, only Paula had not been so ready to forgive.

It was a different girl with him now, sobbing with fear and pain. Together they had managed to pull off her boot and sock and watched in dismay as her ankle seemed to be swelling and turning black and blue before their eyes.

Matthew felt paralysed by fear. They were lost; maybe no one would ever come into this secluded little valley to find them; but Paula couldn't walk, and he knew he couldn't carry her, for she was taller and heavier than he was.

He couldn't leave her there. If he tried to find his way home on his own, he might get even more hopelessly lost. Now at least they were together.

He tried to think about his parents, as if to will them to realise that something was wrong and to send help, but all he could do was think of all the things that his mother might worry about.

Wild pigs! She always talked about that, and of course the highlanders never went far without their weapons, for this danger was very real; and he, big-headed, had sent his bodyguard home. There were cassowary birds too. One thrust of their great claws and they could rip a man in two. He listened, trembling. If they stayed quiet, they were not likely to be attacked. He knew that. It was only when you surprised them with their young that you were in danger.

Just then he heard a rustling in the undergrowth. A snake? He shook himself. Come on, Matthew Kelly, mish kid. You know there aren't any snakes in this area. Maybe it's a lizard, and that won't harm you.

Paula lay limp and quiet. That was better than her screaming or going hysterical or something, but he hoped she wasn't going to die. Why didn't she talk to him?

Maybe they should kneel down and pray, only he wasn't sure what to say. He didn't think Paula was in any state to laugh at him, but you never knew. Almost unconsciously he was holding his fingers, reminding himself of his very special promise from the Lord Jesus, "I will never leave you." If his mother knew they were in trouble, she would pray. Somehow she always knew that if she told her heavenly Father, then everything would come right.

She must have been praying, or the Lord must have known anyway, for it was just then that Matthew saw the little brown face smiling at him from the branches of a tree above him.

"Tundi!" Matthew gasped, a joyous grin breaking over his face. "Where have you come from?"

"We don't go away," he replied, relieved to find that he was welcomed. "We stay. We your friends."

"You certainly are my friends. I don't deserve you," Matthew acknowledged, as Kepa now showed his face. Together they came and tried to help Paula up the bank, but she was bigger than they were, and it was hard going.

"Do you think you should go for help?" Matthew suggested eventually.

"Yes, yes. We go," and the boys scampered off, as if thankful to be relieved of their responsibility. They had helped Matthew and Paula reach a fallen log, where they sat now, huddled together. It seemed to be getting dark, and they shivered as the first patter of the rain turned to heavy drops that fell from the trees and slithered down their necks.

It was as though they had been waiting for hours. Matthew's watch assured them that it was not more than half an hour, but they were convinced that it must have stopped.

"Perhaps they have forgotten where we are. They can't find us." Paula sobbed.

"Of course they will. They'll be coming now." Matthew tried to sound reassuring. He put his arm around Paula as if to comfort her, but he was trying to warm her too, for he knew that the high-landers always ran to their fires when the rains came, in case they died of exposure in the cold.

"Perhaps they can't remember where we are. Suppose they can't find us?"

"Hush! Hush!" Matthew didn't really think he had heard anything, but he didn't want to listen to Paula's supposings. But at last they knew that it was not their imagining. There was the snap of a broken branch, the woosh of bushes thrust aside and the welcome shout, "Here! They are here."

As soon as Paula felt Jim's strong arms around her she began to sob. "Oh, Mr Kenny, I'm sorry. It was all my fault," Matthew heard her blurt out, between her tears. She was clinging to him like a little child.

"Here! Tope will give you a piggyback. You'll be safer with him," Jim explained. Having reassured her and passed on his burden he reached out a hand to Matthew as they began the ascent back to their home.

"Did Kepa and Tundi tell you what happened, Dad?" Matthew asked, after telling his father how truly sorry he was.

"We had already set out. We met them on the way. Your mum heard someone calling out to Andupi and she knew he was supposed to be look-ing after you. I said you wouldn't be so daft as to go on without your helpers, but it seems your mother knows you better." He tweaked his son's ear and Matthew grinned ashamedly, resolving that he would make his peace with the older boy.

"She stayed at home to pray, while I gathered the men to come and search for you."

It was later that afternoon that Matthew found his Bible lying open on his mother's bed. He noticed the picture of the shepherd reaching down over a cliff and pulling up a lamb that had fallen over and become entangled in the briars. He read the words under it, "The shepherd goes looking for the one that got lost until he finds it." How happy he was to be found.

"Will you teach me some words, so I can talk to the people too?" Paula asked, that afternoon, as she lay, showered and changed and with her ankle bandaged up. Jenny thought it was nothing worse than a strain.

It certainly was a different Paula that they had staying with them now.

"She won't be able to go while her ankle is bad, will she?" Matthew asked hopefully.

"We'll see what her mother says," was Jenny's reply.

"Will you be all right without me, Mum?" Paula asked, when her mother came on the radio.

"I don't like to leave my mother too long," she explained. "Sometimes she worries when Dad is away."

Jenny came and sat beside the girl as she lay on the settee.

"We understand," she said gently. "It's dangerous, flying up here in the highlands. Everyone knows that. It's wonderful that your mum is willing for your dad to do it."

Paula's father had known, of course, that she wouldn't be able to meet him at the airstrip, the next time he made his table-top landing. Matthew had a job keeping up with him as, with his long strong legs, he strode over the rough terrain to where their house was perched on the side of the mountain.

"Dad! Dad!" Paula's excited welcome echoed over the valley. They stood back as Ralph bounded up onto the veranda, gathering his daughter into his arms.

"Are you sure you didn't do it on purpose?" he teased, having assured himself that her ankle was mending well. "I can carry you back if you want to come home now, you know."

"Oh Dad, I would like to stay until next week if I may. I— I'm only just getting to know everybody," she said, hanging her head slightly. "And I'm learning to speak the 'true talk' you know."

"True talk? What's this then?"

"That's what these people call their language," Matthew volunteered. "They're so happy that Paula wants to learn. Oh, please, Mr Emerson, do let her stay until next week."

"Well now, let me see." The pilot was sitting, his legs dangling over the edge of the veranda, a sandwich in his hand. Matthew knew he was teasing, enjoying keeping them in suspense. "I think I'll let Paula stay on one condition."

"What's that?" They waited, breathless.

"That Matthew comes out to stay with us soon."

He saw Paula throw her father a kiss and knew that if she had been mobile she would have thrown her arms around his neck. As for himself, he had a strange desire to go off and dance a jig. He really couldn't believe that his feelings could have made such a complete turn-about. To think that just a few days ago he couldn't have got rid of Paula soon enough.

"As a matter of fact," his father was saying, "we'd been intending to ask you a favour. Jenny needs to fly out to the hospital soon for her check-up, and we were wondering whether she might have stayed with you. It would be great if Matthew could come with her for company."

"That's the Jamesons now," Jenny interrupted. She had been standing by on the radio. "They'll be at their strip in half an hour."

"Right! I'm on my way." Giving his daughter a kiss, and handing his mug to Matthew, he bounded down the steps, and was off. A few minutes later the little plane circled above them, dipped its wings, then zoomed out of sight.

Paula had her own school books now, so Matthew was left in peace when it was lesson time, but they were both anxious to finish. Then off they would go, calling out to the local children, who were delighted to teach them their skills.

There was fierce competition between them once Paula had her own bow and arrows, and Matthew was relieved to find he could outshoot her. His mother didn't appreciate it though, when they both came home twanging away on tiny harps.

"We'll call up tonight and find out if your dad is coming for you tomorrow," Jenny volunteered at lunch-time.

"Oh, Mum," Matthew groaned. "Does she have to go?"

"I do have to," Paula answered. "It has been super staying here. I've enjoyed it so much. But I do want to see Mum, and I know she wants me."

"Of course, Paula," Jenny affirmed. "We understand. And it won't be long before we'll be coming out to stay with you. And you'll hear each other on School of the Air."

"Extra trip. Your father has got to do an extra trip before he comes for you." There was a lot of static and Mrs Emerson's voice was hard to understand over the radio.

"What time?" Jenny let Paula speak.

"About ten o'clock. Over."

"Hope the weather stays fine." Matthew didn't mind if it didn't. He'd be sorry to see Paula go.

The next morning Paula had her bag packed ready.

"Shall we go and wait by the airstrip?" she suggested. Now that she was going, she was anxious to be off.

"Better wait," Jenny advised. "No sense sitting out there with nothing to do and getting sunburnt. He'll give us a call on the radio when he has taken off."

It was a long morning of waiting. In the end Jim walked with the children to the strip, for it seemed impossible to settle to anything.

"Nothing!" Jenny told them when, the weather having closed in, the forlorn little group returned to the house. "I managed to get through to your mother, Paula, but she hasn't heard anything from your father."

Paula went white and crumpled up on the settee. Jenny was beside her, holding her tight.

"Now, now! Don't go fearing the worst."

"Could be his radio has conked out," Matthew volunteered. He felt he had to say something, but

Paula turned on him angrily. "He could still fly then, couldn't he? Why isn't he here?"

Suddenly she began to cry. "Oh Matthew. I didn't mean to shout at you. It is just that I am so worried."

"Of course your dad will be all right," Paula's mother assured her when she called up that night. "He's one of the best pilots in the territory. Don't forget that. You pray, and then you'll see. We'll hear some news in the morning. Over."

"Mum's being bright to cheer me up, but she needs me. I should be with her. I should never have left her to come up here."

"Come on now," Jenny comforted, "We'll pray, and you'll see, in the morning we'll hear that everything is all right."

But it was a bleary-eyed, white-faced little company that gathered round the radio the next morning.

Chapter nine

"What time is it?"

Paula was still on the settee, a blanket wrapped around her. She didn't seem to see Matthew as he staggered, bleary-eyed, from his room.

"Not yet, Jen," said Jim as his wife went to switch on the radio. "It's too early. We'll have our Bible reading and prayers before anything else."

Jenny squeezed up beside Paula on the settee, giving her a comforting hug as they settled down to listen. Matthew pulled up a stool. Paula had still not spoken a word and there were great circles under her eyes.

His father stood by the window to get the maximum light. They had been reading through the New Testament from Matthew's Bible and today they had reached the story where Peter was in prison.

"Peter was kept in prison, but all the Christians were praying for him."

It was hard to concentrate on something that happened so long ago when they were worrying about pilots and planes and things, but suddenly Matthew was alert.

"Dad!" he interrupted, "listen!" He ran out onto the veranda. The others joined him.

"It's the Christians. They're singing a hymn, 'That good friend Jesus'," Jenny whispered to Paula. They hushed as now a surge of voices rose from the little church.

"They're praying, Mum." There was excitement in Matthew's voice. "Do you think they are praying for Paula's dad?"

"Of course they are." said Jim. "Good old Masala! He must have called them together. Come on, we'll have our prayers here, and then I'll go and join them."

"Hey! It's just like in the Bible. Peter shut up in prison, and all the people praying for him." The Bible story had taken on a new meaning for Matthew. "And we are all praying for Paula's dad."

"We'd better do our bit of praying then," his father suggested.

Matthew didn't find it hard to add his prayers. He felt sure now that God was listening to them, just as he had listened to the people in the Bible.

It was his mother who suggested that they should read the rest of the chapter. He was so glad it was a story with a happy ending.

"I like the part when Rhoda told the others that Peter was knocking at the door, and they wouldn't believe her. She was a young girl, probably just like you, Paula," his mother commented, when Jim had closed the book.

"As a matter of fact,"Paula began. This was about the first time Matthew had heard her speak.

"Go on," Jenny was encouraging her.

"In the night I couldn't sleep, but then I must have dropped off, for I was dreaming about my dad, and he was talking to me. I don't remember what he was saying—" Paula choked up then, and once more Jenny cuddled her up.

"We know that Jesus is with your dad, whatever has happened. Remember his promise: 'I will never leave you.' Isn't that your special verse, Matt? So come on now, try and eat a little breakfast."

"Isn't it time for the radio yet?" Matthew asked, trying to change the subject.

"Yes," Jim agreed. "We'll switch on now. Maybe we can hear some news from someone."

The other missions were all busy with their messages and didn't seem to hear the faint call from high up in the mountains as now and again they tried to break in. Once Paula thought she heard her mother's voice coming through, but they weren't able to make contact. Then it was time for School of the Air.

"Is Paula still with you, Matthew?" their teacher was asking. "We heard the news about her dad's plane. Tell her not to worry. My husband says if anyone can get out of a bad situation, he can."

"Mrs Barry!" It was Ivor calling in. He always had plenty to say in their news time. The eldest of six, you could be sure that one or other of the family had had some adventure.

"Come in, India Foxtrot."

"My dad says to tell Paula that there was a bad storm over the other side of the range, where her father was yesterday. He can't make contact with our mission station over there. He says it could be that their radio was struck by lightning, so maybe the plane was damaged too."

They were longing for Jim to return from the prayer meeting so they could share this news.

"Could well be," he mused, when they told him, then he asked, "Paula, how is your ankle now? I'm going out to visit one of the men. They've got some cassowary chicks, and wanted me to bring you two to see them. Do you think you're up to it?"

Jenny smiled her agreement. She knew that there would be no lessons done, and this would help to take Paula's mind off her worries.

"Hey! Mum! We got some super photos," Matthew burst out, as they returned at lunch time. "There were two chicks—" but then he stopped short, for there on the table was a parcel, with his name on it.

"What...? How... ?" Matthew stammered.

"It was supposed to be a surprise for your birthday, Matt," his mother explained, "but I thought maybe you wouldn't mind having it early, as it's something you'll all enjoy."

"A jigsaw!" Paula exclaimed. "Oh, I love jigsaws."

"Wonderful idea, Jenny," Matthew heard his dad whisper, when they were all busy. "We all needed something to stop us from worrying."

"Mike Kilo! Mike Kilo! Do you copy!" The radio had been crackling away in the background, but they were all alert now as they heard their call. Jim went to answer, while they clustered around him. It was Paula's mother.

"News from Dad, Paula. They're going to airlift the parts he needs, and he should be home tomorrow. He'll come for you as soon as he can. We'll let you know."

"Come on, Paula. You can't go home until this jigsaw is finished," Jenny laughed, but Paula was walking around the room as if she were dazed.

"We can see now how Rhoda forgot to open the door for Peter," laughed Jim.

"It was rather like a jigsaw, finding out the full story," remarked Jenny two days later as they were walking back home, having seen Paula off at the airstrip.

"We heard about the storm from Ivor first," volunteered Matthew.

"Yes, and then after Paula's mum came on we heard them calling up about the boy who had walked right over the range to take the message."

"And now Ralph has told us of the pilot who flew up from the coast with the spare parts and helped with the repairs."

The house seemed empty with Paula gone, and Matthew didn't know what to do with himself.

"What about your diary, Matthew?" Jenny suggested. "I thought Mrs Barry wanted you to keep one. You've had lots of adventures that you could write about."

"Hey! Good idea!" Jim joined in. "You could type it out for him, Jen, and we'll illustrate it with photos. We got some good ones of the cassowaries, and of Paula and the plane."

"Would you, Mum?" Matthew liked writing. He had given up sending letters to Tim as he so seldom received an answer.

"You could call one chapter: The Perils of Paula," Jenny laughed. "I never knew a girl to have so many adventures. I don't think she'll be coming back in a hurry though. She was too upset at not being with her mother when she needed her."

"Have you written about our literacy classes in your diary?" Jim asked Matthew, a few weeks later. "I've got six of the men ready to go out and start classes in other villages. They are full of enthusiasm. And one or two want to start writing some of their own folk tales."

"My women are doing quite well too," Jenny joined in.

"You help me take some photos then, Dad, and I'll write about them," agreed Matthew. He was enjoying this literary effort.

There was great industry when the photos were eventually returned and duly stuck into the diary, but after that the book was put away for a few weeks, and once again Matthew was complaining that he was bored. "Nothing exciting ever happens round here," he grumbled.

"I've nothing against a quiet life." Jenny laughed. "I'd rather you didn't give me any more frights. It's not good for the baby," she added, patting her tummy.

"Listen to how the dogs are howling," Jim called as he came in for his morning break, the following day. Matthew came and joined his parents on the veranda. There was a hush in the air. It gave him an eerie feeling.

His mother shivered. "What can it be?"

"Jim – don't go," she pleaded, when he rose to leave them. "I don't know – everything seems so still – as if nature were holding its breath, waiting for something to happen."

Matthew had reluctantly returned to his lessons, but suddenly he ran out. He had an awful feeling his legs were turning to cotton wool. "The table, Mum – it's moving," he gasped.

The dogs were barking in unison now. A cup tumbled off the shelf and crashed onto the wooden floor. They could hear screams coming from the women in their houses as they hurried out into the air.

"Outside!" his father was shouting, pulling Jenny down away from the house.

"What is it, Dad?" Matthew felt as if everything he had always relied on was suddenly giving way.

"Just an earth tremor," Jim replied, after they had huddled together some yards from the house, waiting. "There! I think it's over now. Thank God it wasn't any worse."

But just then one of the men ran up.

"Mr Jim, Mr Jim! Come quick!"

"What is it?" Jim asked, already on his way.

"Paella's house fell down with the shaking, and the king post is crushing his leg."

"My first aid box, Matthew," Jim called. He ran up with it promptly, proud to be of assistance, but he was disappointed when his father took it from him.

"No, Matt. Stay with Mum. I'll send a message if we need you," he called back to his wife as he ran off in the direction of the village.

"Come and sit down, Mum. I'll make you a cup of tea." Dad was right. She shouldn't be left. She was trembling as he helped her into the house.

"Shall we walk across to Paella's house and see how he is?" Matthew suggested, when she handed him her empty cup.

"Yes, good idea. I'm fine now," she assured him. But they had hardly closed the door when they heard someone screaming. Matthew, to his horror, saw one of the women running towards them, and her husband, axe in hand, in hot pursuit.

His one thought was to protect his mother, but suddenly it was as though she had been turned to steel.

"Here! In here!" she called to the woman.

"Fetch your dad – Quick!" she commanded. Matthew didn't need telling twice. He heard a slam and knew that his mother had locked herself in with the woman. But their door was poor protection from an axe-wielding madman.

"Dad! Dad!" he screamed as he ran. He was supposed to be looking after his mother, keeping her quiet, and now it seemed they were in the middle of a nightmare.

"What is it Matt?" Their bush telegraph had relayed the cry, and Jim was already running to meet him.

"Quick, Dad! Quick!" He couldn't stop to explain as they ran together to the house. He was imagining the door already cleft in two and the women being chased in circles around the table.

No, the door was still intact. The man stood there, his axe raised above his head, ready to strike a blow. Jim strode up to him.

"Oh Dad! No!" Matthew felt his strength draining away. What could his dad do if the man turned on him? But even as he spoke, some of the men came and stood beside him, taking the axe and holding the man firmly.

"It's all right now, Jen," Jim called. Matthew saw his mother open the door and then, in slow motion and very gracefully, collapse onto a bench.

"Sorry," she laughed, when Matthew had fetched her some water, and the colour was returning to her cheeks. "I was all right until you came, and then suddenly my legs turned to jelly."

"Oh Jim," she went on, "Do ask Masala to come and help us. This poor woman talks so fast I can't understand a word she says – except something about a pig, of course."

Masala came in now. The husband, shame-faced, was standing with him.

"It seems that with the earth tremor this man's prize pig ran away, and he was blaming his wife," he told them.

"Looks like another long session, Jen," Jim laughed, as they called the village elders and went outside to sort it out.

"Come here, young Matthew Kenny, Missionary Kid," called Jenny, trying to sound severe, but giving him a playful shake. "Don't you ever, ever complain that things are quiet and that you have no news for your diary. From now on I'm all for a quiet life. What with earthquakes, houses falling down and wife-chasing, I feel as if I've had enough excitement to last me the rest of my life."

"I promise, Mum," Matthew laughed. "It's going to take me a week to write all this up. And we haven't even heard how Paella is yet."

Paella was rescued from the ruin without any bones broken. Matthew enjoyed getting photos when the whole clan turned out to build him another house, and then he decided to fill his pages with some nature notes, for life would surely be quiet from now on. What more adventures could there be?

But one day, as he returned to the house from a game with his friends, he heard his father on the radio. "Roger, Colin. I'll call up Ralph and get her out to you as soon as possible. Over."

What could it be? Was his mother ill?

Chapter ten

"There's news of your mum, Matt," Lucy Emerson called to Matthew as she returned from taking a telephone call, a few days later. "She's going to be all right, the doctor says. Yes – and the baby."

Matthew couldn't help feeling anxious when his mum had to be flown out to the hospital urgently. He was pleased, all the same, when it was arranged for him to stay at Paula's.

Lucy began quietly laying the table. "I expect it was the fright she had with the earthquake." Her voice was soothing. Matthew was glad to hear her talk about it. "They want her to rest there for a few days, but she is going to be fine. You'll soon be back with your dad."

He sat quietly, watching her as she continued preparing the meal.

"It must have been quite a shock for you all to find there was a baby on the way," she commented after a while.

"It sure was." Matthew thrust his head in a magazine, not noticing that it was upside-down. It was easier to talk somehow without having to look at Mrs Emerson.

"I won't be here to enjoy the baby, anyway," he

blurted out at last. "I'm going to stay at home with my grandparents next year, so I can go to high school."

Paula came in at that point and started talking to her mum. Matthew was glad. Somehow he found it painful to talk about the new baby. But the next day Lucy brought up the subject again.

"You are very special to your mum and dad, Matthew," she told him. "You know that. Of course they're thrilled about the new baby, but he, or she, won't take your place, even if you are away at school. You have your own place in their hearts. No one else can take that. You remember that, Matthew." He felt himself wrapped in a hug. Of course he was too old for such things, but there was comfort in it, all the same.

"You'll never guess who's coming to town," Ralph called as he came in from his session on the radio.

"Who, Dad?" Paula asked.

"It's Ivor, your class-mate. His father is bringing him in to see the dentist."

"Oh, will we be able to see him?"

"If the weather holds, yes. You'll be able to see him, and someone else. Your teacher heard he was coming, and that you're here, Matthew, and she wants me to fly you all out to her place. I'm due there tomorrow and I can arrange to leave you with her for a couple of hours."

"Are you going to take your diary to show her, Matthew? Paula, you had better get your camera ready. We'll be making an early start in the morning if the weather's OK. Lucy, do you have a cake in the deep freeze they could take to Mrs Barry?" Ralph was trying to think of everything to save any last minute panic. Matthew was excited. He could forget about mothers and babies and schools, if only for a few hours.

The next morning Ivor was at the strip waiting for them.

"He looks like a professor, with those round glasses," Paula whispered to Matthew.

"Looks like he forgot to comb his hair," he giggled, but there was no time for more comments.

Ivor greeted them politely enough, but he seemed to be more interested in the plane than in them.

"Could I sit in the front, beside you?" he asked Ralph. "I want to ask you about the different instruments and how they work."

The pilot did not answer straight away. "He has to think of weight distribution," Paula explained knowledgeably.

"Let's see. You're pretty heavy. Yes, right you are," and Ivor scrambled in, immediately full of questions.

"Where would you land, if your engine failed?" he asked suddenly. The town was well behind them now, and they gazed at the dense jungle below, clothing the mountains as closely as the fur of an animal.

"Hey, Ivor! That's not a nice thing to say." Paula spoke in her best schoolteacher voice.

"My dad told me that good pilots always look for somewhere to land in case of an emergency; and if there isn't anywhere within reach then they call it 'unforgiving territory'."

"See that village down there?" Ralph called. Matthew sensed that he wanted to change the subject. They all knew that flying in these single engine planes was dangerous, and that there was always the possibility of a crash, but it didn't help any to talk about it.

"And the river. Look!"

"We're going to climb up over this mountain now and then you'll see the lake. See which of you is first to spot your teacher's house."

"Now let me see if I know you," Mrs Barry laughed as she rattled up to the airstrip in her Land Rover. Matthew was surprised to see that she looked older than his parents. She always sounded so young on the radio. "Paula – no doubt about you. Now, let me see – which is Ivor and which is Matthew?"

No talk about school work. Mrs Barry had a lovely lunch prepared for them and then they were off to the lake. There was a raft that they could swim out to, and then a brown-skinned boy paddled by in a dug-out canoe.

"Oh, Mrs Barry," they called to their teacher, "would he take us in it?"

"Yes. Steady how you get in," she cautioned, "or it will roll over. He's going to take you out to that island. It's a floating one, so don't try walking on it. You might go through."

"I think I can see a nest," Ivor exclaimed, as the boy manoeuvred his lengthy craft around it.

"Sit still, Ivor!" Fear made Paula speak sharply. "You nearly tipped us over," she scolded.

"Oh, please!" he begged. "I want to see if there are any eggs in it," but Matthew yelled a warning.

"Look out!" A water-fowl was skimming over the lake to protect its young. Their navigator gave a shriek and dived into the water.

"Heads down and hide your faces." This was Paula taking command.

Cautiously Matthew lifted his head. The canoe swung gently, one end caught in the vegetation. From the nest came a pathetic cheeping, while the mother bird swooped around, ready to make another attack. But where was their oarsman?

Suddenly the canoe swung free, there was a lurch and there was the boy, paddling them back towards the shore, as if nothing had happened.

"Get dressed, quickly!" Mrs Barry was urging, almost before they had landed. "Your father has just called, Paula. He'll be here in a few minutes."

"It was a great day, Mum," Matthew told his mother, when he went to see her the next afternoon.

"What was Ivor like?"

"All right, I suppose."

"What do you mean?"

"Well – he didn't seem a bit interested in Paula or me. He just wanted to know all about the plane; and then he was making notes about the plants and birds and things." There was a trace of disappointment in his voice, but his mother laughed.

"Seems like he's quite a professor." She paused, then went on, "I suppose with all those brothers and sisters he doesn't bother so much with other children. Not like you, Matt. You're glad enough of some company," and she patted her son's hand.

"Well, I'll have a brother to play with soon, won't I?"

"Would you mind if it was a sister?" Jenny asked. He knew he'd pleased his mother. This was the first time he had been able to talk as if he were looking forward to the baby.

"Course not Mum." There was warmth in his voice, but then he added, "Not that it makes much difference." There was still a lot of hurt inside. He hadn't wanted it to, but somehow it came tumbling out. "I won't be here, will I? If she only sees me once a year she might not even know me."

His mother reached out and grabbed his hand. It was painful for her, too, to think of their parting.

"We'll make sure she knows you," she affirmed. "We're a family, Matt, wherever we are. We all belong to each other. Don't forget that – ever."

"Can Mum come home now?" Matthew asked the doctor. "It's our flight tomorrow."

Dr Janson pulled up another chair and sat down.

"Your mum's fine, Matthew. But we want her to stay here for one more week, just to be sure. After all, this is a very special baby, isn't it? You won't mind, will you?"

"Dad'll be awfully lonely," Matthew said, when the doctor had left them.

"I know, Matt," said Jenny, "but I must do what the doctor advises. But why don't you go back? After all, I've got plenty of company. I'd feel happier if I knew that you were there with Dad."

"It's like being a piece of elastic, pulled both ways," Matthew complained, when the arrangements were made. "I want to be with Mum, and I want to be with Dad. Still, at least I can be with one of them. Next summer I won't be here at all."

"Still, you'll enjoy school, Matthew." Mrs Emerson was trying to sound comforting. "Paula has to do all her lessons on her own. Run and see if Dad's nearly ready, Paula, and we'll come and wave them off." Matthew was already lumping his bag towards the door when Lucy ran to answer a call on their radio.

Paula meanwhile stood in the doorway, watching her father as he made his way back to the house. What could have happened? He looked so worried.

"What is it, Dad?" Ralph didn't answer, but walked straight to where his wife was sitting by the radio.

Paula and Matthew turned to each other for support. Instinctively they realised that something was wrong.

"What... ?" Matthew began to ask, but he knew that Paula didn't know any more than he did. Slowly he unzipped his holdall. He guessed they wouldn't be flying up to the mountains that day.

Lucy was very pale when at last they came out of the office. In a daze, she filled a flask and kissed her husband goodbye.

"It is Arthur Campbell, the new pilot," she told the children, when the plane had roared out of sight. She sat down as if her legs wouldn't hold her any more. "He's missing. They are calling all planes to go out to search for him."

Chapter eleven

"Hey! Paula! See how red the river is? What can it be? Can we go and look?"

"OK. Let's walk down to the bridge. But we mustn't be too long. We don't want Mum worrying about us, on top of everything else."

"The water doesn't look red from here," Matthew commented, but then, "Look! Over there! See that tiny red flower, growing near the bank? That's what we saw. Further down it must have covered the water so that it looks like blood. But come on, we'd better be getting back."

Honk! Honk! They scuttled across the bridge, leaping out of the way as a lorry lumbered across.

"Morny! Morny!" shouted the children who were in the back. The fact that it was well into the afternoon made no difference. This, to them, was the white man's greeting.

"Hey! Aren't they from the mission school near the hospital?" Matthew asked.

"Could be," Paula replied. "Why?"

"There was a boy who came out with a man who had to go to hospital. They said he's at that school. I'd love to see him and find out how he's getting on."

"I'm sure we can arrange something for you,

Matthew," said Lucy when she heard the story of Kamenoo and Brave One.

"There isn't any more news is there, Mum?" Paula asked, the next day. Lucy shook her head. "They thought they'd sighted some wreckage, but it was a false alarm."

"But he couldn't just disappear," complained Matthew. "All those people and planes out looking."

"Of course he could." Paula spoke sharply. "You saw what it was like when we flew over to the lake. It's just dense jungle for miles and miles. Why, there have been tribes who thought that they were the only people on the earth. They didn't know anyone else existed and no one else knew that they did, because these valleys are so remote. That's why they've been living in the stone age all these years." Paula didn't often put on her high and mighty tone with Matthew these days, but she was using it now. He felt his hackles begin to rise, but then her mother spoke more gently.

"People have gone out walking in the bush," she added, "and have never ever been found again, Matthew. That's why you've been told never to go out on your own."

Both of them flushed. They were remembering how they had disobeyed and given Matthew's parents such a fright, when Paula had come up to stay.

The telephone shrilled out a timely interruption.

"That was a message for you, Matt," Lucy smiled when she came back from the office. "One of the teachers is coming this way tomorrow and will drop your friend off for half an hour to see you."

"Good morning. My name is Philip."

Matthew had run out as soon as he had heard the honk of the truck at the gate. He wouldn't have recognised this lad, shining from the application of soap and water, now clothed in shirt and shorts, and speaking in English.

"Do you remember me?"

"Er... yes." Matthew felt quite tongue-tied, but Mrs Emerson sent Paula out with a cold drink and some biscuits and he was able to relax.

"You speak English much better than I speak your language," he said at last, "and you have only been here a few weeks. And you have an English name."

Philip laughed. "We speak English all the time. I had to learn quickly. And most of us have taken English names."

"Are you happy here, Philip?" Paula asked. It was going to be hard for him to go back to the primitive conditions of his own tribe, she was thinking.

"I thought you were so brave to be willing to go on the plane and amongst people that you didn't know, and Kamenoo not even your own family," Matthew told him. He had to remember to speak slowly, as his highland friends had to when they spoke to him in their language.

"Yes. Nothing would have made me go at first." He sat quietly for a while, and they listened to a government plane circling overhead before it came in to land.

"So, what made you change your mind?"

"Say you would go," Paula prompted, seeing Philip looking puzzled at this phrase.

"One day," he began, "when I was a small boy,

two men came to our village. We didn't know where they came from, but they told us that we must get ready. We must stop fighting and killing and stealing and doing bad things and get ready because the great spirit was going to send somebody from the sky to show us how to serve him.

"My father always remembered this and tried to teach us to be good. When he was dying, he told me not to forget, and that I must be ready and listen when they came to teach us.

"Then, when everyone was shouting and arguing and no one wanted to go with Kamenoo, suddenly I remembered this. The air plane had come from the sky, and that was what these men had said. And then you and your mother came out of the crowd, walking close by me – and I looked at you. You were a different colour, and you had strange clothes and things, but somehow I felt that you were just like me underneath, and I didn't feel afraid to tell you that I would go."

"And has someone taught you about God?" Matthew asked, after a pause.

"Oh yes, indeed." Philip's face lit up. "Why, only last Sunday I stood up in the big church and told all the people how I had come to trust in Jesus."

Lucy had come out and joined them on the veranda where they were sitting.

"You are enjoying it here, aren't you Philip? Are you going to go back to your own people when Kamenoo is well enough to return?"

"Oh, yes, madam. For Kamenoo is a Christian now too, and he says I must go with him to teach all our people about the Lord Jesus."

When Philip had gone, Matthew slipped away

and lay quietly on his bed. He was remembering a dream that he'd had, back when there was all that trouble about the airstrip and they had first known about the baby. He had forgotten all about it, but now it had come back to him clearly. It was Philip who had brought it back to him: Philip and the bridge.

It hadn't been a bridge like that in his dream, one strong enough for a lorry to cross, for it had been somewhere up on their mountain. He had been climbing, climbing. There had been so much confusion, as there usually is in dreams, but the part that was so clear to him was the bridge – a vine bridge. It wasn't even finished. The men were working on it, as he had seen one day when he was out trekking with his dad, but in his dream it had been so important that it should be finished. Something to do with the mountain. The men were pushing saplings firmly into the bank so that they reached out across the river. They were then tying long vines and branches to these until they were about to meet from either side. Matthew had been amazed at their skill and daring, as he and his dad had sat and watched the bridge being made, but in his dream he had not been an onlooker. He had been there, reaching out above the swirling waters, trying to link up with the one who, also risking his life, was seeking to make that vital contact.

Matthew shivered as he remembered the fear of letting go of his slender foothold in order to reach out.

There had been more to the dream that he couldn't remember, but the end was before him now. They weren't over the river. They were standing on firm land, but they had joined hands. He and this other one coming from the other side of the river – they were grasping hands. Yes, it was Philip who had brought the dream back to him. He had the strange feeling that Philip, Brave One, was the one to whom he had been reaching out.

He had always thought that it was just people like Joseph and Daniel who had special dreams, because of course they didn't have a Bible to read in their day. But did God still give people dreams like that? Could it be that this dream, that he hadn't been able to forget, was in some way a message from God?

It was as they were seated at breakfast the next morning that Lucy heard their call sign and ran to answer the radio. When she returned she had a whimsical look on her face.

"What is it, Mum?" It was Paula who asked.

"I don't know if it's good news or bad," she answered.

"Well, tell us the good news, anyway."

"Dad will be home tonight."

"They haven't found the missing plane?" Lucy shook her head. "They've called the search off. I suppose they've decided that there's no hope."

"We're going to fetch your mum this afternoon, and Paula's dad will take you both home tomorrow,"·Lucy told Matthew the next morning.

Matthew was relieved. It had been bad enough while the search was on, but since the message had come it was as though a cold wet mist was covering them. He and Paula had been sent to bed early the night before, for when Ralph arrived home he had looked strained and withdrawn.

"What happened, Mum? What made them

decide to call off the search?" Paula asked, when they had her to herself.

"Arthur's wife made the decision."

"But why, Mum?"

"She said she knew he was dead, and she didn't want us to go on searching."

"Oh, Mum." She ran and hid her face on her mother's shoulder and they wept together. "Poor, poor Mrs Campbell."

Matthew went out onto the veranda. He could see the river winding in the distance, and the stretch that seemed to be blood red.

There was so much in life that he couldn't understand. They were up in this strange, dangerous land because they felt God had asked them to come, and yet these awful things happened. Couldn't God have looked after Arthur Campbell and kept him safe? How could this terrible thing be turned into something good?

Paula came and stood beside him.

"It looks as though the river is turned to blood," Matthew remarked, not wanting to talk about the tragedy.

"I'm trying to remember what my mum said, when I told her about the beautiful red flowers in the river," said Paula after a pause. "She said, sometimes life is like that. We think some things are all sad and horrible, but later on we find there is something beautiful after all. Oh dear – I don't know. Life is so hard to understand."

It certainly was. Matthew was on the plane with his mother now. He had felt quite sick and ill that morning at the thought of flying, but now they were up in the blue sky, puffs of fleecy white clouds floating beneath them, it wasn't so bad.

"We'll soon be home," Jenny whispered, giving Matthew's arm a squeeze.

Matthew didn't answer. He had never thought that he could think of this remote spot, high among the grandeur and fierceness of these mountains, as home. But of course it was, for they would be together. There was his dream too, and Philip – Brave One. Somehow he knew at last that he belonged up here. After all the adventures, and the tragedy, while he had been with Paula, it was good to be coming back to their mountain. Only, for how long? A few more weeks before the baby came, and then they would have to start thinking about his going back to school. Just a few more months and he would be far away, and they would be here with the new baby. They wouldn't miss him so very much, would they?

Chapter twelve

"Were you lonely without us, Dad?" Matthew asked as they sat down together for the meal Jim had prepared for them.

"I can see that I can hand over my job as cook," Jenny teased. "Just as well, as I'll be away for a week or two before the baby arrives. The doctor says I must come out in plenty of time. He doesn't want a last minute panic if the baby comes early and the plane can't get out here because of bad weather."

"We'll make sure you do get out in time, won't we Matt?" Jim got up and fetched a jelly from the shower. That was the coolest place in the house.

"But weren't you awfully lonely, Dad?" Matthew persisted.

"Well, to be quite honest," Jim began slowly, struggling to dish out the jelly with a dessert spoon, "I don't think I've had time to be lonely."

Matthew got up and fetched a serving spoon, trying to hide the hurt he was feeling.

"Oh – thanks, Matt," his father laughed, taking the spoon. "Why didn't I think of that?" Then suddenly a great warmth melted away all the pain as Matthew felt himself wrapped in a bear hug. "But don't you worry," Jim went on. "It's great having you back. I'd never choose to be without you."

"Tell us what you've been up to, then." Matthew sensed that his mother was anxious to change the subject.

"Masala's been helping me to check through the Bible lessons I've been working on," his father began, his meal forgotten. "We got quite a lot done, but there seemed to be more interruptions than usual. I had another husband chasing his wife with an axe. And there were the usual endless arguments over gardens and pigs. Hey! And didn't you notice the new bridge?"

"Yes, I noticed, Dad." It was a good strong plank bridge, not like the one in his dream.

"I'd meant to ask you," Jenny interrupted. "There wasn't a gully there before. There was no need of a bridge. Tell us, what happened?"

"It must have been the earthquake. It made a crack then, and whenever it rains the water rushes through and makes it deeper. We needed to make a strong bridge, for without it our house could be cut off from the airstrip.

"Oh, and I forgot to tell you," Jim went on, "Aipi's new wife has not been well. I wished you'd been here, Jen, to give her some advice. I told them to carry her down to the aid post."

"That's two days' trek away, Jim, and you know what they are like. They'll do it for a man, but they won't bother for a woman."

"It isn't that they won't bother. It's to do with their taboos. But we must ask again to have a medical assistant up here. And a school teacher too. They promised to try to send someone."

"Dad, listen! I can hear crying." Matthew, one

ear on his parents' conversation, had stepped onto the veranda, but now he ran in to call them.

"It's coming from Aipi's house. Run and ask, Matt, would you?" Jim and Jenny exchanged anxious glances.

"It's Kaiyuna, Aipi's wife. She has died." Matthew returned, panting out the news.

"We'd better go and see. Do you feel up to coming, Jen?" Jim asked.

"Aiy! Aiy! Aiy!" the people wailed, as they sat in a circle around the body that lay on a bed of branches.

"Why didn't you carry her to the clinic, as I told you?" Jim demanded.

No one answered. Matthew noticed that a few of the Christians hung their heads but others were defiant. "A curse could have come on us from her blood," they mumbled.

Matthew watched his mother seat herself among the women. She was crying unashamedly. "Oh, poor Aipi. His beautiful young bride, and they were both walking as Christians."

He felt his father's hand on his shoulder. "Take your mother home, will you, Matt?" he asked. "I won't be long."

The eerie wail of the mourners continued long into the night. The Kennys had gone to bed, each convinced that it would be impossible to sleep. They must have dozed off though, for it was well past midnight when they were awakened by a tapping at the door.

Matthew lay quietly, thinking that he had been dreaming, but then he heard his father call out.

"Who is it?" No answer. Matthew held his breath. Perhaps, after all, it was just a rat that had disturbed them. But then it came again, gentle but persistent.

As soon as he heard his father move, Matthew was out of bed, and slipped in beside his mother. They watched as Jim, grabbing his torch, made for the door.

"Who is it?" he asked again.

"Me, Mr Kenny," was the muffled answer, against the background of the mourning wails.

"Why, Aipi?" they heard Jim exclaim, as he opened the door. Pulling on some clothes, they joined Jim as he pulled Aipi into the house.

"Oh, look at you," his mother exclaimed. She wrapped her arms around the lad, in spite of the ash that he had rubbed over his body and the wildness of his eyes. She cares as much as if it had been me, Matthew thought.

Aipi began to shiver violently.

"What is it, Aipi?" his father asked, but they could get no answer.

"He seems to be afraid," Jenny commented, more to break the silence than anything. "Aipi, we know that you are very sad because Kaiyuna has died," she went on.

At this big tears rolled down his cheeks, but still he trembled violently.

"Aipi! Tell me – why have you come to us? Are you afraid?"

"Afraid." He nodded.

"Do you want to stay here?"

Once again the only response was a nod, but the shaking grew less. Matthew was grateful when his mother began to pull some old blankets out from under the bed and he was able to help her. He hated standing round "nothing" as these people called it.

He was grateful, too, when his father suggested that he stay with his mother for the rest of the night. It all seemed so scary.

"I'll sleep here on the settee, so that Aipi isn't alone. I think he'll sleep better with someone near him."

The fire was already alight when they emerged the next morning, Aipi sitting close beside it. He had his own sweet potato with him and was not interested in their food, as they gathered for breakfast.

"It's Kaiyuna's clan," Masala explained, when, having been called in, he had exchanged a few words with their refugee. "They are accusing him of murdering her."

"But would they really kill him?"

"Maybe they are just trying to frighten him."

"Anything to do with the bride price?" Jenny asked afterwards.

"Could well be. Aipi still had more pigs to pay. He wouldn't want to give them now, and he might even want them to return the ones he has paid; but if they accuse him of killing her he would have to pay the lot."

"So what are they going to do?"

"Masala is going to call the elders of each of their clans, and see if they can work out something fair. We'll keep Aipi here for a day or two until we know that it's settled. If he thinks there is danger, then we'll arrange for him to go away, but he seems to think it can be sorted out."

"Do you want me to do any more typing for your diary?" Jenny asked, a few weeks later.

"Oh, I don't think so, Mum. I haven't written

106

much recently. Not since that trouble with Aipi."

"Well, if you want me to do any, you'd better hurry. It's only another two weeks and I'll be off to the hospital."

"Oh, Mum!" Matthew didn't say any more, but he slammed his book shut and stomped out of the house.

He hadn't meant to hurt her. She was the best in the world, only – he was upset. He knew he should be excited about the baby, but somehow it was spoiling everything, even before it had come. And, and – oh, he felt all mixed up.

Life was so complicated. His dream had been comforting, as if God had been telling him that he had brought him up here into these mountains for a purpose. But could he really believe that God would give a dream specially to him?

And then there was school. Even if he could have stayed up here with his parents and the new baby, he would miss out on so much schooling. But if God was telling him that he had brought him here, didn't that mean that he was meant to stay? He felt as if his head would burst with all these questions.

"We'll have to do something about strengthening that bridge," Jim mentioned, a few days later when he returned from the airstrip. "It seems as though a river is making its course through that gully. We don't want to be cut off."

"We certainly don't," Jenny answered. "Lucy has been on the radio. Ralph can come for me on Thursday and I shouldn't delay much longer.

"I'm sorry to be leaving you," she went on, seeing the dismay on their faces, "but we'd better be sensible, hadn't we?"

There was much planning and packing, but on Thursday the mountains were cloaked with cloud throughout the day.

"Ralph will come first flight tomorrow if the weather permits," Jenny told them. But that afternoon they were all huddled round the fire as the rain poured down. The sky was black. Every now and again there was a sizzling and hissing around the radio, and then suddenly there was a blinding flash and crash.

"It's OK, Mum," Matthew said, seeing how white she had gone. But Jim groaned.

"That's done it. The radio is broken for sure. No contact, and just when we need it so much."

"Ralph will guess what's happened," Jenny said hopefully, once they had recovered a little from the shock. "We know that he's coming tomorrow. We must be down there on the strip ready."

Matthew went to the door and looked out.

"The rain, Dad! It's sheeting down. I hope it won't wash away the foundations of the house."

Jim stood beside him, watching the rain like a wall before them. Suddenly Matthew felt his father stiffen, and even in the half-light he could see the colour draining from his face. In a flash he realised what he was thinking.

"The bridge!"

"Yes, the bridge, Matt! It will never stand up to this."

Jenny was with them now. They huddled together for comfort.

"What will we do? I've got to get out to have the baby. Oh Jim? What can we do?"

She was nearly crying. The rain showed no sign

of letting up. What were they going to do?

The next morning the family and most of the clan had gathered by the river, which now intruded between their home and the path to the airstrip. The sun was shining now, and the plane was already on its way. There had been no time for the men to fix the proper bridge. Hastily they had felled a tree and thrown it across the gully.

"Come on Jen, I'll hold you." Jim stepped onto the log and reached out for his wife to take his hand. Trembling she stretched out toward him, but then drew back.

"No, Jim. It won't hold us both."

"Let the children help you then." Jim named two of the lads, but their parents called them back. They were afraid that if anything should happen to the white woman that they would be blamed.

Matthew saw his mother hide her head in her hands, and his dad came and put his arm round her shoulder.

"It's for the baby, Jen. You've got to do it."

"I know. I know. Oh, dear Lord, help me," she sobbed. It was then that the boy had appeared.

"Give me your hand!" That was all he said. No one called him back. Matthew and his dad watched breathlessly as Jenny stepped forward and gave her hand to the boy who was standing on the log that stretched over the swirling torrent. Would she dare to cross with him, and would he be able to lead her safely over?

Chapter thirteen

Matthew had already crossed the log. Thankfully he reached out to grasp his mother. She was almost fainting, but they got her safely to the airstrip.

"There was four inches in the rain gauge, Dad," Matthew called to his father, the next day. "It's no wonder the bridge was washed away."

"We've had four inches in a night before, Matthew," Jim responded, "but it all seemed to come in one hour. That's what caused the trouble. A good job Masala had sent the men to search for a tall tree to throw across. It'll be a couple of days before they have a proper bridge fixed."

Matthew sat quietly, reliving the scene as they had set out for the airstrip; his mother trembling as she looked at the raging torrent and the slender tree trunk she had to cross.

He was remembering how that boy had stepped up and, taking her hand, had calmly led her across. She was over. Well, they had seen her safely onto the plane. Now all they had to do was wait.

"Dad?" Matthew asked, as they prepared their meal, "Do you remember, back home, how Mum said that if God wanted her to go over any log bridges, he'd have to send an angel to help her?"

Jim paused, knife in hand. "That's right, Matt. She did." There was a clatter as the knife fell to the floor.

"I say, you don't think... Could it have been? I didn't know that boy, did you?"

Matthew handed his dad the knife and, having wiped it, he continued cutting the bread, but every now and then he paused to shake his head, as if in disbelief.

"Well," he said, as at last they sat down to eat, "God certainly helped her somehow. She will be settled at the hospital by now."

"Hey, Dad! This is an interesting letter," Matthew exclaimed. His dad had been busy shoring up the house, where the foundations had been weakened by the storm, but when one of the men carried up the mail-bag from the airstrip he decided it was time for a tea-break.

"Oh, I thought it must be something I wasn't allowed to see," Jim teased. "Wouldn't have been from your girl friend, by any chance, would it?"

"Paula's not my girl friend," Matthew emphasised. "Well – of course we're good friends. I like her a lot, but she's older than me." He spoke matter of factly, but the flush that was creeping up his neck gave him away.

"So – did she have some news, or did she just write to say she misses you?" Jim teased.

"I won't tell you if you're going to laugh at me," Matthew threatened. He ruffled his father's hair to show there were no hard feelings.

"Here it is." He began to read. "She says, 'Next year they are going to start a school specially for missionaries' children. It's on the coast, so it will still be quite a way away, but instead of long terms and long holidays, we will come home every six weeks for a fortnight. Mum thinks I should go, and we hope you might too. It would be fun if we were there together." Matthew stopped abruptly, and again felt the colour sweeping up his cheek.

Jim didn't notice. He was hastily sorting through his letters until he found an official looking envelope. Having read in silence to check the news was confirmed, he let out a long drawn-out "Well," and tipped his chair back, running his hands through his hair. The next moment he rocked forward again and leapt to his feet.He was clearly excited.

"That gives us something to think about, doesn't it, Matt? Six weeks is a different matter from a whole year. We might be able to face it better. We'll let your mum know, and we had all better start praying about it."

"Ye-es." Matthew needed time to think.

It was the next day before he felt he wanted to talk about it again. "I'd still be away from you, wouldn't I?" It was as though he was thinking aloud. "If I go back to New Zealand I'll be able to go home to Gran and Gramps each night. And the sports will be better than at the mission school."

"Yes, you won't have the same facilities or specialist teachers over here. It's all right for Juniors. Well, there is still time to decide."

"I'm off to see how they are getting on with the bridge," Jim called, a little later. "Want to come?"

"I'll just finish this lesson, Dad." From the veranda Matthew watched Jim walk towards the gully, but then he saw a band of men approaching. They were running and chanting tonelessly, and

They were running and chanting tonelessly, and something about them filled Matthew with a sense of unease.

Poor old Dad. More trouble. Just then their call sign came on the radio. They were keeping it on all day in case there should be a message about Jenny.

"Dad! Dad! The radio!" Matthew called, but there was far too much hubbub going on for his voice to be heard. He hesitated.

"Tundi!" he called. "Go and tell my father to come," and with that he went and picked up the receiver. After all, it might be about the baby.

"Mike Kilo here," he answered. "My father will be here in a minute."

"Hello Matthew." It was one of the leaders of their mission. "Tell your dad there will be a school teacher coming next month. I called now so he can start work on a classroom. Over."

"Roger, Mr Jennings," Matthew answered and ran out to share the good news. Dad would be glad. But as he set out he saw that the crowd had grown and seemed in angry mood. He felt anxious, but knew he had better keep out of the way.

Tundi was standing helplessly on the edge of the crowd.

"Tundi-o!" he called, and the boy returned to him.

"What is the trouble, Tundi?" Matthew asked.

"It is over the pandanus nuts," he explained. "Kaki's clan say that Masala's clan have stolen their nuts and they want to make war."

"Oh dear!" There was often fighting over the nuts. "Poor Dad," he thought, and sat down, his head in his hands.

he reminded himself. I sure hope he will tell Dad, that's all. Mum isn't here to do the praying – guess I'd better ask God myself. He left his books and went into his bedroom.

"Please, God, will you tell my dad what to do, so that there won't be a war, Amen."

It wasn't much of a prayer. Perhaps he should have stayed there on his knees for a long time but he didn't know what else to say.

He tried to get on with his lessons but gave up and was busying himself preparing lunch, when suddenly he was aware that everything was quiet. He stepped out to see his father walking towards him.

"What happened, Dad?" Matthew asked, pouring a cup of tea.

"Thanks, Matt. I'm sure ready for that." He sat, his hands wrapped around the mug, gazing out over the cloud-tipped mountains. Matthew waited patiently.

"They were very angry about these nuts that had been stolen, and everyone was accusing everyone else. I felt so helpless. They were so excited that I couldn't understand half of what they were saying. And then, quite suddenly, the whole atmosphere changed. I don't know who suggested it, but they asked me to speak. They were all quiet and I was able to tell them about being peacemakers and forgiveness. It was as though somehow God had come and was speaking to us. Now, instead of a fight, we are going to have a feast. Somebody must have been praying."

Matthew didn't say anything, but joy bubbled up inside. He was only up here because he wanted to be with his parents; he hadn't been very good at praying; but God must have heard him!

114

"Oh Dad! I nearly forgot. Mr Jennings was on the radio. They're sending a school teacher up here. He said to get a classroom ready."

"Why, Matt!" Jim jumped up and gave Matthew a bear hug and then exclaimed again, "Why, Matt!" as if he could find no words to express his excitement.

"It looks as if we are going to be too busy to miss your mother." Jim ran to fetch paper and pencil to write the news for their bulletin board, until Matthew suggested they have lunch first.

"It seems everything is working out right," Jim remarked, munching a sandwich. "Most of the people are reading well now, so they should be happy for their children to have schooling."

"Mike Kilo! Mike Kilo!"

Matthew was at his side as Jim rushed to answer the call. Two weeks had gone since Jenny had been flown out. Was there some news at last?

"Jenny wants to know if you are all right." It was one of the nurses at the hospital.

"She says to tell you that they are both fine too."

"Is it—?" Jim could hardly get the words out. "Is it a boy or a girl?"

"She says, tell Matthew that he has a lovely little sister."

Matthew had put on a shirt and tie and now they were waiting at the airstrip. He felt as nervous as he had when they were waiting for Paula's arrival. It would be marvellous having his mother back. But would she be the same mum now she had the baby?

The little yellow plane had once again landed safely. Ralph jumped down and opened the door, but it wasn't Jenny they saw clambering out.

"Philip!" Matthew exclaimed, welcoming his friend. "I thought you were going to stay at school?"

"Kamenoo is well now," he explained, as they helped the older man down. "Because you are having a school here, they said I should come back."

Mum was there now, a tiny bundle in her arms. Jim took the baby, holding her for Matthew to see. They would wait until they were back home to welcome Jenny as they longed to, but they were happy just to be beside her.

"Ei! Ei!" The women were gathering around, putting their fingers to their mouths and then shaking them. "White baby, white baby." They followed the family home, and sat themselves down on the grass in front of the mission house, as if they were waiting for church.

"What are they waiting for?" Jim asked Masala, who had brought some of their luggage into the house.

"Why, they want to know if you have really had your baby in the same way that they have."

Jenny laughed. "Oh yes, I've heard they used to think that the white man was not really human as they are. Well, surely now they will believe."

She picked up the baby and went out, walking among the people so that they could see the tiny hand waving at them, and the little rosebud mouth. Some of the women reached out to touch her, but Jenny pushed them gently away.

"You must wash first," she told them. "Go home now. I'm going to feed the baby."

There was a buzz of expectation. They settled

116

down, showing no sign of dispersing. Jim came into the bedroom where Jenny was.

"Masala says they won't really believe the baby is human unless they see you feeding her as they do."

Matthew was shocked when he saw his mother go out onto the veranda, the baby at her breast.

"Mum!" was all he said, but she understood the wealth of meaning in the word.

"You know, the Lord Jesus was a tiny baby, fed in the same way," she assured him. "If this is what it takes to help them realise how much God loves them, well – we'll do it for his sake."

Matthew went then and sat beside his mother. How proud he was when, her hunger satisfied at last, the baby was placed in his arms.

"Why, Matthew, our little Marianne will miss you so much when you go away to school," Jenny exclaimed one evening. "See how her eyes follow you."

Matthew began to laugh. "I've just realised. Marianne Kelly: MK. She's a mish kid too, isn't she? She's growing so quickly, Mum. Why, almost every week there's something new to write in my diary. Even if I go to this new mission school, I'll miss so much – and if I go back to New Zealand she may not even know me when I come back."

"Well, Matt, as your parents, we have to make the decision. You know that we had planned for you to go home to Gran and Gramps, but with this new school opening over here, it seems so wonderful that we can't just dismiss it out of hand, and we must consider what you would like to do."

Matthew stood there, shaking his head.

"I don't know what to think," he said at last. "Gran and Gramps will be disappointed if I don't go to them. And Paula will be disappointed if I don't go with her – and – oh Mum, I do wish we could have stayed together, especially now Marianne has come to live with us."

"Yes, Matt." Jenny stroked his hair. "Well, let's just tell the Lord how we feel, shall we?"

"Do you think you can look after your mother and sister for a few days, Matthew?" Jim asked one evening.

"Why, Jim?" Jenny asked.

"Kamenoo and Philip have been visiting some of the other clans, telling them how to be Christians, and they want me to go and do some teaching.

"It's wonderful how wise Kamenoo is. With some training, he could take over here as pastor."

"Why Jim, that's wonderful. Of course we'll be all right, won't we Matthew?"

Matthew felt so different from the little boy who had trekked with his parents through the bush to come and live up here on this mountain. That was eighteen months ago. He knew the language now, and these strange-looking people had all become his friends; and yet – he couldn't help a feeling of foreboding as his father strode away into the distance. So many things could happen up here, and he had his mother and a baby sister to look after. He did hope nothing would go wrong.

Chapter fourteen

Matthew staggered out of bed to join his mother.

"I just thought you might like some company," he explained. "I heard you up with the baby."

"Are you worried with your dad away?" He took the baby from his mother as she poured a cup of cocoa. She always knew when something was wrong.

"Or is it the school?"

Matthew had been worrying. Somehow after that terrible time when the pilot had gone missing, and meeting up with Philip, he had had a wonderful warm feeling that he was meant to be up here.

But his schooling was important. It was such a big decision to make.

"It's a few weeks yet before we have to let the schools know, Matt. Try not to worry. I'm sure we'll all know what to do when the time comes. Dad may be back tomorrow and we'll all feel better then. Come on, our little mish kid is asleep. Let's go back to bed."

"See those men coming, with those huge wigs!" Matthew remarked. It was a few days after Jim's return and they were together at the airstrip. "They're from Philip's tribe."

They turned to greet them. Men seemed to be coming from all over, these days, not only to trade and receive cargo from the plane, but for special church celebrations too. Some of their feasts, when they cooked the food in earth ovens, were a sight to behold. It was marvellous that these different tribes, once so full of fear and suspicion, always ready to make war, were living at peace with each other.

Once the plane had gone and the people had dispersed, Matthew's father grabbed his hand, pulling him up to their favourite look-out place.

"Just think," he began, after standing in silence for a few moments. "On almost all of those mountains there is a church now." He squatted down, a blade of grass between his teeth.

"I was thinking about that day when the plane came to take Kamenoo out to hospital. He would probably have died if Philip hadn't had the courage to go out with him. And now it's through them that the work has opened up. It's as though that was the key."

The key. Matthew remembered his dream – joining hands over the rushing river. He was sure now. Philip had been the one in his dream; but not just Philip. Matthew had played his part in reaching out to this boy. If he hadn't been there then maybe his Brave One wouldn't have gone in the plane; and this had proved to be the key to God's work.

Of course, God could have used someone else. Matthew knew that, but all the same, it was a marvellous feeling, that in some small way he had played his part.

He felt so contented as they walked home, then

suddenly the nagging worry was there again. School! What am I going to do? I've got to come to a decision.

"It's so good having John with us," Jim exclaimed one day. "He's an excellent teacher. He is doing well with the adult Bible classes too. I sometimes wonder if we haven't worked ourselves out of a job."

Matthew was busy writing up his diary, but he looked up now to see dismay on his mother's face. "Oh, but Jim. Just when you have made the house so nice and comfy. We've got to know the people, and the language. We belong here. Besides, where would we go?"

Jim had his arm round her. "Now, don't go crossing bridges, Jen. It was just a thought. But we mustn't think that because the Lord asked us to come here, he wants us to stay for ever."

Parents are funny, thought Matthew. Would he ever understand them? He set this memory aside, as he might a piece of jigsaw that he couldn't fit in.

"I'm worried about the baby, Jim," Matthew heard his mother say, a few days later. "Marianne seems to catch cold so easily, and she isn't putting on weight as she should. I'm wondering if I should take her out for a check-up."

"Well, have a chat with the doctor over the radio and see what he says. We can manage for a few days without you, can't we, Matthew?" It felt good when his father treated him as an equal.

"Marta could take the women's class," his mother went on. "She often leads if I'm busy with the baby."

"Like I told you. We've all been working ourselves out of a job."

"Oh Jim."

Matthew felt as if this was another piece of the jigsaw that would have to be fitted in.

"Dr Grant thinks you should bring Marianne in for tests, Mrs Kelly," came the message over the radio. "We're arranging a flight for you on Monday, over."

"Do you want to visit Paula, Matthew, if there's room on the plane?"

"No. They've only just arrived back. It wouldn't be fair. In any case, Mum will have Marianne. We men had better stick together, hadn't we?" He gave his father a friendly nudge.

"They've made a good job of this bridge," Jim exclaimed, as they returned from the airstrip. "It's wonderful how many skills they have learned."

"Dad," ventured Matthew, as they took their lunch to eat on the veranda.

"Yes, Matt?"

"You'll have to let the schools know by the end of this month, Dad."

"Yes, I know. Look. Mum's made a note on the calendar." Jim made as if he would say more, but then he sighed and returned to his sandwich.

"What, Dad?"

"I don't know if I should talk to you about it with your mum away, but, well, you'll soon be a man. Why shouldn't we have a heart to heart?"

A slow grin spread like sunlight over Matthew's freckled face. He felt ten feet tall. But what could it be that his dad had to say?

"You see, I really do feel that it might be better

for these people if we leave. These people have got to learn to stand on their own feet."

"Where would you go, Dad, if you didn't stay up here?" A great hope welled up inside him but he pushed it down again. He couldn't bear to be disappointed.

"Well, Matt. I really feel it would be best for all of us if we went back home. It's a risk having a young child up here without medical attention. And we don't like the idea of you being far away from us. After all, God made us a family."

"But what would you do, Dad? You couldn't be a missionary there could you?"

"Course I could. 'Across the street or across the sea.' Do you know that song? You can be a missionary anywhere that God sends you. Do you remember that Gramps wrote that they are thinking of getting an assistant pastor at their church? I wondered whether they would consider me."

"But Mum wants to stay here, doesn't she?"

"Yes, Matt, your mum had a missionary call for years and years. I just felt that this was a job that the Lord wanted me to do, and that I was the right man in the right place at the right time. But it is no use going home if Mum is all the time thinking we should be up here. Oh dear – I shouldn't have burdened you with this. Forget I said anything, Matt, will you? Have you got lessons to do, or are you coming with me to see Masala?"

Matthew couldn't concentrate on his lessons. He was thinking about what his father had said. It would be wonderful if they could all return home together. But he knew God had to come first in their lives. If his mother felt they should stay – well, then, they still had the great decision to make; to have six weeks away at a time, or go south on his own, and not see any of them for a whole year.

He knew that Paula would be disappointed if he didn't go with her. They had become good friends. Oh dear! Life was so difficult.

He heard the babble of voices as the children tumbled out of school. Thankfully, he threw down his pen, and ran to join in a game of football.

"Have you had the doctor's report yet? Over."

Matthew stood beside his father at the radio as they listened for the answer.

"We're flying home on Monday. Don't worry. Tell you about it then. Over."

Jim left the radio crackling in the background and they began to prepare their meal.

"We'd better cook something special for Monday and have a good clean up, too."

"What's the matter, Dad?" Matthew came and stood with his hands on his father's shoulders where he had slumped in his chair.

"I suppose—" Jim began slowly, "I was really hoping that the doctor might have said that we shouldn't stay up here. Then the decision would have been taken out of our hands."

"But we don't know. Perhaps Mum didn't want to say it over the radio."

"Dad!"

"Yes, Matt?" It was the following morning, and neither had had much sleep, even with no Marianne to disturb them.

"I've made up my mind. Even if you stay here, I think I should go back to high school. I'm not a kid any more. I'll have to stand on my own feet. And I'll have Gran and Gramps."

"What made you decide?" Jim asked.

"I was reading in my Bible about Elijah. He said to the people, 'How much longer will it take you to make up your minds? If the Lord is God, then follow him.' I realised then that God had already shown us what to do. We had made the decision before we came up here, and somehow, I just know that although the other school sounds good, it isn't for me."

Jim reached across the table and grabbed his son's hand, shaking it heartily. A spoon went flying, but neither of them noticed.

"I'm proud of you," was all he said.

"This little piggy went to market,
   This little piggy stayed at home..."

Marianne squealed with delight as, once again, she had her big brother to play with her.

"Oh, Jim. It's great to be back," Jenny exclaimed. "Oh, I feel I've come home."

Matthew noted the swift glance his father threw him.

"By the way, Matthew," Jenny began, once they had sat down for their meal, "I saw Paula in town. She was asking if we had decided yet about you going to this school with her. She's really hoping that you will come. Ralph needs to know because of arranging your flights."

Matthew was struggling with his last mouthful of rice. Eventually he was able to speak.

"Mum, I don't think I should go with Paula. I've told Dad. I don't think we should change our plan for me to go back to New Zealand."

It was Jenny who was flustered now.

"Paula will be so disappointed—" she began, but his father interrupted.

"It's no good us making our decision because of Paula, Jenny. Ralph could be moved at any time. You know that. By the way, did you know that Paula's married sister lives not far from Gramps? I'm sure that, somehow, the Emerson family are going to stay in our lives.

"Matthew has prayed about it, Jen," he went on, "and he believes this is what God wants him to do. That's what matters, isn't it?"

To his dismay, his mother put her head on her arms and began to sob. He didn't need his father's signal. He made himself scarce.

He walked along, scuffing at the turf, as if it were responsible for his misery, when he heard Tundi calling. Gratefully he ran to join in a game of marbles.

When night crept up, driving the children back to their homes, Matthew returned to find the table still spread, but this time there were some chocolate biscuits that had been saved for a special occasion. No sign of tears now.

"Your mother has something to tell you," Jim began, but Jenny picked up Marianne, holding her on her shoulder.

"No, Jim, you tell him," she smiled.

"It's about your sister," he began.

Matthew shifted uneasily. Surely it wasn't a bad hospital report. He had thought that everything was fine. Jenny stretched out a reassuring arm.

"She's got a slight defect of the heart, Matt. No, it isn't serious, and the doctor says that if we go home to New Zealand, she might never even need to see a doctor. But you know what it is like up here. Living at eight thousand feet puts a strain on anyone. If she were taken ill we couldn't always get out to a doctor quickly, and of course there are better hospitals back home. The doctor says we are taking a risk in living up here. He has advised us to return home."

Matthew tried to press down the joy that was surging in his heart. He was afraid to hope.

"Mum didn't say anything at first," Jim continued. "She believed God would heal Marianne, so we could stay. Go on, Jen. You explain," Jim said, taking the baby now. Matthew was looking puzzled.

"You know, a lot of missionaries come for a year or two, and then go home. I used to think that they weren't real missionaries. and that we were going to be different. We would live and die here. The Lord opened a way so you could go to school up here, and I believed he would heal Marianne, and nothing would prevent us staying for a long time."

"And then I threw a spanner into the works?" Matthew suggested. That was one of his father's expressions.

"You certainly did," Jim laughed.

Jenny was laughing too.

"When you said you were going home to school, I remembered that God had asked me to be willing to go anywhere for him. That means being willing to go back home, and serve him there, too.

"I suppose in my heart I've known for a long time, only I didn't want to listen."

The family had gripped hands, thinking of what

it would mean to each of them to leave this mountain, and the people they had grown to love.

Matthew had learned to climb mountains, and in climbing he had become strong. There were so many things he had learned. He had faced many difficulties and that too had helped to make him strong. He knew that wherever he went, there would be plenty of difficulties for him to face. He sat quietly, thinking. He had often grumbled about the tough conditions up there, but he had loved it too. It would be hard to leave. But then a smile that had somehow started on the inside lit up his eyes, and then curled his lips as he asked,

"You'll still be missionaries, back home, won't you?"

"Yes, we'll still be missionaries," his father answered. "We'll serve God as a family, and later on, who knows, he may send us to some other land."

"Then I'll still be a mish kid?"

Jim and Jenny laughed.

"Matthew Kenny. I'm afraid you are stuck with that. You'll be a missionary kid for the rest of your life, and I guess there will always be mountains for you to climb."